THE ELEGY
LADY FIAMMETTA

THE ELEGY OF
Lady Fiammetta

GIOVANNI BOCCACCIO

Edited and translated by

Mariangela Causa-Steindler

and

Thomas Mauch

With an Introduction by

Mariangela Causa-Steindler

The University of Chicago Press

Chicago and London

...sa-Steindler is visiting assistant professor in the Department
...anguages at the University of Vermont. Thomas Mauch is
professor of English at Colorado College.

The University of Chicago Press, Chicago 60637
The University of Chicago Press, Ltd., London
© 1990 by The University of Chicago
All rights reserved. Published 1990
Printed in the United States of America

99 98 97 96 95 94 93 92 91 90   5 4 3 2 1

Library of Congress Cataloging-in-Publication Data

Boccaccio, Giovanni, 1313—1375.
[Fiammetta. English]
The elegy of lady Fiammetta / Giovanni Boccaccio; edited and
translated by Mariangela Causa-Steindler and Thomas Mauch; with an
introduction by Mariangela Causa-Steindler.
    p.   cm.
Translation of: Elegia di madonna Fiammetta.
Includes bibliographical references (p. 173).
ISBN 0–226–06275–9 (cloth). — ISBN 0–226–06276–7
(pbk.)
I. Causa-Steindler, Mariangela. II. Mauch, Thomas. III. Title.
PQ4272.E5F38   1990
853′.1—dc20   90—11057
                                                CIP

CONTENTS

PREFACE   vii

ACKNOWLEDGMENTS   ix

INTRODUCTION   xi

PROLOGUE   1

ONE   3

*In which Fiammetta describes who she was, by what
signs her future miseries were foreshadowed, and
when, where, how, and with whom she fell in love,
along with the pleasure that followed.*

TWO   28

*In which Lady Fiammetta tells why her lover left her and
describes his departure and the suffering it caused her.*

THREE   42

*In which is demonstrated how many and what kinds of
thoughts and pastimes this lady engaged in while waiting
for the time when her lover had promised to return.*

FOUR   53

*In which this Lady tells of the thoughts she had and
of the life she led when the date of Panfilo's return
arrived without his coming back.*

FIVE   58

*In which Fiammetta shows how she heard that Panfilo
had taken a wife and then tells of the anguish in
which she lived while despairing of his return.*

SIX   100

*In which Lady Fiammetta tells how she came to extreme
desperation and wanted to kill herself when she heard that
Panfilo was unmarried but was not returning because
he was in love with another woman.*

SEVEN   130

*In which Fiammetta shows how she rejoiced in vain
when she was told that a certain Panfilo had returned to the
place where she was, and how she eventually fell back into
her earlier melancholy when she discovered that it
was another Panfilo, not her own.*

EIGHT   142

*In which Lady Fiammetta, comparing her pains to those
of many ancient ladies, demonstrates that hers are
greater and then finally concludes her lamentation.*

NINE   156

*In which Lady Fiammetta makes an end by speaking to
her book and enjoining it in what dress it must go forth,
when, to whom and against whom to be on guard.*

GLOSSARY   161

SELECTED BIBLIOGRAPHY   175

PREFACE

Giovanni Boccaccio's *Elegia di Madonna Fiammetta* has been previously translated into English twice. Bartholomew Young (or Yong) did a rather free rendering of the work in 1587, entitled *Amorous Fiammetta*. A translation by James Clark Brogan, published in 1907, turns the Italian into a quaintly archaic English and frequently omits passages in the original. A slightly revised version of the Young translation, done by Edward Hutton, was privately printed for the Navarre Society in 1926 and reprinted in 1970. In making this present translation it has been our hope to give as literal and faithful an equivalent of Boccaccio's complex and intricate style as is possible in modern American English. In that spirit we have avoided the practice of some previous English translators of Boccaccio of introducing archaisms into the language in a misguided attempt to give the translation a medieval fragrance. The original language of the *Elegia* is unmistakably a contemporary fourteenth-century Italian, and archaisms have no business being in a translation of that language. We also have nearly always resisted the temptation of cutting up Boccaccio's characteristically lengthy and involuted sentences into a sequence of shorter ones which today's reader might have found more manageable. After all, it is through that complex sentence structure that Boccaccio explores the full possibilities of the medieval rhetorical tradition and introduces a wealth of word play and ambiguity. The translator of the *Elegia* is hard pressed to find a way of rendering into English this rich ambiguity of the original. Since it may be impossible to do so, the best principle for such a task is a spirit of dedication, akin to love, to a process the end result of which is admittedly a new work. We have based our translation of the *Elegia* on such a principle, knowing full well that complete faithfulness is an unrealizable goal and ever mindful of the Italian saying, "Traduttore, traditore."

In making this translation of Boccaccio's *Elegia di Madonna Fiammetta,* we have consulted three modern editions of the work: that in Bruno Maier's edition of Boccaccio's works (Bologna: Zanichelli, 1967); that in Segre's edition of Boccaccio's works (Milano: Mursia, 1978); and the edition of the *Elegia* by

Salinari and Sapegno (Torino: Einaudi, 1976). This last edition is an exact reproduction of the earlier and widely accepted edition of the *Elegia* in the *Decameron, Filocolo, Ameto, Fiammetta,* edited by Bianchi, Salinari, and Sapegno (Milano-Napoli: Ricciardi, 1952). Many discrepancies exist between this last edition and that of Segre, whose text closely follows Maier. Our translation is based on Segre and Maier.

ACKNOWLEDGMENTS

Mariangela Causa-Steindler extends her thanks to Helen Carroll, Donna Disch, William Doty, George Eastman, Joan Mallonee, and Meg Worcester; to David Berkowitz, who first introduced her to the *Elegia* at Brandeis University; to Elizabeth Petroff and Janet Whatley, whose trust helped her through hard times; to Brigitte DeGennaro, who had the courage to read through a draft of the translation all in one afternoon; to Donald Cheney, whose interest and pertinent touches added luster to dull areas; to "Hephaestus," for the joy he brought into her life in a year of trials; and above all to Alice L. Steindler, who never gave up trying to lead her through the mazes and mysteries of the English language.

We would also like to express our gratitude to Mark Stavig, who gave the whole translation a careful reading and made numerous helpful suggestions, and to Marcia Dobson, who alertly caught a number of errors and oversights in the glossary. Salvatore Bizzarro and Herving Madruga helped to disentangle certain knotty passages in the Italian, and Owen Cramer's classical erudition proved eminently useful on several occasions. Our special thanks go to Joan Cooper, Nancy Nicholl, and Betty Welch for providing a flawlessly typed manuscript.

INTRODUCTION

Mariangela Causa-Steindler

I. The Life of Boccaccio

Boccaccio was a medieval man whose secular interests and keen belief in the insuppressible laws of nature gave to his writings astoundingly modern characteristics. Quietly rebellious, he accepted Western literary tradition as a creative construct to be subverted and transformed with a minimum of pomposity and a maximum of formal precision. From both the recognized and the apocryphal writings of that tradition he borrowed freely as from a collective treasure, heeding mostly the demands of his imagination. He had a keen sense of the paradoxical aspect of reality and introduced irony even in his most serious works, particularly through the use of understatement. At the same time, his trust in the freedom of fantasy made him unafraid of the overstatements of the grotesque. In what has been called the first psychological novel in a modern language, *The Elegy of Lady Fiammetta,* he successfully bridged the gap between allegory and introspective narrative by giving shape to a character who encompasses realistic and archetypal qualities.

Boccaccio's interest in the feminine aspect of human nature is evident in most of his writings. But the adoration of woman often evident in his characters turned to bitter hatred in the *Corbaccio,* one of the most virulently misogynous writings of all times. He frequently celebrated marriage in his writings, but he himself fathered five children without ever marrying. He praised Italian as a literary language and ended his career writing almost exclusively in Latin. He denied the value of his earlier writings, but labored until his death on the *Decameron,* the work which he suggested not be read by women because of its corrupting effect. And finally, although his many literary and psychological preoccupations focused on the feminine, his deepest and most meaningful affections were for two men, Dante and Petrarch, the writers who most influenced his own writing.

Giovanni Boccaccio was born either in Florence or in the nearby village of Certaldo between June and July 1313. The identity, place of birth, and social status of his mother are still unknown. Although seemingly autobiographical, the passages found in his early works suggesting that his mother was of noble birth and of French nationality are now considered by scholars to represent the self-aggrandizing fantasy of an illegitimate youth in a French courtly milieu. Since his father, Boccaccio di Chelino, had another son in 1320, from his wife Margherita de' Margoli, Giovanni Boccaccio had a stepmother at an early age, and another later, because his father appears married to another woman, Bice de' Bostichi, in documents dated 1343 and 1350. At a young age Boccaccio trained to become a businessman, and along with the basic rules of Latin grammar he learned mathematics and perhaps accounting. He practiced commerce under the supervision of his father and other relatives, and it was during this period of apprenticeship—presumably before the age of fourteen—that he followed his father to Naples.

Boccaccio's father moved to Naples in 1327 as a representative of the Florentine banking house of Bardi. Until 1331, the elder Boccaccio's position was closely connected to the economic affairs of King Robert of Naples, who in 1328 named him counselor and chamberlain. Under the rule of the French house of Anjou, Naples emulated the court of France in its cultural ambitions and the luxury of its entertainments. Robert of Anjou was a man of no particular talent, but he was interested in culture and in the natural sciences in particular. His library and the Neapolitan "Studio," the equivalent of a university, flourished under his patronage and became the meeting place for many scholars. Through his familiarity with the faculty of the Neapolitan Studio and the intellectual and literary circles of the Angevin Court, Boccaccio made the acquaintance of a number of leading writers and scholars of the time.

In *The Genealogy of the Gentile Gods,* which he began writing when he was in his mid-thirties and carefully revised in 1373, shortly before his death, Boccaccio tells us how for six years he wasted time as an apprentice to a merchant, and then for another six years as a student of canon law, to prepare himself for a profitable career. It is not known when he stopped studying law, but we may surmise that during the last few years of university studies, he dedicated more time to writing than to addressing legal complexities. In fact, the *Caccia di Diana* (1336–38), the *Filos-*

trato (1335–?), and the *Filocolo* (1336–38) were written when he was still a law student, during his last years in Naples. It was also during this time that the character Fiammetta began to appear in Boccaccio's writings. It is impossible to establish whether he created Fiammetta entirely out of his imagination or based the character on someone he really knew. In any case, Fiammetta became the inspiring presence of the *Filocolo*, and later reappeared in the *Teseida*, *The Vision of Love*, and *The Comedy of the Florentine Nymphs*. Later still, Fiammetta recounted her own story in *The Elegy of Lady Fiammetta*, acted as one of the noble story tellers in the *Decameron*, and finally inspired the last sonnet Boccaccio ever wrote.

Boccaccio's father's association with the Bardi ended in 1338, and it is possible that following this break, his economic and professional situation at the court of Naples may not have been as secure as it had been in the past. What is known is that Boccaccio returned to Florence from Naples at the end of 1340 or early in 1341, most likely as a result of his father's professional problems. In his late twenties, still dependent financially on his father and without a career, the young poet found it difficult to begin a new life in a city which was by then foreign to him, and which could hardly compare with the dazzling elegance of Naples.

These lines of *The Comedy of the Florentine Nymphs* (also known as *The Ameto*) written soon after his return to Florence, reflect his dejection:

> There, laughter seldom rings,
> the sorrowful dwelling
> opens dark and silent,
> holds me reluctant
> where the vulgar, hideous sight
> of a coarse and cold
> miserly old man always
> fills me with woeful anxiety.
>
> . . . .
> How happy can be said to be the one
> who lives free and self-sufficient!
>
> *Li' non si ride mai se non di rado;*
> *la casa oscura e muta e molto trista*
> *me ritiene e riceve, mal mio grado;*

dove la cruda e orribile vista
d'un vecchio freddo, ruvido e avaro
ognora con affanno piu' m'atrista

. . . .

Oh quanto si puo' dir felice quello
che se' in liberta' tutto possiede!

(49:76–83, 85–86)

Notwithstanding the hardships of Boccaccio's first few months in Florence, and a profound desire to return to live in Naples, which lasted for the rest of his life, there are clear indications that already in 1341 he was becoming part of the cultural circles of Florence. He befriended writers of popular vernacular literature, such as Antonio Pucci and Giovanni Villani, and other poets and humanists. His interest in Italian as a literary language and in the works of Dante is well established, as is his ever-increasing admiration for Petrarch.

What Boccaccio wrote at this time reflects his assimilation into both the wealthy bourgeois society of Florence and a circle of intellectuals who looked at the classics as ancestors to be rediscovered and reinterpreted. In *The Comedy of the Florentine Nymphs* and in *The Vision of Love,* allegories in which he developed the theme of love as an ennobling force, he incorporated characters and stories of Florentine contemporary life. The truly innovative work of this period is *The Elegy of Lady Fiammetta,* which represents a turning point both in his career as a writer and in the history of the romance as a genre. The *Ninfale Fiesolano,* a pastoral poem composed in eight-line stanzas, may have followed The *Elegy* sometime during the year 1344–45, but the exact date of its composition is still a matter of debate.

We know very little of Boccaccio's life during the decade 1340–50. For Florence this was a time of major changes and crisis. The Guelfs lost power to the Ghibelline faction; the friendship with King Robert of Naples was severed and, under the so-called Duke of Athens, the city suffered a regime of harsh dictatorship; the poor revolted against the power of the rich by burning and sacking their homes; the banking houses of Bardi and Peruzzi went bankrupt, and the famine of 1347 was followed by the plague of 1348. During this long succession of social and civil calamities, Boccaccio created his masterpiece, the *Decameron,* which he finished between 1348 and 1351.

In 1345 Boccaccio had been living in Ravenna at the court of Ostasio da Polenta, where he translated Livy. In 1347 he was a guest of Francesco Ordelaffi in Forli'. But sometime in 1348 he was back in Florence, which had lost about two-thirds of its population because of the plague. His father, his father's second wife, and many of his friends and relatives had died, and when the epidemic was over, the poet found himself at the head of his family and in charge of his father's modest estate.

In the years following the plague, Boccaccio was involved in Florentine politics as an ambassador of the republic and traveled on various diplomatic missions. On one such mission to Ravenna, the poet met Becchino Bellincione, who urged him to compile a mythological genealogy in the name of his king, Hugh of Cyprus. The idea resulted in *The Genealogy of the Gentile Gods*. It was in the autumn of 1350 that Boccaccio met and became friends with Petrarch, with whom he was to maintain a lifelong friendship and correspondence.

One scholar, Vittore Branca (*Profilo,* p. 107), attributes to the year 1355 the conception and first drafting of some of the works Boccaccio wrote in Latin, such as *De Casibus Virorum Illustrium, De Montibus,* and perhaps sometime later *De Mulieribus Claris.* On these works he toiled until the end of his life; they would give him fame as a moralist and a humanist. The *Corbaccio,* his last work of fiction in Italian, may have been written at this time as well, but some critics, Branca included (*Profilo,* p. 140), believe that it was written in or around 1365, nearly ten years later. The *Corbaccio* can be seen as the other side of the coin of the *Elegy.* In the latter, love, seen from a youthful and feminine point of view, is the passionate source of Fiammetta's creative fantasies; in the former, love becomes a destructive, corrupting, hateful power of which woman is the personification.

The year 1360 represents a turning point in Boccaccio's civil and political career. A conspiracy against the Florentine government was discovered, many people were executed, and others fled a climate of repression and suspicion. Many of these people were Boccaccio's friends. To Pino de' Rossi, who was one of those exiled, he wrote a famous consolatory letter in which he condemned the factionalism that was destroying their city. His critical views of the government, and his connections with the conspirators, may have been a cause of his ostracism from public affairs. In fact, he was not assigned any other diplomatic mission until 1365, suggesting that his financial position too may have become increasingly problematic. Be that as it may, in July 1361 Boccaccio abandoned Florence and moved to Certaldo, leaving his house to his half-brother.

In the spring of 1362 a monk visited Boccaccio, saying that he was sent by Pietro Petroni, a Carthusian brother who had recently died and who was considered a saint. The monk reminded the poet that his death was approaching and urged him to abandon poetry and profane studies so as not to incur the wrath of God. Boccaccio was so deeply disturbed by this visit that he began contemplating drastic actions, such as burning some of his manuscripts, setting aside his wordly interests, and dedicating himself to works of faith. He wrote of his concerns to Petrarch, offering to sell him his library. Petrarch's cautious and sober reply questioned the good faith and sincerity of the pious visitor, and reminded his friend that only an ignorant person prejudiced against culture and learning could suggest he abandon his poetic studies. He also encouraged him to prepare himself mentally for death, though without undue apprehension, by freeing himself of his perhaps too passionate attachment to earthly things. On the matter of the library, Petrarch suggested that they live together in order to share not only their books but all their possessions. Several times he extended this offer to Boccaccio, who never accepted.

In 1365 Boccaccio's diplomatic activities resumed with his reinstatement as a comptroller of the army and armaments of the city of Florence. He was also sent to Avignon, with the mission of urging Pope Urban V to return to Italy, and to assure him of Florentine support. In the spring of 1367, the pope returned to Italy, and Boccaccio went to Rome to welcome him. There he renewed old acquaintances and friendships with high prelates and dignitaries he had already met in Avignon. In 1368 he paid what was to be his last visit to Petrarch in Padua, and in 1370 he made his last trip to Naples. Unlike the previous two journeys to the city he loved so well, this last visit was very successful. He went no longer in the hope of being supported by his powerful old friend Niccolo' Acciaiuoli, who had died in 1365, but because he was invited, and was in fact warmly welcomed by Queen Joanna I and by many of his friends.

Back in Certaldo in the early 1370s, Boccaccio wrote numerous letters and was occupied with his last work, the commentary on Dante's *Commedia*. In 1373 the government of Florence decreed that the *Commedia* should be read in public, and Boccaccio was asked to deliver the first public lectures on Dante. He lectured for several months, but his health soon failed him. In July 1374 Petrarch died, leaving Boccaccio a fur blanket meant to keep his good friend warm during the long winter nights in which he worked late. In a letter (Epistle 24) and a sonnet (124), Boccaccio mourned the man he considered his friend and master. Although plagued by various illnesses, he never ceased to study and work till his death on 21 December 1375.

II. *The Elegy of Lady Fiammetta*

Scholars agree on the date of composition of *The Elegy of Lady Fiammetta,* established between 1343 and 1345. Boccaccio was in his early thirties and was trying to make a name for himself in Florence, as a citizen and as a poet, after having spent many years in Naples. The work is generally recognized as a turning point in his career. The large number of manuscripts of the *Elegy*—over seventy—scattered around the world, seems to prove its popularity in the fourteenth and fifteenth centuries. As the first psychological novel in a modern language and a forerunner of stream-of-consciousness fiction, *The Elegy of Lady Fiammetta* is one of the earliest and most remarkable, if still largely unexplored, artistic achievements of European literature. Considered psychologically, it represents an early attempt at creating an image of a self becoming conscious of its uniqueness, ambivalence, and multiplicity.

The extraordinary nature of the *Elegy* stems partially from the crucial fact that it was created by a man who writes pretending to be a woman. Furthermore, this woman, the Lady Fiammetta, writes in the first person and announces herself from the very outset as an outspoken feminist. In fact, Fiammetta says that she writes for women only, and in the first page of the *Elegy,* as well as close to the end of the book, she rejects men as readers and, by implication, as lovers, by calling them the "ungrateful sex," unsuited to perceive "godly things."

Fiammetta tells women how, while married to a loving and dear husband, she fell in love with a charming young foreigner by the name of Panfilo and, driven by an irresistible passion, became his lover. She recounts how the young man later abandoned her to return to his native land and to the duty of caring for his old father. Panfilo promises to come back within a given time, but does not return, and the rest of the story is the interiorization of Fiammetta's suffering and of her consuming doubts. A multitude of opposite sentiments form the increasingly desperate dialectics of a frustrated love that drives Fiammetta to attempt suicide. Having survived self-destruction, with the help of her old nurse, she wishes to go in search of her lover because, as she frequently says, life is not worth living without him. From that moment on, Fiammetta lives hoping to see him return to Naples or to be able to search him out in his own land. She would spare no means to this end, even that of enlisting her own husband's help with a lie.

Betrayer and betrayed, Fiammetta gives more importance to the betrayal of sentiments than to the betrayal of a social convention such as marriage. Her reality is the reality of romantic/sexual love, which Boccaccio relates to femininity and to artistic creativity. From this point of view the only true betrayal is the betrayal of love. It is for this reason that Fiammetta rejects men as lovers and as readers. For her, the masculine propensity to laugh at woman's love woes is an indication of man's lack of understanding of love's universal powers.

Like everything else in the *Elegy*, Fiammetta's rejection of men must be taken with a grain of salt, because Boccaccio is, after all, the semicovert but ubiquitous narrator of the story. His presence as storyteller is directly observed only in the brief summaries, written in the third person, that precede each chapter. By this means he ostensibly distances himself from Fiammetta's narrative. But Boccaccio remains present throughout the *Elegy* "in absentia," much as Panfilo lives in the narrative through Fiammetta's memory and imagination.

Three predominant relationships structure the *Elegy*, the one between Fiammetta and Panfilo, the work's protagonists, that between Fiammetta as protagonist and Fiammetta as narrator, and that between Fiammetta as narrator and Boccaccio as author. The first relationship mirrors the last. What connects Fiammetta and Panfilo—and by implication Boccaccio and Fiammetta—is a love-hate relationship that constantly keeps opposite points of view in play. Lacking the physical presence of the other, Fiammetta's dialogue with Panfilo becomes internalized, nourishing her imagination and making of her the artist we are ultimately meant to see her for. The relationship between Fiammetta as protagonist and Fiammetta as narrator is based on a chronological difference: an older Fiammetta recounts the story of how she, as a self-conscious young woman, became a writer.

The narration of the *Elegy* issues at once from male and female points of view. It is the representation of a consciousness aware of its own hermaphroditic nature and of its capacity to give form to a reality in which change, transformation, and ambiguity seem to be the only rules. As the narrative proceeds, this consciousness becomes more and more aware of the limits and of the unbounded possibilities of narrative form. In its hyperbolic, melancholy, repetitive, emotional style, the *Elegy* is reminiscent of the traditionally plaintive style of the *Heroides*. In the *Elegy* Boccaccio, like Ovid, moves into the emotional indefiniteness of a feminine psyche—or into the darkness of his own psyche, recognized as feminine—and maps it dialectically, erotically, and ironically.

The relationship between Fiammetta as narrator and Fiammetta as protagonist extends to the women readers for whom the narrative is ostensibly meant. It presupposes a feminine sensitivity from which men are excluded, symbolized by the "circle" formed by women talking about love, an image found more than once in the text. More fundamentally, this relationship suggests the image of a narrator watching her younger weeping self, laughing. The laughter of the present contains the tears of the past, and makes of it a lesson for the future. Laughter and tears have a rippling effect that finally reaches and implicates the author. In fact, the more critically we read the *Elegy*, the more the masculine presence we are supposed to forget asserts itself.

The difference fundamental to the ironic tone of the *Elegy* is established by this masculine interruption of the feminine point of view. On one hand, the constant presence of "the other author" peeking over Fiammetta's shoulder undermines the seriousness of her overabundant tears. On the other hand, the *Ele-*

gy's extremely accurate, eloquent rhetorical style, in which every word is placed where it is needed, bespeaks the close co-operation of a determined mind and a suffering soul. Told from a feminine viewpoint, and ostensibly composed for women's benefit, the *Elegy* bespeaks a double meaning, which invites the reader—especially the male reader—to consider it as an insight into the nature of femininity as a creative principle.

In chapter 1 Fiammetta says: ". . . quantunque io scriva cose verissime, sotto si fatto ordine l'ho disposte che, eccetto colui che cosi' come io le sa essendo di tutte cagione, niuno altro, per quantunque avesse acuto l'avvedimento, potrebbe chi io mi fossi conoscere (". . . even though I am writing things that are very true, I have arranged them in such a way that, except for the one who knows everything as well as I do—for he is the cause of them all—no one else, no matter how sharp his intellect, could discover who I am."). Close to the center of this sentence appears the word *colui*. *Colui* is a masculine pronoun translatable as "the one who" or "he who." Fiammetta does not tell us who this *colui* is; she merely whets her reader's appetite. A reader inclined to take things at face value would say that *colui* and Panfilo are one and the same. But readers curious about such a suggestive expression as "the one who knows everything," accepting the challenge of the riddle, will recognize that it leads to a multiplicity of identities. Panfilo is certainly the one who knows everything, as well as Fiammetta, about their love story, and is also the cause of all her troubles. But someone else is in the same position, and that, of course, is Boccaccio. If one remembers that at the very beginning of the prologue Fiammetta indirectly names Love as the cause of all her tribulations, *colui* assumes yet another dimension. If Love knows everything and is the cause of everything, *colui* becomes a sign that ties a passionate sentiment to a mythological image. Finally, if the readers are aware that Panfilo in Greek means "the all loving" or "the one who loves all," and remember that the God of Christianity is traditionally recognized as omniscient and all-loving, another and divine identity is at least suggested. Clearly, the riddle ties the human and personal to the archetypal and divine. This pronoun *colui,* a mere grammatical substitute, signifies the dynamism that unites and separates tangible and metaphorical realities.

Critics have variously seen Fiammetta as an ideal woman, a

tragic character, a victim of destiny, an irrational and irresponsible personality, a sophisticated, cunning and modern female, a faithful believer in the superior rights of love, a compulsive and sick creature, and finally, in Robert Hollander's words, "a fool." In *Boccaccio's Two Venuses* Hollander describes *The Elegy* as a parody, and Fiammetta as a comic character, vain, sick with melancholy, and stubbornly unwilling to be cured. Hollander exemplifies the masculine, reductive point of view—slighting as he does the anguish of feminine love—which caused Fiammetta to reject men as readers. Hollander's invitation to his readers to laugh at the character of Fiammetta seems to provide, six hundred years later, a new cause for her and Boccaccio's mistrust of the "ungrateful sex" that finds in laughter a compensation for its incapacity to "perceive godly things."

Scholars have often observed that, as the idealized lady of one of the three great writers of the early Italian Renaissance, Fiammetta is today more alive, more real than her predecessor, Dante's Beatrice, or her contemporary, Petrarch's Laura. This may be due to the fact that Boccaccio did what Dante and Petrarch could or would not do, namely allow his ideal woman to speak for herself, in her own voice. It is true that the Fiammetta we find later in the *Decameron* is hardly distinguishable from her noble lady friends. This same lady to whom Boccaccio dedicated the *Teseida* is the typical idealized lady of a Renaissance poet. Similarly, the "cara Fiamma," mover of *The Amorous Vision,* is an allegorical beauty whose character is left undefined. It is only in the *Elegy* that Boccaccio has invested Fiammetta with a full—and as some critics say—modern personality.

But one may wonder why not even in the *Elegy* can Fiammetta be identified physically. We do not know whether she is tall and thin or small and plump, nor the color of her eyes. We know that she is beautiful, with magnificent golden hair, and that her beauty fades to become ugliness as her suffering intensifies. Boccaccio described the ladies of the *Ameto* in minute detail. His stylization of Fiammetta's physical appearance must then have had a specific purpose, which may have been that of drawing the reader's attention to her as soul, or as psyche. Seen as a new Psyche, Fiammetta is a symbolic image of the soul. She is a soul with a voice, or the voice of soul. In fact, Fiammetta is not a woman whose glory, according to the Aristotelian belief widely accepted in the Middle Ages, was silence. In the *Elegy* she speaks for herself, and what she says, and how she says it, make her not only the extremely intriguing character she still is after six hundred years, but also the first Western figure of the woman-as-author since antiquity.

III. Sources and Influences

At the beginning of this century, Giuseppe Gigli wrote that it was impossible to speak of concrete sources of the *Elegy*, for they were to be found in the events of the author's life ("ragion materiale") and in his psychological motivations.[1] Gigli's idea that the book is rooted in the events of Boccaccio's life, if not entirely disproven, has certainly been radically modified by recent scholarship. Because they are impossible to prove, the biographical sources of the *Elegy* have been more and more disregarded in favor of a view that stresses a literary background. During the last three-quarters of a century, critics have demonstrated the importance of works by Statius, Seneca, Ovid, Apuleius, and Dante as sources of inspiration or models that Boccaccio transformed or reversed in the *Elegy*.

Vincenzo Crescini has compared Boccaccio to a maker of inlays who takes the pieces that please him most from Seneca's *Phaedra* and places them in the *Elegy* to suit his taste.[2] Cornelia Coulter points out that the last part of the prayer to Sleep in chapter 5 is a translation of a portion of the Chorus from Seneca's *Hercules Furens*.[3] Albert L. Cook, by comparing several passages of the *Elegy* with equivalent passages in *Phaedra* (or *Hippolytus*) draws no firm conclusions, but notes that Boccaccio "imitated" a large part of the chorus at the end of Act 1 in *Hippolytus*, and placed it in the first chapter of the *Elegy*, at the point where Venus appears to dissipate Fiammetta's scruples about Love.[4]

1. Giuseppe Gigli, *Antologia delle opere minori Volgari* (Biblioteca Scolastica di Classici Italiani, diretta da Giosue' Carducci, 1907), 191.

2. Vincenzo Crescini, *Contributo agli studi sul Boccaccio con documenti inediti* (Loescher: Torino, 1887).

3. Cornelia C. Coulter, "Statius, Silvae V. 4 and Fiammetta's Prayer to Sleep," *American Journal of Philology* 80 (1959):390–95.

4. Albert L. Cook, "Boccaccio, 'Fiammetta' Chapter One, and Seneca, 'Hippolytus' Act One," *American Journal of Philology* 28 (1907):200–204.

Pamela Waley stresses the *Elegy*'s dependence on the "construction and emotional atmosphere" of the *Heroides*, and studies the differences between the personality of Fiammetta's old nurse and various old nurses in the *Heroides* as well as in Seneca's tragedies.[5] What emerges from Waley's inquiry is a new image of the old nurse and another facet of Fiammetta's character. In the *Elegy*, as Waley points out, Fiammetta becomes her own counselor and, like her nurse, often speaks the words that in Seneca's tragedies are spoken by the choruses. This, I would add, seems to imply that Boccaccio viewed the feminine as the direct source of a creative wisdom—personal and collective—of which woman is the incarnated, although often unconscious, personification.

Walter Pabst notes that in the *Elegy* the description of the effect that Fiammetta's beauty has on the crowd in the church where she encounters Panfilo is parallel to that caused by Psyche in the story found at the center of Apuleius' *Golden Ass*.[6] One might add that both heroines can be seen as personifications of the psyche, but that the myth of the fourteenth-century lovers seems to be reversed in its intentionality. The overt objective of Venus in the *Golden Ass* is to separate Psyche from Eros, but the effect of her jealousy is opposite to her apparent wishes, since the two lovers are reunited in the symbolic world of the Olympian gods. In the Boccaccian tale, Venus claims that she wants to unite Fiammetta and Panfilo, but she succeeds in separating them, at least on earth. What Boccaccio may have wished to illustrate is another and opposite cycle in the ever-corresponding movement between the human and the divine.

Most critics agree that Boccaccio must have known Andreas Capellanus's *The Art of Courtly Love*. Like the suitors and ladies of *The Art of Courtly Love*, Fiammetta argues for and against love skillfully and at length, but at the same time she is aware not only of its destructive power, but of its inseparability from herself as a creative human being. She cannot be what she is without love; from this realization comes Fiammetta's insistence on two choices: death, or her lover.

5. Pamela Waley, "The Nurse in Boccaccio's 'Fiammetta': Source and Invention," *Neophilologus* 56 (1972):164–74.

6. Walter Pabst, *Venus als heilige und furie in Boccaccio's "Fiammetta" dichtung* (Krefeld: Scherpe-Verlag, 1958).

In chapter 8 of the *Elegy* Fiammetta speaks of "French romances," and refers to the story of Tristan and Iseult. Since he spent his youth at the sophisticated Neapolitan French court of the House of Anjou, it would be indeed surprising if the writings of Chrétien de Troyes and the poetry of the troubadours had not been part of Boccaccio's cultural background.

The connection between the *Elegy* and Dante's *Vita Nuova* may have been noted for the first time when someone wrote "*Vita Nuova*" next to the title of a manuscript of the *Elegy* which belonged to Pietro Bembo.[7] Dante's influence on Boccaccio has been explored by Billanovich in *Prime Ricerche Dantesche,*[8] and the idea that the *Elegy* is the *Vita Nuova* upside down is sustained by several critics. In his essay on the *Vita Nuova,* Charles S. Singleton speaks of a "construction aware of the inner principle of its own being, which is a principle of becoming toward an end."[9] Of the *Elegy* one can say that it is a narrative constantly aware of its own fragmentary nature, and of a reality essentially repetitive in its infinite variety. For Dante there seems to be a prescribed manuscript of the book of memory from which to copy. Not so for Boccaccio, who overtly relies not only on memory but also and predominantly on fantasy.

In the *Vita Nuova* love is represented by a Christ-like figure clad in white. Such an image is remindful of a self-sacrifice that inspires an ever-increasing spiritual purity. In the *Elegy* love leads to violent self-destruction which, if survived, gives life to artistic expression through an expansion of consciousness nourished by desire. Fiammetta is the personification of such a consciousness. When one compares the two main feminine characters in the two texts, what can be said of Beatrice seems to find its opposite in Fiammetta. One is silent, the other speaks for herself; of the first, one remembers only a smile, from the other, one hears a stream of words, tears, and sighs. Beatrice is the prototype of the "donna angelicata," a woman miracle; Fiammetta is a lustful creature made of flesh and bones who wants her man. If

7. Pietro Bembo, *Tradizione delle opere di Giovanni Boccaccio* (Edizione di Storia e Letteratura: Roma, 1958), 32.

8. Giuseppe Billanovich, *Prime ricerche Dantesche* (Edizioni di Storia e Letteratura: Roma, 1947).

9. Charles S. Singleton, *An Essay on the "Vita Nuova,"* (Johns Hopkins University Press: Baltimore and London, 1977).

the *Vita Nuova,* as Singleton maintains, is a theory of love, the *Elegy* is the experience of love. The question posed by Singleton, "Was love of Beatrice good love?" sounds rigidly moralistic if seen from an elegiac point of view that considers love as neither good nor bad, but as a transforming power.

Boccaccio's critics have often referred to the antithetical nature of the *Elegy* and the *Vita Nuova,* but a study relating them as opposite views of the feminine remains to be written. However, it is possible that further studies may reveal degrees of difference more than straight opposition. Dante's presence in the *Elegy* has been more thoroughly studied by Carlo Delcorno, who perceives a "development of [Boccaccio's] 'dantism' towards forms more and more cryptic, subtle and allusive."[10] Delcorno concludes that "the elusive refinement of Boccaccio's refashioning work is particularly evident when the dantesque model which he straightforwardly imitates, in turn indicates a classical archetype, thus bringing about a game thick with interferences, a kind of three levelled reading."[11] Delcorno's opinion is confirmed by Robert Hollander, who writes: "Dante alone is the source of what must be hundreds, or may be thousands of Boccaccio's words, phrases, thoughts. Rarely has an author been so frequently present within another's works."[12] Boccaccio's greatness, then, resides in his capacity to transform what he inherits from the past by lightly weaving into "the form of the eternal return" the most subtle articulations of the present.[13]

After what has been said about Dante and his influence on Boccaccio, it is not surprising to find at the very center of the *Elegy*—and to my knowledge nowhere else in the book—the word *dante,* used as the present participle of *dare,* and meaning "leading into." The word is placed in a passage that describes Baia, a beautiful location near Naples depicted as a paradise on earth. Trying to convince her to cure herself by leaving Naples, Fiammetta's husband entices her with the description of this

10. Carlo Delcorno, "Note sui Dantismi nell 'Elegia di Madonna Fiammetta,' " *Studi sul Boccaccio* (Sansoni: Firenze, 1979), 261.

11. Ibid, 294.

12. Robert Hollander, *Boccaccio's Two Venuses* (Columbia University Press: New York, 1977), 6.

13. Jacques Derrida, *Writing and Difference,* University of Chicago Press: Chicago and London, 1978, pg. 296.

lovely place, unaware that she has been there before with her lover: ". . . quivi vicine l'isole Pittacuse e Nisida di conigli abbondante e la sepoltura del gran Miseno, *dante* via a' regni di Plutone . . . (not far away are the islands of Pithecusae and Nisida, which abound with rabbits, and there is the grave of the great Misenus, *leading into* the realm of Pluto . . .)" (emphasis added). Misenus, son of Aeolus, was first the trumpeter of Hector, and subsequently that of Aeneas. Virgil speaks of him in the sixth book of the *Aeneid,* and Ovid mentions him in the fourteenth book of the *Metamorphoses.* The mythical figure of a herald servant of two masters evokes the image of a poet acknowledging his most meaningful sources of inspiration. In fact, Virgil was Dante's guide through hell, while Ovid's transformative and ironic spirit pervades the *Elegy.* Boccaccio, like Misenus the great trumpeter, may be celebrating here the glory of his heroes with his poetic song.

In the *Elegy*'s narrative, whose reverse side the reader is constantly obliged to consider, the deepest imprint seems to be the one treated most lightly. Few places are indeed less permanently lived in than a passageway, but no place is as necessary, or more central, to the articulation of poetic reality as a place in-between. As Jacques Derrida has said, "The center is the threshold"[14]; the sign on the *Elegy*'s threshold/center is *dante,* a verb/surname that is Boccaccio's affirmation of play. This is what Dante seems to be for Boccaccio: central to the "excentric" poetics of the book, indispensible, ironically unobtrusive in his linguistic disguise.

Fiammetta perceives Baia's earthly paradise as a hell on earth, because whatever she sees reminds her of the absent lover and makes her desire more deeply painful. Baia is where consciousness and the unconscious meet to mark a change, a place where poetry is born. Boccaccio could not have chosen a better place to inscribe the name of the man who seems to be the main source of his inspiration. The Baia episode appears in chapter 5, which, announced at its very beginning as a turning point, represents the structural, psychological, and symbolic center of the book. Such an ironically simple little joke, with such a freighted meaning, is very much in keeping with Boccaccio's style of narration.

14. Jacques Derrida, *Writing and Difference,* University of Chicago Press: Chicago and London, 1978, pg. 297.

THE ELEGY OF
LADY FIAMMETTA

Here begins the book called THE ELEGY OF
LADY FIAMMETTA, *sent by her to women in love.*

PROLOGUE

Unhappy people customarily take greater pleasure in lamenting their lot when they see or hear that someone else feels compassion for them. Therefore, since I am more eager to complain than any other woman, to make certain that the cause of my grief will not grow weaker through habit but stronger, I wish to recount my story to you, noble ladies, and if possible to awaken pity in you, in whose hearts love perhaps dwells more happily than in mine. And I do not care if my speech does not reach the ears of men; in fact if I could, I would entirely keep it away from them, for the harshness of one of them is still so alive in me that I imagine the others to be like him, and I would expect jeering laughter from them rather than compassionate tears. I pray that you alone, in whom I recognize my own open-mindedness and inclination for misfortunes, may be my readers; and as you read, you will find neither Greek myths embellished with many lies, nor Trojan battles befouled with much blood, but stories of love stirred by innumerable desires; in them, there will appear before your eyes the wretched tears, the impetuous sighs, the doleful voices, and the stormy thoughts that have troubled me with constant torment and have taken away from me appetite, sleep, joyful memories, and treasured beauty all at once.

If you will consider these things both one by one and altogether and feel them with a woman's heart, I am sure that your gentle faces will be bathed in tears, something which will cause endless grief to me, who seek nothing else but tears. I beg you, do not refuse to weep, and bear in mind that your fortunes are as insecure as my own, and that if—God forbid—they were to turn out like mine, you would cherish these tears when you remember having shed them. And not to spend more time talking than weeping, I shall force myself to come quickly to what I

1

have promised, and I will begin with those feelings of love which were more happy than enduring, so that by comparing that happiness to my present condition, you may know me to be more unhappy than any other woman; therefore, I shall go on, with a tearful pen and to the best of my ability, to those sad events which I lament with good reason. But first, so grieved as I am and bathed in my own tears, I beg that if the prayers of the wretched are heard, and if there is any deity in heaven whose blessed mind is touched by pity for me, he may aid my afflicted memory and sustain my trembling hand in the present work; and may both be made so powerful that as one suggests the words, the other, more willing than able in this task, may write them down, conveying my mental anguish as I have experienced it and still experience it.

ONE

In which Fiammetta describes who she was, by what signs her future miseries were foreshadowed, and when, where, how, and with whom she fell in love, along with the pleasure that followed.

At that season when the newly clad earth displays her beauty more than at any other time of the year, I came into the world born of noble parents and welcomed by a benign and generous Fortune. Cursed be the day I was born, more detestable to me than any other! How much luckier it would have been if I had not been born or if I had been led from that wretched birth to my tomb, or if I had not lived longer than the teeth sown by Cadmus and if Lachesis had cut her threads as soon as she had spun them![1] Innumerable woes, now the sad reason for my writing, would have found a conclusion at a tender age. But what is the use of lamenting this now? I am here all the same, and it has pleased and still pleases God that I should be here.

As has been said, I was welcomed into the world's most sublime pleasures, and I grew up in them; from infancy to delightful childhood I was raised by a revered teacher from whom I learned all the manners suitable to a young noblewoman. And as my body grew with the passing of time, my charms, which were the specific cause of my troubles, multiplied. Alas, what pride I took in them, although I was still young, and how I improved on them with care and artful means upon hearing them praised by many people!

But once I had passed from childhood to a more mature age, trained by nature stirring within me, I learned of the desires lovely young women can arouse in young men, and I became aware that my beauty in particular, an unwelcome gift to anyone who wishes to live virtuously, set afire young men my own age as well as other noblemen. By various means which I then hardly understood, they tried countless times to kindle in me

---

1. Fiammetta attributes both the spinning and cutting of the individual life span to Lachesis, roles customarily given to, respectively, Clotho and Atropos.

the same fire which was burning in them, and which in the
ture would not only warm me but would consume me m
than any other woman. I was also insistently urged by man
them to enter into marriage; but when among those many,
suitable to my station in every respect obtained me, the pe
ing throng of suitors lost nearly all hope and stopped pursu
me with their behavior. Therefore, duly satisfied with suc
husband, I lived in bliss until the raging passion later took h
of my young mind with a fire I had never felt before. Alas, t
was never anything which might please me or any other wo
that was not quickly granted to my satisfaction. I was my yo
husband's sole good and only joy, and I loved him just a
loved me. Oh, how much happier than any other woman I c
call myself, had such love lasted in me forever!

While I was living contentedly, and as I was being cont
ally entertained, Fortune, who is quick to overturn human
fairs, became envious of the very gifts she had bestowed
wished to retract her favors, but not knowing where to place
venom, with subtle guile she made misfortune find its
through my very own eyes, since at that time there was no o
avenue but the one through which she entered. But the gods
favored me and were more concerned about my affairs th
was; and since they were aware of Fortune's hidden snares,
wished to offer me weapons to protect my heart—had I
known how to take them—so that I would not go unarmed
that battle where I was to fall. And on the eve of the day that
to be the beginning of all my troubles, the gods made the fu
clear to me by means of a revealing vision which came i
sleep in the following manner.

As I lay on a grand bed, with all my limbs abandoned to
sleep, for some unknown reason it seemed that I was fe
more joyful than ever and that the day was extraordin
lovely and brighter than any other; and in this state of deli
seemed to be sitting alone amid the tender green grass in a
protected from the brightness of the sky by the dappled sha
of newly leafed trees; there, after picking many of the flo
that gave color to the entire place, I gathered them into a fo
my dress with my pure white hands, and choosing them on
one, I wove them into a graceful little garland with wh
adorned my head. Bedecked like this, I stood up, and went

ing through the fresh spring as Proserpina did when Pluto stole her away from her mother; then, tired perhaps, I lay down to rest where the grass was thickest. But just as the lurking beast pierced the tender foot of Eurydice, a serpent slithered unseen through the grass in which I lay and seemed to bite me under the left breast; when its sharp teeth first pierced my flesh, the bite seemed to burn, but then, as if I had feared something worse, I felt reassured, and I seemed to place the cold snake into my bosom, imagining that by offering the warmth of my bosom I would make it kinder toward me. The snake, made bolder and fiercer by my gesture, fastened its evil mouth onto the bite it had given, and after a long time, having swallowed much of this blood of ours,[2] it seemed to leave my bosom against my will and go away sinuously through the young grass, taking my spirit with it. As it was leaving, the clear day grew cloudy; its turbulence came after me and surrounded me entirely; and it followed the path of the beast as if all the clouds were tied to it and drawn by it; soon thereafter it disappeared from my view, like a white stone which slowly fades from the observer's sight when it is thrown into deep water.

Then I saw the sky enclosed by the most profound darkness and the sun nearly disappear, and I thought night had returned, just as it fell on the Greeks at the sin of Atreus; lightning rushed through the sky in great confusion, and crackling thunder terrified me and the earth alike. But the wound, which until then had only stung from the biting, was left full of viper's poison and incurable by medicine; it seemed to spread throughout my body with a most dreadful swelling; at first, and not knowing how, I seemed to be left lifeless, but then, as I felt the strength of the venom searching most intimately for my heart, I thrashed about in the tender grass and longed for death. Believing that I was already close to death and troubled by fear of the hostile weather, I felt such an unbearable pain in my heart as I waited to die that it shook all my sleeping body and broke the deep sleep; immediately after, still terrified by what I had seen, I ran my right hand over the bitten side, searching in the present for what had been prepared for me in the future; finding it without any

2. this blood of ours: *nostro sangue*. Here and frequently elsewhere Fiammetta uses the plural possessive pronoun when referring to herself.

wound, I felt somewhat pleased and reassured and began mocking the foolishness of dreams; and thus I rendered useless the efforts of the gods. Miserable me! How appropriate that since I scorned dreams at that time, I should have come to believe later in their truthfulness through great pain and wept over them in vain! But I complain no less about those gods who reveal their secrets to obtuse minds in such obscure ways that they can be said to be almost unrevealed until they have come true. Thus awakened, I lifted my sleepy head and saw the morning sun peering through a tiny hole into my room; I then set aside all other thoughts and arose at once.

It was a solemn holiday for nearly everyone, so I dressed most carefully in robes resplendent with much gold and adorned every part of myself with a masterful hand, since I considered myself similar to the goddesses whom Paris saw in the valley of Ida, and I prepared myself to attend the solemn celebration. While I was admiring myself all over, just as the peacock preens its feathers, and thinking to please others as I pleased myself, a flower in my crown was somehow caught on the curtain of the bed, or perhaps it was plucked by an unseen heavenly hand that pulled the crown from my head, and so it fell to the ground; but being indifferent to the secrets revealed by the gods, I picked it up as if nothing had happened, put it back on my head, and went out. Alas, what clearer sign than that could the gods have given me of what was to happen? Surely none. This was enough to show me that my soul, free and until then mistress of itself, would that day renounce its sovereignty and become a slave, as indeed happened. Oh, if only my mind had been sound! Then I would have recognized what a black day that was for me and would have spent it without leaving the house. But the gods deprive those who have angered them of the understanding they need, although they may offer them a sign of their salvation; in this way they show that they are doing their duty but satisfy their anger at the same time. It was my luck then, that drove me out, vain and unconcerned; and in the company of numerous ladies, I slowly reached the sacred temple where the solemn ceremonies of that particular day were being celebrated.[3]

3. temple: *tempio.* Fiammetta uses this word rather than the more specifically Christian *chiesa.*

By long-standing tradition and because of my nobility, a very special place had been reserved for me among the other ladies; and as soon as I was seated, I looked around as usual and saw the temple filled with men and women alike, doing different things in separate groups. While the holy service was being celebrated, no sooner was my presence noticed in the temple than what had happened in the past happened again: not only did men turn their eyes towards me, but so did women, just as if there had appeared before them miraculously and for the first time Venus or Minerva, instead of me. Oh, how often I laughed to myself about this, being pleased with myself and taking no less pride than a goddess in such an occurrence! So almost all the bands of young men ceased to admire other women and grouped themselves around me; they stood encircling me, nearly forming a crown, and as they chatted among themselves about my beauty, they concluded by praising it with virtual unanimity. But as for me, I turned my eyes elsewhere and pretended to be occupied with other matters while I listened to their discussions and felt a sweet yearning; and since I seemed to feel somewhat indebted to them, I looked at them from time to time with a friendlier eye; more than once I realized that some of them were deriving a vain hope from this and boasted of it vainly to their friends.

While I went on in this way, seldom looking at others but much admired by many and believing that my beauty captivated other people, it happened that someone else's beauty unfortunately captured me. And as I was already close to that fateful moment which was to be the cause of certain death or of a life more wretched than any other, I was moved by an unknown spirit, and with my eyes raised in due solemnity, I gazed piercingly through the crowd of surrounding youths, and apart from everyone else, alone and leaning against a marble column, exactly opposite me, I saw a young man; moved by an inevitable fate, I did something I had never done before with anyone else: I began to take mental stock of him and his manner. I must say that according to my judgment, which was still free from the influence of love, he was very handsome and very pleasing in his gestures, and he was dressed most nobly; his soft curly beard still barely shadowed his cheeks as a clear sign of his youth, and he stared at me, no less adoring than cautious, across the crowd of men. To be sure, I had the strength to refrain from looking at him for long, but neither the estimation of the other things just mentioned, nor any other incident could dissuade me from thinking about him, even if I made an effort. Since his image was already imprinted upon my mind, I observed it within myself with a certain quiet delight as if I were adducing new reasons to confirm the judgment I had made of him.

But during these intermittent looks, since I was not protecting myself from love's snares, at one point I stared into his eyes much more intently than usual, and in them I seemed to read words that said, "O woman, our blessedness lies in you alone!" I would certainly lie if I said that these words displeased me; on the contrary, they pleased me so much that they drew from my breast a soft sigh, accompanied by these words: "And mine in you." But I became conscious of myself and deprived him of them. To what avail? What had not been said, the heart understood by itself, and it kept within itself that which might have allowed me to remain free, if it had been said.

So from that moment on I granted more power of judgment to my foolish eyes and indulged them with more of what they had come to desire; and certainly if the gods, who draw all things to their predetermined end, had not deprived me of understanding, I could have remained my own woman, but I put off to the very end all consideration and followed my appetite, and I immediately became susceptible to being caught; for not unlike fire which leaps from one spot to another, a most subtle ray of light left the young man's eyes and hit my own, and it did not rest there satisfied, but by some mysterious route it suddenly reached my heart and penetrated it. Terrified at this sudden visitation, my heart drew all its vital powers to itself, leaving me all pale and chilled. But I did not remain this way for long before the opposite happened; and not only did I feel my heart grow warm again, but as my energies returned to their proper places, they brought with them such a heat that it drove away my pallor and made me very red and as hot as fire; and as I looked at the one from whom this came, I sighed. From that moment on, I could not have any other thought than to please him.

Without moving from his place he watched cautiously these changes in my appearance, and like an expert in many struggles of love, apparently he knew which weapons had to be used to capture the desired prey and continued to show with greater humility how very devout and how full of passionate desire he was. Alas, how much deceit was hidden under that devotion, which (as the consequences demonstrate) left his heart, never to return, and then appeared in its falsity on his face! And without going on to describe every one of his deeds, each of which was filled with masterful cunning, whether it was he who did this or the Fates who permitted it, things went on in a way that is beyond my capacity to recount, and I found I was caught in a sudden and unexpected love, and I still am.

Therefore, compassionate ladies, of all the noble, handsome, and valiant young men who were available not only there but in my entire beloved Parthenope, he was the one my heart chose with insane judgment to be the first, last, and only lord of my life; he was the one I loved and still love more than anyone else, the beginning and cause of all my troubles and, as I hope, of my wretched death. This was the day I first became the lowest of servants, after having been a free woman; this was the day I first knew the love I had never known before; this was the day the poisons of Venus first contaminated my chaste and pure heart. Alas, miserable me, how much harm came into the world because of me on such a day! Alas, how much trouble and anguish I could have avoided if that day had been changed into night! Alas, miserable me, how hostile was that day to my virtue! But after all, things badly done in the past can be more easily regretted than corrected. As was said, I was caught anyway, and whether it was an infernal fury or a malevolent fate that, envious of my innocent happiness, undermined it, on that day it could rejoice in the hope of certain victory.

Therefore, surprised by this sudden passion, I sat among the ladies, nearly stunned and beside myself, and I let the sacred service, as well as my companions' various conversations, go by me, barely listening to them and much less understanding them. So entirely had this new and sudden love occupied my mind that either my thoughts or my eyes were constantly on the beloved young man. and deep inside me I hardly knew what an end I was demanding for myself from such a fervent love. How many times, wishing to see him closer to me, did I blame him for staying in back of the others and interpret as indifference what he was doing out of caution! The young men standing in front of him also annoyed me, because as I sometimes looked past them at the object of my interest, some of them thought that my gaze alighted on them and believed that it was they whom I loved. But while my mind was dwelling on these matters, the solemn ceremony had ended and my friends were already standing and about to leave when I became aware of this and recalled my soul to myself, which was wandering around the image of the young man I liked so much. Then I too stood up with the other ladies, and when I turned my eyes towards him, I seemed to perceive in his gestures what I was about to show him in mine, and in fact I indicated that it was painful for me to leave. Nevertheless, after a sigh or two and without knowing who he was, I left.

Ah, merciful ladies, who would believe it possible for a heart to change at once in such a manner? Who would say that one could love so desperately at first sight a person never seen before? Who would think that the desire to see such a person could flare up so much merely by desiring to see him that upon losing sight of him, one would feel the deepest grief? Who would ever imagine that everything which had been pleasing in the past would become worthless when compared to this new thing? Surely no one can understand this except someone who has experienced it—or is experiencing it, as I am. Alas, just as Love is now showing unheard-of cruelty toward me, so when he first caught me, it pleased him to use a different rule from the one he used with other people. I have often heard that in people his delights are at first very slight but that later they become stronger and more serious as they are nourished by thought, but this did not happen to me; on the contrary, such pleasures entered my heart with the same strength they had later, and still have now. On the very first day Love took complete possession of me; what happened to me is exactly what happens to green wood, which catches fire with great difficulty but, once lit, burns longer and with more intense heat. I had never been overcome by any pleasure before although many had tempted me, but I was ultimately conquered by one and I burned, and still burn; and I tended, and still tend, this fire more than any other woman ever did before, now that it has been kindled.

Leaving aside the many thoughts I had in mind that morning, as well as other incidents besides those mentioned, I will only say that I returned to the place where my soul used to be free, burning with a new passion and with a new soul now enslaved. Once I found myself alone and idle in my room, I felt moved by various desires, full of new ideas, and excited by innumerable concerns which had as their only object the image of the beloved youth; and I thought that if love could not be put to flight I should at least keep it hidden in my wretched heart; no one can know how difficult this is unless one has tried it; indeed, I believe that it is no less troubling than love itself. Firm in such a resolution but not knowing yet with whom I was in love, I told myself that deep inside me I was in love.

It would take too long to try to describe the nature and extent of the ideas which this love generated in me, but I feel nearly compelled to describe some of them, along with other matters that began to give me more delight than previously. So I will say that after I set aside everything else, only the thought of the beloved young man was dear to me; and since I felt that, as I persisted in this, what I intended to hide might be suspected, I frequently reproached myself. But what was the use? My own scoldings left ample room for my desires, and since they were ineffectual they flew off like the wind. For several days I felt an intense desire to know who the beloved young man was; new information made this possible, and I prudently learned his identity, to my great pleasure. I also began to appreciate the ornaments of apparel which I had disdained in the past, having thought that I had little need of them, and I now felt that the more adorned I was, the more admired I would be; therefore, I valued clothing, gold, pearls, and other precious things more than before. Until then, I had gone to the temples, to social gatherings, to the seashore, and to the gardens, with no other thought in mind than to meet with my lady-friends, but now I began to seek out such places with a new wish in mind, believing that I could see and be seen to my delight. To tell the truth, however, I lost the confidence I used to have in my beauty; and never did I leave my room without first having the trusted advice of my mirror: my hands, guided by some unknown teacher, each day found prettier ornamentations by which to add art to my natural charms and make me the most splendid of all women.

I also began wanting (as if they were my right) the homages the other ladies had in the past offered me spontaneously, although they may also have been appropriate to my nobility; and I thought that if I appeared magnificent to my lover, he would have more reason to appreciate me; the avarice innate in women fled from me, and I was left in such a state that I regarded my own things as if they were not mine and I became prodigal; my daring increased, and my feminine reserve diminished, since I foolishly believed that I had become rather more precious than before; and besides all of this, whereas up to that time my eyes had been used to gazing around innocently, they now changed their ways and became wondrously artificial in their behavior. Many other changes in addition to these became evident in me; but I shall not take the trouble to describe them all, both because it would take too long and because I believe that you who are as much in love as I am know how many and what kinds of changes take place in anyone put in such a situation.

As experience proved many times, he was a shrewd young man. As if he too had reached the same decision as I had, namely, to conceal all amorous feelings, he rarely and very decorously approached wherever I was and was very discreet in looking at me. Of course, I would be belying the truth if I denied that whenever I chanced to see him, Love (although already more powerful in me than anything else could be) forced my soul to grow as if he were enlarging it. He then made the flames which he had already kindled in me burn more brightly; and whatever ones, if any, had been dead he lit anew; but in this matter the beginning was never so joyful that the end was any the less wretched whenever I was deprived of his sight, so that my eyes, deprived of what made them happy, caused my heart to ache and my sighs to become greater in number and intensity, and since desire occupied nearly all my feelings, it estranged me from myself, as if I had forgotten where I was, so that I often astonished those who saw me and accounted for such incidents in deceptive ways suggested by Love himself. And besides this, Love frequently deprived me of nightly quietude and daily nourishment; he led me to utter strange words and made me do things that were mad rather than just impulsive.

Eventually my growing affectation, deep sighs, strange behavior, wild gestures, restlessness, and all the other changes provoked in me by this new love astonished one of the household servants, a nursemaid of mine, old in years and not young in wisdom, who, already knowing within herself about the wicked flames of love but pretending to be ignorant of them, scolded me more than once for my changed behavior.

But finally one day, she found me as I was lying melancholy on my bed and saw my brow burdened with cares; as soon as she noticed that we were alone, she said to me:

"My daughter, dear to me as my own self, what has been bothering you lately? You don't even get through an hour without sighing, whereas before I used to see you always cheerful and free from all melancholy."

Then, after a deep sigh, as my face changed from one color to another more than once, I pretended to be asleep and not to have heard her, and tossing back and forth to gain time for a response, hardly able to bring my tongue to form a word correctly, I finally answered:

"Dear nurse, nothing unusual is bothering me, and I am no more sensitive than I normally am; what makes me more pensive is only the natural ebb and flow of things which keeps people from being always the same."

"Surely you are deceiving me, my dear girl," answered the old nurse, "and you do not realize how serious it is to make elderly people believe one thing in words and show something else in deeds; there is no need to hide from me what I have clearly recognized in you for several days now."

Alas, when I heard this, with a mixture of grief, hope, and worry I replied:

"Then, if you know it, what are you asking for? One needs to hide only what one knows."

"Indeed," she said then, "I will hide what others are not allowed to know; and may the earth open up and swallow me before I reveal anything that brings you shame; long ago I learned to keep secrets. So rest assured, and be careful to keep anyone else from learning that which I recognized from your countenance without being told by you or by others. But if you cannot avoid that folly into which I see you have fallen, and if you were as shrewd as you used to be, I would leave you alone to worry about it, quite sure that my advice would be out of place. But because that cruel tyrant to whom you—being young and unwary—have naïvely submitted yourself usually deprives one of discernment as well as freedom, I want to remind you and beg you to uproot and banish all wickedness from your chaste heart, to stifle these dishonorable flames, and not to become a slave to the basest of hopes. Now is the time to resist with all your might, because those who have strongly opposed this mean kind of love from the beginning have banished it and stood secure and triumphant, but for those who nourish it with lingering thoughts and enticements it will be too late to reject the yoke to which they have almost willingly submitted."

"Alas," I replied, "how much more easily are these things said than done!"

"Even if they are difficult," she retorted, "they are nevertheless possible and should be done. Consider whether you wish to risk losing, because of this one thing, the nobility of your family, your reputation for virtue, the flower of your beauty, the respect of this world, and all the other things that a noble lady must hold dear, above all the good will of that husband whom you love and who loves you so well. Of course, you must not want this, nor do I believe that you do want it, if you give yourself wise counsel. So, for God's sake, stop yourself and banish those false delights promised by filthy hope, and with them the passion that has seized you. In the name of this bosom, old and weary from so many cares, from which you drew your first nourishment, I beg you to take care of yourself; look after your reputation, and do not refuse my advice in this matter; keep in mind that a good part of health is the desire to be cured."

Then I began:

"My dear nurse, I realize that what you say is true, but this madness constrains me to follow worse things, and my conscious mind craves your advice, but in vain because of its uncontainable desires; the dictates of reason are overcome by this ruling madness. Love takes possession of our entire mind, and lords it over us with his divinity, and you know that it is not safe to resist his powers."

After saying this, I fell forward on my arms, nearly exhausted. But my nurse, much more troubled than before, said more sternly:

"You are all nothing but a mob of senseless young women burning with a fiery lust, and being driven by it you have discovered that Love is a god who should more appropriately be called madness, but you call him the son of Venus and say that his powers come from the third heaven,[4] as if you wished to plead necessity as an excuse for your folly. You are all mistaken and entirely out of your minds! What are you saying? This being, who is moved by an infernal fury and visits all lands in his swift flight, is no god but a madness in anyone who accepts him, although he mostly calls on people who enjoy an overabundance of worldly pleasures and whose empty minds he knows are ready to receive him; and this is very clear to us.

"Now don't we often see the most blessed Venus dwelling in very modest homes, useful for the exclusive fulfillment of our own procreation? We do indeed, but he who is called Love by reason of his madness is always craving wanton things and goes only where a prosperous fortune is present. Scorning the food and clothing that merely suffice for nature's needs, he encourages delicate meals and splendid apparel and mixes his poisons with them, thus taking hold of naughty souls; and since he prefers to cultivate lofty dwellings, he is rarely or never found in poor homes because he is a pestilence that chooses only refined places as being better suited to the purpose of his evil operations. We see healthy affection in humble people; but everywhere the wealthy, with their resplendent riches, are insatiable in this as they are in other things and always seek more than is necessary, and the powerless always desire the power of the very powerful; and I see that you are one of these wealthy people yourself, my very unlucky young woman, for your excessive well-being has brought you into a shameful and new kind of trouble."

After having listened to her for a long while, I said:

"Be quiet, old woman, do not speak against the gods. Because by now you are incapable of such responses, and are accordingly rejected by everyone, you speak almost deliberately against him, blaming what you once enjoyed. If other women, more famous, wiser, and more powerful than I am, have called him and still call him Love, I cannot rename him; I am truly his subject,

4. third heaven. In Dante's *Paradiso* the sphere or realm of Venus.

whatever the reason for this may be, and whether he is my happiness or ruin, there is nothing more I can do. My forces have often opposed his own, but having been vanquished, they have retreated. Therefore, the only end to my sorrows rests either in death or in the man I desire, and you should lessen such pains by giving counsel and help (and I beg you to do so), or desist from aggravating them by finding fault with the one toward whom my soul, unable to do anything else, tends with all its might."

So, indignant, and deservedly so, without answering me and muttering I know not what to herself, she walked out of the room, leaving me all alone.

My dear nurse, whose advice unfortunately I had spurned, had already left without a word, when I found myself alone with her words churning in my troubled heart, and although my judgment was already blinded, I felt that her words were fruitful and began having doubts about what I had assertively told her I wanted to pursue; with an uncertain mind and full of regrets, I was already thinking about the possibility of deciding to let go of things that are justifiably considered dangerous, and wanted to call her back to comfort me, but a new and sudden event dissuaded me from it, because in my secret bedchamber, coming from I know not where, a magnificent lady, surrounded by a light so bright that the sight could hardly bear it, offered herself to my view. Although she was still standing silently before me, I focused my eyes as sharply as the light allowed, until her lovely shape reached my consciousness; and I saw her naked, except for an extremely fine purple veil which covered some parts of her pure white body so scantily, to be no more an obstacle to my admiring gaze than if it were an image placed under glass; and her head, with hair that surpassed the brightness of gold as much as our own golden hair surpasses the blondest, was covered by a garland of green myrtle beneath whose shadow I saw two eyes of incomparable beauty, extremely enchanting to behold, which sent forth a marvelous light, and the rest of her face was so beautiful that no other like it can be found on earth.[5] She said nothing, but perhaps pleased with my

5. the rest of her face: *tutto l'altro viso,* literally, "the entire other face," perhaps an allusion to the two aspects of Venus, sacred and profane love.

admiration or observing the pleasure I derived by looking at her, little by little she uncovered more clearly her lovely aspects in that brilliant light, so that in her I experienced beauties impossible to express in words and inconceivable among mortals if not seen. When she realized that I had viewed her from all sides and saw me astounded by her beauty and her presence there, with a happy face and with a voice sweeter than our own human voice, she spoke to me in this way:

"Young woman, you are much more fickle than any other. What are you getting ready to do because of the advice of your old wet-nurse? Don't you know that it is much more difficult to follow such counsels than the very love you wish to avoid? Do you not realize how much and what kind of unbearable anxiety they will procure you? You are very foolish; you have just surrendered to us, but like someone still unaware of the quality and quantity of our pleasures you wish to run away from us. You unwise one, hold to your resolve, search our words and see whether what has been sufficient for the heavens and for the world is enough for you. Although Phoebus presides over the light of day from the moment he rises from the Ganges until he dives into Hesperia's waters to give rest to his weary chariot, he is under the power of our winged son,[6] along with everything that lies between cold Arcturus and the burning pole, without exception. And in the heavens not only is he a god unlike the others, but he is also more powerful than they are because there is not one of them that has not already been wounded by his weapons. With utmost ease he flies with his golden wings instantly throughout his domains and visits all of them, carrying his strong bow and fitting on to the stretched cord the arrows made and tempered in our waters; and when he summons to his service someone more worthy than others, he sends him in a flash wherever he wishes.

"He stirs the fiercest flames in the young, revives those extinguished in tired old people, and ignites with an unknown fire the pure hearts of virgins, and he equally warms wives and widows. In the past, after having inflamed the gods with his torches, he ordered them to leave the heavens and inhabit the earth in disguise. After all, was not Phoebus, who destroyed the great

6. our winged son: Cupid (see Glossary).

Python and tuned the zither of Parnassus, conquered more than once by him at sundry times through Daphne, Clymene, Leucothoe, and many others? He certainly was! And finally, enamored and with his splendor shut into the paltry form of a young shepherd, he tended the flocks of Admetus.

"Jupiter himself, ruler of the heavens, was forced by Love to assume a lesser form. Once, in the shape of a white bird fluttering its wings, he made sounds sweeter than those of the dying swan; another time he became a horned bull and bellowed through the fields, lowered his back for a frolicking virgin,[7] and by using his cloven hooves as oars, he kept himself afloat with his powerful chest as he swam to his brother's kingdom, where he enjoyed his prey. Let us not mention (for it would take too long) what he did with Semele in his own shape, with Alcmene by becoming Amphitryon, with Callisto by changing into Diana, with Danae by transforming himself into gold. Under Love's power, the fierce god of battles whose bloodiness still frightens the giants,[8] tempered his harsh effects and became a lover. And Jupiter's blacksmith,[9] who is accustomed to fire and is the maker of the three-pronged lightning, was cooked by the more powerful fire of Love. And we too, although we are his mother, could not defend ourselves from him, as the tears we shed for Adonis' death well demonstrate. But why do we labor with so many words? There is no god in the heavens who has not been wounded by him except Diana, who alone escaped from him by amusing herself in the forests, although, according to some, she did not actually escape but kept her love hidden.

"However, if in your diffidence you shun the examples of the heavens and look for someone who may have had such experiences in the world, there are so many that we need only choose where to begin, but we can truly tell you this much: they have all been heroic. Let us first look at the very strong son of Alcmena,[10] who after having set aside the arrows and the frightening skin of the great lion, tolerated having his fingers adorned with green emeralds and his untidy mane groomed and who,

---

7. frolicking virgin: Europa (see Glossary).
8. fierce god of battles: Mars (see Glossary).
9. Jupiter's blacksmith: Vulcan (see Glossary).
10. son of Alcmena: Hercules (see Glossary).

with the same hand that had earlier carried the hard club and killed the great Antaeus, dragged out the infernal dog,[11] spun the woolen thread fed by Iole onto the turning spindle; and his shoulders, which had carried the high heavens while Atlas changed sides, were first embraced by Iole's arms and then, to please her, were draped in sheer purple garments. Everyone knows what Paris did because of Love, or Helen, or Clytemnestra, or Aegisthus; and the same is true of Achilles, Scylla, Ariadne, Leander, Dido, and many more I need not mention. It is a holy and very powerful fire, believe me!

"Now that you have heard that my son conquered heaven and earth through gods and people, what have you to say of his powers which extend to reasonless creatures in the skies and on land? Because of him the female turtledove follows her mate, and our own female doves keep after their mates with the warmest affection, and not one would ever break this habit; in the forests the shy deer become ferocious with one another when touched by him and fight for the desired doe, bellowing and showing signs of Love's heat; in their rage, the cruel boars foam at the mouth and point their ivory tusks; and touched by love, the African lions shake their manes. But, if we leave the wilderness, I can say that even the cold waters of a multitude of sea gods and running rivers feel the effect of our son's arrows. And we do not believe that you ignore the proof which Neptune, Glaucus, and Alpheus have given of it, since they were unable to dampen, let alone extinguish his flame with the wetness of their waters; and such a flame, already experienced by everyone on the earth and in the waters, also came to penetrate the earth, making itself felt even by the king of the dark marshes.[12]

"Therefore, heaven, earth, sea, and the underworld have known through direct experience the weapons of Love, but in order for me to encompass in a few words all there is to say about his power, I will say that while all things are subjected to Nature and no power is free from her, Nature herself is under the power of Love. When he orders it, ancient hatreds are quelled, old angers and novel ones retreat before his fire, and fi-

11. infernal dog: Cerberus (see Glossary).
12. king of the dark marshes: Pluto (see Glossary).

nally, his power is so widespread that at times it makes step-mothers kind towards their step-children, and this is no small wonder! So, what are you looking for? What are your doubts? What are you running away from so madly? If so many gods, so many men, and so many animals have been conquered by him, will you be ashamed to be conquered by him? You do not know what you are doing to yourself! If you expect to be reprimanded for submitting yourself to him, do not let it become our concern, because a thousand greater failures justify you, for you, who have failed in a small measure and are less powerful than those just mentioned, have but followed your betters in their footsteps.

"But if these words do not stir you, and you still want to resist, remember that your power is unlike that of Jupiter, nor can you be equal to Phoebus in intellect, nor to Juno in riches, nor to us in charms, and all of us are vanquished. Do you believe that you alone can win? You deceive yourself and in the end you will also lose. Let what has been enough for the whole world be enough for you, and do not become indifferent to this by saying: 'I have a husband, and the sacred laws, as well as the promised faith, forbid me these things,' because these are very empty arguments against Love's power. Since he is the strongest, he annuls the laws of others by disregarding them and gives his own. Pasiphaę, Phaedra, and I too still had a husband when we fell in love. Husbands themselves most of the time fall in love while they have a wife; look at Jason, Theseus, the strong Hector,[13] and Ulysses. Therefore, it is not an offense if they are treated according to the same rules by which they treat others; they are not given more privileges than women, so let go of these foolish thoughts and love confidently as you have begun doing. In sum, if you do not wish to be subjected to this powerful Love, you should run away, but where will you run so that he may not follow you and reach you? He has the same power everywhere; wherever you go you are in his domains, where no one whom he wishes to wound can ever hide from him.

"Be it enough for you, young woman, that he did not molest you with a wicked fire as he did with Myrrha, Semiramis, Byblis,

---

13. Hector. The presence of Hector's name among a list of unfaithful men is perplexing.

Canace, and Cleopatra. Our son will not do anything new to you; like any other god, he too has rules which you are not the first to follow (nor must you hope to be the last). If at present you believe you are alone, you believe in vain. Let us not even consider the rest of the world, which is full of people like you; just look at your own city, which can show you an infinite number of women like you, and remember that nothing which is done by many people can rightly be called disgraceful. Then follow us and give thanks to our much admired beauty and true godliness, for we have drawn you out from among innocent women to learn the pleasure of our gifts."

Ah, compassionate ladies, may Love happily fulfill your wishes! What could I do or what answer could I give but, "May it be as you wish" to such and so many words, and from such a goddess? Thus, I say that she no sooner became silent than, having gathered her words in my mind and feeling within myself that they were full of innumerable "reasons,"[14] and being already acquainted with her, I prepared myself to do her bidding. I immediately rose from bed, kneeled down with a humble heart, and began timidly:

"Oh, remarkable and eternal beauty! Oh, celestial goddess, only mistress of my mind, whose power is felt more fiercely by those who most resist it, forgive me for innocently resisting the weapons of your son, who is unknown to me; do with me as you wish and as you promised: reward my fidelity at the proper time and place so that by praising you among other women, I will infinitely increase the number of your subjects."

I had no sooner pronounced these words than she moved from where she was and, most fervently desirous in her appearance, kissed my forehead and embraced me. Then, as the false Ascanius kindled Dido's hidden flames by breathing into her mouth, she too, by breathing into mine, made me feel my original desires more intensely. By opening her wide purple mantle, she showed me the image of my beloved young man in her arms between her delicate breasts and enveloped in her thin veil, and with concerns not unlike mine, she said:

---

14. innumerable "reasons": *infinite scuse*. The word *scuse* could mean excuses as well as reasons or arguments. The quotation marks suggest the ironic tone of this sentence.

"Look at him, young woman; we have not given you as a lover a Lyssa, or a Geta, or a Byrria, or someone like them; in every respect he is worthy to be loved by any goddess; as we wished, he loves you more than he loves himself, and he always will; so surrender, trustful and joyful to his love. Your pious prayers sound worthy to our ears, so hope that what you do will be rewarded without fail according to its merit."

Then without saying another word, she suddenly disappeared from my view.

Oh, miserable that I am! Seeing what followed, I do not doubt that she who appeared before me was not Venus but Tisiphone, who after concealing her horrible hair, just as Juno concealed the luminosity of her godliness, and after assuming a splendid form, as Juno assumed an elderly one, she appeared before me as that goddess appeared before Semele, offering similar and ultimately destructive advice, in which I unfortunately believed, and this made me turn against you, most merciful Faith, reverend Shame, and most holy Chastity, unique and precious treasure of virtuous women. But if penance given to and borne by the sinner can sometimes obtain forgiveness, do forgive me.

After the goddess had disappeared from my sight, I remained wholeheartedly inclined towards her pleasures, and because the furious passion I was experiencing deprived me of all judgment—I do not know through what fault of mine—I was left with only one of the many gifts I had lost, that is, to know that seldom or never is a happy ending granted to openly revealed love. But as one of my foremost thoughts (although very difficult to put into effect) I decided I would not subject to rational judgment my wish to carry such a desire to the end. Of course, while I was often very strongly constrained through various incidents, I was blessed with enough strength to withstand this anxiety like a man, without trespassing the limit.

In all truth, I have still enough strength to comply with this decision, because even though I am writing things that are very true, I have arranged them in such a way that, except for the one who knows everything as well as I do (for he is the cause of them all), no one else, no matter how sharp his intellect, could discover who I am. If by chance this little book should fall into the former's hands, I beg him, in the name of the love he felt for me, to hide what could bring him neither benefit nor honor if it were revealed. And even if he had deprived me of himself without my deserving it, may he not want to take away from me that reputation which, even though undeserved by me, he could never give back, just as he could never give himself back to me, even if he wanted to.

So, trying to be true to my intention, and to control my desires, which were urgently pressing to manifest themselves, and heavily burdened by sorrow because of it, I did all I could (but secretly and whenever I had the opportunity) to kindle in the young man those same flames that were burning in me and to make him as cautious as I was. And indeed, this did not take much effort on my part, because if it is true that appearance reflects the quality of the heart, I soon understood that my wish had had its effect, and I noticed with great pleasure that he was filled not only with burning love but also with perfect caution. Fully aware and anxious to protect my virtue and fulfill his desires whenever time and place would allow it, he did his best (and, I believe, not without great trouble and by using much cunning) to become familiar with anyone related to me and ultimately with my husband; and not only did he succeed in this, but he also achieved it with so much charm that no one took a liking to anything unless they consulted him about it. How this pleased me I believe you know without my writing it; in fact, what woman could be so naïve as not to believe that it was especially from such familiarity that the opportunity arose for him to speak with me and I with him in public from time to time?

Since he thought that the time had finally come for more subtle things, whenever he noticed that I could hear and understand him, he spoke with one person or another of things that taught me (and I was very eager to learn) that an affection for others can be demonstrated and reciprocated not only through speech but also through various gestures and facial expressions, and since I enjoyed this immensely, I understood him so keenly that there was nothing whose meaning he wanted to make known to me and I to him that we would not conveniently make understandable to each other. Not fully satisfied with this, by speaking figuratively he managed to teach me to speak in the same way; and in order to be sure that I understood his desires even better, he named me Fiammetta and himself Panfilo. Oh, how often in my presence and even before my dearest ones, inebriated with gaiety, love, and food, pretending that Fiammetta and Panfilo were a Greek couple, he recounted the manner in which we had been taken with one another, along with all the incidents that had followed, giving convenient names to places and people in the story! Indeed, I often laughed at this, and no less at his cleverness than at the innocence of the listeners; and many times I also feared that too much heat would inadvertently carry his tongue where it did not want to go, but he was shrewder than I thought, and he guarded himself very astutely from telltale language.[15]

Most compassionate ladies, is there anything that Love does not teach his subjects and which he does not make them capable of learning? I was a very innocent young woman barely able to speak of simple and concrete matters with my women friends when I picked up his manner of speaking with such enthusiasm that in a short time I could have outdone any poet in speech and fiction; and once I understood his approach, there were few things to which I could not give a proper answer by inventing a fictitious story.

I have recounted many things which in my opinion are difficult to learn and for a young woman harder to put into practice, but they might seem utterly trivial and of no account if, the present subject demanding it, I were the one to write about the subtle cunning with which we tested the fidelity of an intimate servant of mine to whom we had decided to entrust the secret fire we were still hiding from everyone else, feeling that, there being no other way, it could not have been kept secret for long without the greatest of efforts. Besides this, it would take a long time to tell of the many different tactics we both used in various matters, tactics which I believe may never have been put into practice or even have been conceived by anyone else before; and although I am now aware that they have been used to my own detriment, I do not regret having learned all of them.

If my imagination is not mistaken, my ladies, our hearts' courage was not small, if we consider with full consciousness how difficult it is for two young minds in love to endure being

---

15. telltale language: *falso latino,* a traditional phrase denoting an error or blunder.

pushed about for a long time, driven by overwhelming desires, and not deviate from the path of reason; on the contrary, this courage was such, and so great that the strongest men would receive worthy and high praise for doing the same.

But my pen, less honest than graceful,[16] is about to write of those ultimate limits of love which no one is given the power to surpass in desire or deed.[17] However, before reaching that point, I invoke, as humbly as I possibly can, your compassion and that loving power which draws your desires to such an end by dwelling in your tender hearts, and I beg both these feelings to rise immediately in my defense, if what I am saying sounds serious to you—of the deed itself I make no mention, since I know that if you have not done it, you wish to do it. And you, honest Shame, whom I have known so late, forgive me, and I earnestly beg you to leave timid women alone so that, not threatened by you and trusting in me, they would read about what they desire for themselves when loving.

His desire and my own made each day drag on one after the other, tense with expectation, and each of us bore this with bitterness because one would show it to the other by speaking cryptically, and the other would appear extremely disdainful, just as you ladies do, who may be looking for the strength to do what you would like to do most and which you know women who are loved usually do. Thus, somewhat mistrustful of me in this matter, and more lucky than wise in what happened to him and with more impudence than talent, he found a convenient time and place and obtained from me that which I wanted just as much as he did, although I feigned the contrary. Surely, if this were the reason for my loving him, I would confess to feeling a sorrow unlike any other every time this came back into my mind; but (and may God be my witness in this) this incident was and is the least important reason for the love I carry for him; however, I don't deny that I cherished it then, as I do now.

And what woman would be so unwise as not to want something she adores close by rather than far away? And the greater

---

16. my pen, less honest than graceful: *la mia penna, meno onesta che vaga.* The phrase directly conflicts with the view of her own writing which Fiammetta expresses elsewhere in the work of being an unpolished but truthful story teller.

17. ultimate limits of love: *ultimi termini d'amore. Termini* can mean, among other things, "limits," "words," or "phrases."

the love, would she not wish it all the closer? I say then, that after such an event, which in the past I had imagined but had never experienced, and under these circumstances, fate and our wits helped us to solace ourselves at length and with immense pleasure not once but many times, although it seems to me now that the time then flew by faster than any wind. But while we were living those happy moments, as Love, whom I can offer as my only witness, can truly tell, he was never allowed to come to me without fear, since he came to me only in secret. Oh how he adored my chamber and how cheerfully it always welcomed him! I have seen him revere it more than any temple. Oh how many tender kisses and amorous embraces, and how many nights were spent talking more than if it were daytime, and how many pleasures, dear to each lover, we had there during those joyful hours! Oh most blessed Shame, most obdurate obstacle to dreaming minds, why don't you go away when I implore you to do so? Why do you hold back my pen, which is ready to show the gifts received in such a way that, fully described and compared to the unhappiness that followed, they would be more powerful in arousing pity for me in loving hearts?

Alas, how you offend me, O Shame, believing perhaps that you are helping me! I wish to say more, but you do not allow it. Therefore, those women who are so endowed by nature to understand those things left unsaid by the things that have been said should reveal them to the ones who are not so wise. But no one may call me foolish as if I did not know that much, because I know quite well that it would have been more honest to keep silent than to reveal what I am writing; but who can resist Love when he opposes you with all his strength?

At this point I have put down my pen several times, but harassed by him, I picked it up again, and ultimately the one whom I was unable to resist when I was still free decided that I should obey as a servant. And he also taught me to prize concealed delights as much as the treasures hidden inside the earth. But why do I revel so much in these words? Let me say that at the time I repeatedly thanked the blessed goddess who had promised and granted those pleasures. Oh, how many times, crowned with her leafy branches, I offered incense at her altars, and how often I blamed the advice of my old nurse! And besides this, being happier than all my women friends, I made fun of their love affairs, reproving with words what was most dear to my heart, and frequently saying to myself:

"No one is loved as much as I am or has as worthy a lover as I have, or gathers as joyfully the fruits of love as I do!"

In brief, I took no notice of the world and seemed to be touching the sky with my head, for I believed that I lacked nothing to reach supreme bliss, except being free to show openly the reason for my happiness, for I was convinced deep inside that whatever pleased me had to be pleasing to everyone else. But you, O Shame, on the one hand, and you, Fear, on the other, held me back by threatening me, one with eternal disgrace, the other with the loss of what was later taken away by adverse Fortune. So, as was Love's wish, loving happily and not envying any other woman, I spent more of my time utterly fulfilled and not considering that the pleasure I was then wholeheartedly enjoying would be the root and seed of future misery, as I, now fruitlessly, am painfully aware.

TWO

In which Lady Fiammetta tells why her lover left her and describes his departure and the suffering it caused her.

As I whiled away my time in the pleasant and delightful life I have just described, dearest ladies, giving little thought to future things, my inimical Fortune was surreptitiously mixing her poisons and pursuing me with relentless animosity, though I was utterly unaware of it. As if it were not enough for her to have made me a servant of Love after I had been my own woman, when she saw that I was already enjoying such servitude, she strove to afflict my soul with more stinging nettles. As you will soon hear, when the time which she was awaiting had arrived, she prepared for me those poisons that I had to swallow against my will, and that changed my joy into sadness and my sweet laughter into bitter tears. Not only while undergoing the experiences but also whenever I think that I must reveal them to others in writing, I am assailed by such self-pity that it drains nearly all my strength away and brings innumerable tears to my eyes, scarcely allowing me to carry on with my task, which I shall do my best to accomplish, no matter how badly.

As it happened, when the weather was tediously cold and rainy, the two of us were in my bedchamber resting together in my sumptuous bed while the night was silently paying one of its longest visits[1]; and since we had already exhausted Venus, the goddess, who was nearly vanquished, offered us a brief respite: his eyes took delight in my loveliness as my own did in his by the light of a great fire lit at one end of the room. But as I was talking of this and that, my eyes drank too much of that sweetness and their sight was nearly inebriated by it and they were—I know not how—surreptitiously overcome by a sleep which stole away my speech, and for a short time my eyes remained shut. When sleep vanished as gently as it had come, my ears

---

1. the night was silently paying one of its longest visits. It is near the winter solstice (December 22).

heard my darling lover's moaning whispers, and because I was immediately concerned for his well-being, I wanted to ask, "What is troubling you?" But a new idea silenced me, and I kept quiet, watching him carefully and keenly, and for some time I listened to him with a sharp ear as he lay on the other side of our bed with his back to me. But my ears could not catch any of his words, although I knew that he was sobbing desperately and breathlessly with his face and chest alike covered with tears.

Alas, as I watched him in such a condition, what words can express adequately what happened to my soul, not knowing the reason for it? In one instant a thousand thoughts raced through my mind, and almost all reached one and the same conclusion, namely, that he loved another woman and remained in his present condition against his will. More than once it was on the tip of my tongue to ask what troubled him, but fearing that he would feel ashamed that I had found him weeping, I swallowed my words; and several times I turned my eyes away from him so that their burning tears would not fall and give him cause to know that I was observing him. Impatient as I was, I thought of innumerable ways to make him believe that, although I was awake, I had not heard him, yet none was satisfactory. But finally I was so eager to learn the source of his weeping that in order to make him turn towards me, I did what people do when in a dream they are frightened by a fall or by a cruel beast or by anything else: they suddenly shake themselves in fear and break off dream and sleep at the same time; so in that fashion I suddenly shook myself, and speaking in a fearful voice I threw one of my arms over his shoulders. And to be sure, the deception succeeded, for he forgot his tears, and feigning cheerfulness, he turned quickly toward me and said in a compassionate tone:

"Beautiful soul of mine, what were you afraid of?"

To which I answered without hesitation:

"I seemed to be losing you."

Alas, I know not what spirit forced these words out of me, which were an omen and a truthful herald of the future. But he replied:

"My young beloved, nothing but death could make you lose me."

These words were immediately followed by a deep sigh, and no sooner did I hear it and inquire about it (since I wished to know the reason for his original lament) than an abundant flow of tears began falling from his eyes—as if from two fountains—and onto his chest that had not yet dried, soaking it even more; and he was sobbing so hard that he kept me in suspense for a long time, during which time I was in great pain and in tears, before he could answer my many questions. When finally he felt somewhat relieved by the rush of his emotion, with words often broken by tears he answered me this way:

"My dearest and most beloved lady, as my reaction clearly shows you, if my tears deserve some trust, you must believe that I do not weep so profusely without a dire reason: whenever there returns to my mind the thought I had just now while I was here with you in such joy, namely, that I cannot divide myself into two as I would like to do, so as to satisfy at once the demands of Love by staying here and of proper compassion by going where a compelling need forces me to go. Since this is impossible, my deeply afflicted heart aches, as does the heart of one who on the one hand is pulled and dragged out of your arms by compassion and, on the other, is held in them with the greatest force by Love."

These words entered my wretched heart with a bitterness I had never felt before, and although my mind had not yet fully comprehended them, the more they were taken in by my ears, which were attentive to their destructiveness, the more they transformed themselves into tears and poured out of my eyes, leaving, however, their poisonous effect in my heart. This was the first time I felt pains so very contrary to my pleasure; this was the time that saw me shed the kind of tears I never had wept before; and none of his words nor any consoling gestures (of which he had many) could restrain me.

But after I had wept bitterly for a long time and as much as I could, I begged him again to explain more clearly what kind of compassion was taking him away from my embraces, at which he said, without ceasing to weep:

"Inexorable death, which is the ultimate end of human things, has recently left me the only survivor among my father's several sons; he is old and without a wife, and I am the only one of my brothers left to care for him; he is also without hope of having other children and is calling me back to see him since he has not seen me for several years, and to be of comfort to him.

For several months I have found various kinds of pretexts to avoid leaving you, but lately he has become unwilling to accept any of them, and he continually implores me to go see him for the sake of my childhood, when I was tenderly raised on his knees, the love he has always felt towards me and that which I must feel for him, the filial obedience I owe him, and every other weighty consideration that could be thought of. Besides this, he pressures me through the formal pleas of friends and relatives, saying that his grieving and disconsolate soul will abandon his body if he does not see me. Alas, how strong the laws of nature are! There was and still is nothing I could do to keep this compassion from becoming lodged amidst my great love for you; and so because my mind is made up to go see him, with your permission, and to stay with him and comfort him for a short time, I keep weeping with good reason whenever I recall this intention, since I do not know how I can live without you."

And here, he fell silent.

If among you ladies whom I am addressing there was ever one to whom such a thing has happened while deeply in love, she alone will, I hope, be able to understand what was my sadness then; to the others I shall not try to explain it, since any other example besides the one I gave would be insufficient for us, as would any further talking. I will simply say that when I heard these words, my Soul tried to run away from me, and I believe that she would have undoubtedly done so had she not felt embraced by the one she loved above all else, but left nonetheless afraid and filled with heavy sorrow, she deprived me of the capacity to say anything for a long time. But then she slowly became accustomed to feeling this unprecedented grief and restored to my wretched senses their timid powers so that my eyes, which had become transfixed, wept abundantly and my tongue was able to form some words. And so I turned toward the master of my life, and said:

"O my mind's ultimate hope, may my words enter your soul with a force that will alter its decision, so that if you love me as you say, your life and mine will not be driven from this wretched world before the allotted time has come. Torn between pity and love, you cast doubts on the future; of course, if you spoke the truth in the past when not just once but many times you affirmed that you loved me, no other kind of devotion should be able to resist such power and pull you elsewhere so long as I live, and now if you follow through with what you said you would do, it is clear to you in how much doubt you will leave my life since in the past I was barely kept alive during that time when I could not see you; therefore you can be sure that once you are gone all happiness will leave me. And if only that were all! Who can doubt that all sorts of melancholy will befall me, and perhaps—no, most certainly—will kill me? You must know by now how much strength there is in delicate young women to sustain such adversity with a toughmindedness. If perhaps you wish to argue that I faced greater adversities in the past when I loved both prudently and passionately, I would certainly agree in part, but the reason then was very different from the present one, since my hope rested in my own will and made it easier to bear what is now burdensome to me because of a dependence on someone else's will. Who denied me the right to have you even though my desire would have driven me beyond all limits, since we were so much in love with each other? No one, certainly, but this choice will not be mine if you are far away from me.

"Besides, although at that time I knew who you were only by sight, I thought much of you, but now I really know you, and I understand by what you can do that you are even more precious than my imagination showed me then, and you have become mine with that certainty women can feel for lovers they consider their own. Who can doubt that it is much more painful to lose what one now holds than that which one hopes to gain, even if the hope is likely to be fulfilled? But all things considered, my death can be very clearly foreseen. Therefore, it is your pity for your old father, placed before that pity you should feel for me, which will be the cause of my death, and if you do this, you will be an enemy instead of a lover. Alas, would you or could you, even if I allowed it, really put the few years of life still left to your father to live ahead of the many years I most likely have coming to me? Alas, what wicked pity would this be?

"Do you believe, Panfilo, that anyone, however closely he wants to be or can be joined to you in kinship or by ties of friendship, can love you as much as I do? If you believe that, you are wrong, because no one can indeed love you as much as I do. So if I love you more, I deserve more compassion; therefore, let me properly be your first choice, and by feeling sorry for me you may forget any other pity that may detract from this, and let your father remain without you; since he has lived without you for so long, let him continue to do so if it pleases him, and if not, let him die. If I understand correctly, he has escaped the mortal blow for many years and has lived longer than he should; and if he is weary of living, as old people are, it would be much more compassionate of you to let him die than to prolong his weary life through your presence.

"But I am the one who should be helped, since I have scarcely lived without you and would not know how to live without you, and because I am still very young, I expect to live many happy years with you. Oh, if your visit could have the same effect on your father that Medea's remedies had on Aeson, I would say that your devotion was right and, however reluctantly, would call for it to be carried out, but this will not be the case, and could not be, and you know it. So look, if you, who are perhaps more cruel than I believe, care so little about me (whom you loved and do love unconstrained and of your own free will) as to place ahead of your love for me this useless compassion for your old father (who is just as destiny gave him to you), at least feel more sorry for yourself than for me or for him, because, if first your looks and then your words did not deceive me, you seemed more dead than alive whenever by accident you spent any time without seeing me. Do you believe now that you can live without seeing me for as long as this untimely pity demands? Oh, for God's sake, look carefully and see that you are liable to be killed by this trip (if it is true that a man can die from prolonged grief, as I understand from the lives of others), since your tears and the fast and irregular heartbeat I hear in your worried breast show how painful it is to you; and if your death does not result from it, you will not fail to have a life worse than death.

"Alas, how my enamored heart is driven both to the pity I feel for myself and to the pity I feel for you simultaneously! For this reason, I beg you not to be so foolish as to choose to face a great danger to yourself, out of compassion for another person, no matter who it is. Keep in mind that he who does not love himself possesses nothing. Your father, for whom you now feel pity, did not put you into the world so that you should become the instrument for removing yourself from it. And who doubts that if it were possible for him to discover our situation, he would say, since he is wise, 'Remain' instead of 'Come'? And if discretion did not allow him that, pity would drive him to it, and I think that this is quite clear to you. If he knew our situation, it is reasonable to assume what his judgment would be; so it is also reasonable to pretend that he has known it and has made such a judgment, and because of this forget this departure, which is harmful to you and me alike.

"Of course, my beloved lord, the reasons I have just given are strong enough that they should be followed, and you should stay if you also consider where you are going, because since you are going where you were born, which is the place that one loves most of all but which (as I have already heard you say) you happen to find irritating because (as you yourself have also said) your city is full of pompous talk and cowardly deeds, is ruled not by a number of laws but by as many opinions as there are men, is torn by strife and war within and without, and is turbulent and filled with haughty, avaricious, and envious people and with innumerable troubles; and all these things are ill-suited to your spirit. I realize you know that this city you are about to leave is joyful, peaceful, rich, magnificent, and under a single ruler; and these are qualities (if I know you at all well) which are very pleasing to you. And in addition to all the things I have enumerated, I am here, and you will not find me anywhere else. Therefore, abandon this distressing project, change your mind, and take care of your life and mine while we stay together, I beg you."

My words had greatly increased his tears, many of which I swallowed, mixed with kisses; but after countless sighs he answered:

"O sublime good of my soul, I know that your words are true and exact, and I am aware of all the dangers you have recounted, but to answer you briefly (not as I wish but as the present need requires), I will say that I believe that you should allow me to repay a great debt with a brief sacrifice. You must believe and be certain that while I am duly and strongly pressed by the compassion I feel for my aged father, I am not less but much more strongly compelled by the pity I feel for ourselves which, if it were possible to reveal, I would seem to be justified (supposing that what you said were to be judged not just by my old father alone, but by everyone else) and because of which I could let my father die without his seeing me again. But since this kind of devotion must be kept hidden, I fail to see how I could fall short of fulfilling the demands of the kind that is visible, except with extreme criticism and shame.

"If I avoid such blame by doing my duty, Fortune will deprive us of three or four months of pleasure, after which (or even before they are over), you will see me here again without fail, to each other's joy. And if the place to which I am going is as unpleasant as you make it out to be (which it is if compared to this place, since you are here), you should be very pleased to think that if there were no other reason to make me leave there, I would be forced to leave and return here because of the characteristics of a place so hostile to my spirit. So allow me to go; and as you have been concerned with my reputation and well-being before, be patient now concerning this matter, so that because I am aware of how important this incident is for you, I will be more sure than ever before that you will value my reputation as you have valued me under any circumstances."

When he had finished speaking and was quiet, I began to speak up again in this manner:

"I see clearly what you hold fast in your inflexible mind, and it seems to me that in that mind of yours you hardly wish to take into consideration how many and what kinds of concerns you fill my soul with by leaving; no day, or night, or hour will be without a thousand fears; I will constantly worry about your life, which I pray God will extend in length beyond my own and for as long as you wish. Ah, why do I want to continue talking so much by enumerating such fears one by one? In brief, there are not as many grains of sand in the sea or stars in the sky as there are uncertainties and dangers that can happen each day to the living, and when you are gone, all of them will undoubtedly hurt and terrify me.

"Alas, how wretched my life is! I am ashamed to tell you what passes through my head, but because it seems almost possible from what I have heard, I am really obligated to tell you about it. If in your country (which I have often heard has innumerable beautiful and charming ladies ready to love and be loved) you should find one you like and forget me for her, what kind of life would I have then? Ah, if you love me as much as you claim, think of what you would do if I changed you for someone else! But this will never be, because I would certainly kill myself with my own hands before that could happen.

"But let us forget this, and not tempt the gods with some wretched forecast of something we do not wish to happen. If your mind is firmly set on leaving, it is necessary that I prepare myself to accept your departure, since nothing else pleases me more than to give you pleasure. But if it is possible, I beg you to do one thing that I wish, namely, that you let some time elapse before you leave, so that during such a time I could learn to endure being without you by imagining your departure and thinking about it constantly. And certainly this will not be difficult for you; even the weather is in my favor, since it is so foul at this time of the year. Do you not see the dark sky always threatening the earth with such calamities as rain, snow, winds, and terrifying thunder? And as you must know, every little brook has now become a great and mighty river because of the continual rain. Who would care so little about himself as to begin a journey in such weather? Therefore, please me in this matter, and if you do not want to, at least do your duty and let the uncertain weather pass; wait for a change, when your travelling will be smoother and less dangerous, and I shall by then be accustomed to melancholy thoughts and await your return more patiently."

Without hesitating to give an answer to these words, he said:

"Dearest girl, may the joyful hope of my future return soften the distressful suffering and the various troubles in which, against my liking, I am leaving you and all of which I am certainly carrying with me; but it is not wise to worry about something which, sooner or later, here or elsewhere, will come to me anyhow, that is, my death, or about future events that may be harmful or helpful. God's wrath or grace reaches man everywhere, and he must learn to bear the bad and the good, since he can do nothing else. So let these things rest in God's hands without worrying, since He knows our needs better than we do; only pray to Him that they turn out well. Love has bound my heart to your governance so powerfully that not even Jupiter could allow me ever to belong to another woman besides Fiammetta, even if I wanted to. And be sure of this because before Panfilo could belong to a woman other than you, the sky will be ploughed by oxen and produce ripened grain, and the earth will bear the stars.

"If I believed that you and I could derive some advantage from delaying my departure as you have asked, I would consent to it more promptly than you ask; but the longer the delay, the more we will suffer. If I leave now, I will be back before the time you have requested to learn to endure my absence; and in the meantime you will have the same suffering for my being away that you would endure from contemplating my imminent departure. And as for the bad weather, I will take suitable precautions against it, as I used to do at other times, and may God grant that I know how to do the same on my way back as I shall on leaving. Therefore, prepare yourself to accept this courageously, since when something must be done, it is better to do it at once and be done with it, rather than, wretched and fearful, to wait and do it later."

My tears, which had almost let up while I was talking, multiplied as I heard this answer, since I was expecting a different one; I placed my weary head on his chest, and resting silently for a long time, I considered various responses in my mind, not knowing whether to accept or deny what he was saying. But, alas, who would have answered those words other than by saying, "Do what you wish, as long as you come back soon"? No one, I believe. And after a long hesitation and not without much pain and many tears, I answered him that way, adding that it would certainly be a surprise if he were to find me alive when he returned.

After saying this, we comforted each other, dried our tears, and put an end to them that night. Before his departure, which took place a few days later, he kept to his usual habits and came back to see me several times, even though he found me much changed from before in appearance and disposition. But when that night arrived, which was to be the last of my pleasurable ones, we spent it in various talk and not without tears, and although it was one of the longest nights of the year because of the season, I had the impression it passed very quickly. And the daylight, that enemy of lovers, had already begun stealing away the starlight, and when the sign of its coming reached my ears, I embraced him tightly and said:

"My sweet lord, who is taking you away from me? Which god is turning his wrath against me with such force that it can be said while I am alive that Panfilo is not where his Fiammetta resides? Alas, I do not know where you are going! When will I ever embrace you again? I doubt that I ever will. I do not know what my darkly divining heart is telling me."

And so, comforted by him, I wept bitterly and kissed him several times. But after many tight embraces, each of us was reluctant to rise, but we did so, forced by the light of the new day. He was about to give me his final kisses when I began saying through my tears:

"You see, my lord, you are leaving, and you promise to return soon. So please, give me your solemn promise of this, so that your words may not seem futile to me and so that while I am waiting I may derive some comfort from this as if it were a future certainty."

Then, with his arms hanging heavily around my neck (I believe because of his weary spirit) and with his tears mixing with my own, he murmured:

"My lady, I swear to you by the brilliant Apollo, whose rays I await to guide me and who by rising now very rapidly causes all the sooner a departure contrary to our wishes; I also swear by the indissoluble love I bear for you, and by that filial devotion that separates me from you, that (almighty God permitting) not even four months will go by before you see me back here."

Then, after taking my right hand in his, he turned toward that corner of the room where the sacred images of our gods were seen to be represented, and said:

"Most holy gods, rulers of heaven and earth alike, be witness to this promise as well as to the oath I am making with my right hand; and you, Love, who know about these things, be our witness; and you, most beautiful bed chamber, more pleasing to me than the heavens are to the gods, as you have been the secret witness of our desires, also keep these words, and if I should break their promise by my fault, may the wrath of God fall on me, as in the past the anger of Ceres fell upon Erysichthon, that of Diana on Actaeon, or that of Juno on Semele."

After he said this, he impetuously embraced me and finally with a broken voice bade me farewell.

After he had spoken, I felt so miserable and so overcome by tears that I could hardly give any answer, but I forced my mouth to shape these wretched, tremulous words:

"May Jupiter confirm in the heavens, with the same effect that Telethusa's prayers to Isis had, the faith I just heard you promise and which was sworn with your right hand placed into mine, and may he make it whole on earth, as I wish and as you request."

Then I accompanied him as far as to the door of our palace, wishing to say, "Farewell," but suddenly my tongue could not speak and my eyes could not see the sky. As a rose cut by the scythe falls in the open fields under the green branches and loses its color even while it feels the sunlight, so I fell nearly lifeless into the arms of my maidservant,[2] and only after considerable time, helped by that faithful woman, did I feel that I was being called back to this wretched world by cold water; and thinking I was still at my door, I rose in a daze like an infuriated bull that rises and jumps wildly after receiving the mortal blow; hardly able to see, I ran and embraced my maid, believing that I was taking my lord into my arms, and with a faint voice broken into a thousand parts by tears I said:

"Farewell, my soul."

Aware of my error, my maid kept silent; but then when my eyes could see more clearly I became aware of my mistake and nearly fell into the same swoon again.

Every corner was illuminated by daylight, and when I realized I was in my room without Panfilo, I looked around for a long while not knowing how this had occurred, and when I asked the maid what had happened to him, she answered weeping:

"It is already a long time since he carried you here in his arms, and then the approaching daylight forced him to separate himself most tearfully from you."

So I asked:

"Then, he has already left?"

"Yes," my maid answered.

---

2. maidservant: *serva*. Not the nurse (*balia*) who appears earlier in this chapter and who will figure prominently in subsequent chapters.

And I continued:

"How did he look when he left? Distressed?"

To which she replied:

"I have never seen anyone more sorrowful." And I inquired further:

"What did he do? What did he say as he was leaving?"

And she replied:

"As soon as he saw you lying nearly dead in my arms, with your soul wandering I know not where, he took you gently into his arms, and with his hand on your breast he tried to find out whether your frightened soul was still with you,[3] and when he discovered your heart was beating fast, I believed that he called you in tears more than a hundred times to respond to his last kisses. But when he saw that you were as still as marble, he brought you here, and fearing the worst, several times he covered your face with tears and said, 'Most powerful gods, if there is any sin in my departure, may the punishment fall upon me and not on this innocent woman. Bring her lost soul back to where it belongs so that both of us may derive comfort from this pleasure, which is to say, that she should see me as I leave and give me some final kisses as she bids me farewell.'

"But when he realized that you were not recovering consciousness, he nearly lost his mind, and not knowing what to do, he put you gently on the bed, and like a sea wave tossed back and forth by wind and rain, he would leave you and reluctantly walk as far as to the doorway of the bed chamber, then would look through the windows at the threatening sky, hostile to his delay, and then would suddenly turn towards you, calling you again, and pour more tears and kisses onto your face. But after he had done this several times, realizing that he could no longer stay with you, he embraced you and said, 'Sweet lady, you are the only hope of my wretched heart, and I am forced to go away and leave you in danger of your life. May God restore your lost peace, and may He keep you safe for me so that we can joyfully see each other again, just as we are sadly separated by this bitter parting.' While he was pronouncing these words he was continually crying so loudly that his sobbing made me fear

---

3. frightened soul: *paurosa anima*. In this passage the soul is identified with the heart and so is placed in the chest.

more than once that he could be heard not only by our household but by the neighbors as well. Then, unable to stay any longer because of the hostile daylight that was upon us, he bade farewell with even more tears and leaving our home as if he were pulled away by force, stubbed his toe hard on the threshold. Once he was outside, it could have been said that he was nearly unable to walk, but he looked back at each step, as if he were hoping that I would have to call him back to see you because you had been revived."

Then she stopped talking, and as you can imagine, ladies, I was left disconsolate and tearful, to lament the departure of my dear lover.

THREE

*In which is demonstrated how many and what
kinds of thoughts and pastimes this lady engaged
in while waiting for the time when her lover
had promised to return.*

You have heard already, ladies, how I was left after my Panfilo departed, and I grieved and lamented over this departure for several days, and although I kept silent, nothing was on my lips but this question: "How can it be that you have left me, my Panfilo?"

Indeed, that name gave me some comfort as I remembered it amidst my tears. There was no part of my room which I would not regard with great longing, saying to myself:

"Here my darling Panfilo used to sit, here he used to lie down, here he promised to come back soon, and here I kissed him."

In brief, I cherished every spot. At times I pretended to myself that he had returned and was coming to see me again, so I turned my eyes toward the door of my room as if he had really come, and fooled by my conscious fantasy, I was thus left sulking as if I had been deceived with the truth. Several times, to stop these useless backward glances, I started out wanting to do many things, but I soon let them be, overwhelmed by new fantasies. My wretched heart tormented me with an unaccustomed throbbing. I remembered the many things I wished I had told him and those I had said to him, and I repeated to myself what he had said to me, and in such a manner I remained grieving for several days without concentrating on anything.

Once the worst pain for this recent departure had begun to subside somewhat with the passing of time, I started having more steady thoughts, and having come, they made a plausible case for themselves. A few days later, when I was in my room alone, it happened that I began talking to myself in this way:

"So, now your lover has left; he is gone, and you, miserable one, not only were unable to bid him farewell, but you could not even give back to him the kisses he gave to your lifeless face

42

or watch him leave; it could be that if he keeps this in mind whenever something harmful should happen to him, he might interpret your silence as a bad omen and complain about you."

At first this thought weighed heavily on my mind, but a new idea displaced it; hence I thought to myself:

"No blame can possibly derive from this because he is wise and will interpret what happened to me as a favorable omen and will say: 'She did not bid farewell as one usually does to people who are leaving for a long time or are never to return, but with her silence she may have believed that she had me near her and imagined that my journey would last a very short time.' "

So I consoled myself in my own mind, and I let go of this idea and turned to others.

At other times it occurred to me to give more serious thought to his having stubbed his toe on the threshold of our bed chamber, as my faithful servant had reported, and remembering that Laodameia had not taken any other sign as seriously as this one, which indicated that Protesilaus would not return, I wept many times. But because at that time it did not enter my mind what future was in store for me, I imagined that these thoughts might be useless and would have to be abandoned. However, they did not leave when I wanted them to, but sometimes I would forget them when others took their place; and as I thought about those that had just come and about no others, I found they were so many and such that it would be difficult to remember their number.

Not just once but as many times as I recalled to mind that he was on a journey, I remembered having read in Ovid's verses that physical exertion made young people forget love. Feeling that travelling takes no small effort, especially for one who is used to resting or who does it unwillingly, I greatly feared first that this could take him away from me and next that the undesired exertion and bad weather might cause him to be ill—or worse. And I remember dwelling on this matter longer than on any other, although, often judging from the tears I had seen pouring down his face and from my own weariness, which never changed my determination, I argued that it was not possible for such a small difficulty to extinguish so great a love, and I also hoped that his youth and prudence would keep him from any other unpleasant accident.

So I argued with myself, gave answers, and found solutions, and I spent so many days in this fashion that not only did I think that he had reached his country, but also I was reassured about this by a letter from him. Because this letter disclosed to me that he was more passionately in love than ever and revived my hope in his return with greater promises, I had several reasons for welcoming it.

From then on, as soon as one thought left my mind, a new one was born from the previous one. Once I said to myself:

"As the only son of an old father who has not seen him for many years, Panfilo is now being received by him with great festivities, and I believe that not only has he forgotten me but he also curses the months he stayed here under various pretexts for love of me; and as he is being nobly received by this or that friend, he perhaps blames me, who could do nothing but love him when he was here. Minds filled with merriment can easily be taken away from one place and become attached to another. Oh dear, could it be that I might lose him now this way? I can hardly believe it! May God forbid that this should happen! And as He has kept and keeps me for him among my people and in my city, may He keep him for me among his people and in his city!"

Alas, how many tears were mixed with these words, and how many more would have been shed had I believed as true what they foretold as being true, although I later wept in vain those tears that, multiplied many times over, still remained unshed at that time.

Besides reasoning in this manner, my soul often foresaw her future misfortunes and trembled violently, seized by I know not what fear, and such fear ended more often than not in this thought:

"Now in his city Panfilo is visiting its many splendid temples that are lavishly decorated for grand ceremonies, and he visits those which are undoubtedly filled with ladies who, as I have often heard, are not only very beautiful but also surpass all others in grace and charm, and among these ladies some are unequaled in their net-throwing dexterity at capturing hearts. Ah, who can be so strongly in control of himself, where so many things converge, that he cannot be captured sometimes by force, even against his own will? Even *I* was taken by force! Furthermore, new things are usually more attractive than others; therefore, it is quite possible that because he is a novelty for them as they are for him, some might like him, and he might like some of them."

Alas, how hard it was to imagine something which might not have happened, but which I could hardly dismiss by saying:

"How could Panfilo, who loves you more than he loves himself, let another love into his heart, which you occupy? Do you know of any woman here who was quite worthy of him and who with enticements stronger than looks tried to penetrate into his heart but could not find a way? It is indeed hardly possible that he would fall in love as quickly as you say, even if he did not belong to you (as he does) and even if these ladies surpassed goddesses in beauty and cunning. Moreover, how can you believe that he would want to break the word he gave you for another? He would never do it, so you must also trust his discretion. You must reasonably think that he is not so unwise that he does not know it is insane to abandon what a person has in order to obtain what he has not, unless what he leaves behind is worthless, what he hopes to have priceless, and the hope of reaching it unfailing; but this cannot happen because if you have heard correctly, you would be among the beautiful ones in his land, which holds no other woman richer or more noble than you, and besides this, how could he find anyone who would love him more than you do? Since he is an expert in this kind of thing, he knows, in the case of a woman one begins to like, how difficult it is to encourage her to let herself be loved, because while women may love (which seldom happens), they always show the opposite of what they desire. Even if he did not love you, since he is hindered by other matters of his own, he could not think of cultivating new women now; so do not think about this, but count on the law that you are loved as much as you love."

Oh, how falsely I was arguing and quibbling with the truth! But in spite of all my arguing, I could never free my mind from the wretched jealousy which had taken over, in addition to my other troubles. However, as if I were conjecturing correctly, I felt greatly relieved and succeeded in moving away from this line of thought.

Dearest ladies, not to waste time telling you about each one of my ideas, just listen to what were my most urgent activities, and do not marvel at their novelty, for they were not as I wanted them to be, but since Love presented them to me, I was obliged to follow them. There were few mornings when, after rising, I did not climb to the highest part of my house, and from there I scanned the whole horizon as sailors do from the crow's nest of their ship to speculate on whether the rock or land they see nearby might be an obstacle. Then I would concentrate on the eastern sky and calculate how much of the new day had passed, judging by how high the sun was over the horizon, and the higher I saw it, the closer I would say was the time of Panfilo's return. I often watched the sun rising in the sky, almost with pleasure, but when I did not see it, I estimated its position by observing my shadow, sometimes made smaller and sometimes larger in relation to the distance of the sun's mass from the horizon; and I would say to myself that it was moving more lazily than ever, making the days of Capricorn longer than those of Cancer, and when it reached its zenith, I also said that it enjoyed lingering so it could look at the lands below, and even if it set quickly in the west, it seemed slow to me. After depriving our world of its light, the sun allowed the stars to show their own, and as I happily counted to myself the days gone by, I marked the one just passed, as I did the rest, with a little stone and distinguished the happy ones from the sad by means of black and white pebbles, as the ancients used to do. Oh, how many times I remember placing a little stone ahead of time, believing I could bring the promised date closer the sooner I added one to the time gone by; although I remembered the number of each perfectly well, sometimes by counting the stones that stood for the days gone by and other times those for the days still to come, I almost invariably hoped to find the former increased and the latter diminished. In this manner desire led me willingly forward to the end of the given time.

So after employing this useless pastime, most often I returned to my bedchamber, where I preferred being by myself to being with people. When I found myself alone there, to escape dangerous thought I opened a coffer, and one by one I took out many of the things which belonged to my lover, I looked at them with the same desire with which I used to look at him, and after having admired them, I kissed them sighing, hardly able to hold back my tears, and as if they had been intelligent creatures, I asked them:

"When will your lord be here?"

Then I put them away and took out the numerous letters he had sent me, read almost all of them, and because I had the impression that I was conversing with him, I was somewhat comforted. It often happened that I called my maid and spoke with her about him, either asking whether she believed that Panfilo would return or questioning her about what she thought of him, and sometimes about whether she had heard something of him. And because she answered me truthfully, either to please me or to express her opinion, she gave me no small comfort, and in this manner a good part of the day often passed with little boredom.

Compassionate ladies, no less than these things I have just mentioned, I enjoyed visiting the temples and sitting by the door of my house with my women friends, where while chatting of this and that, I forgot my countless troubles, and in such places I chanced to see more than once those young men I had seen many times with Panfilo, and it never failed that whenever I saw them, I looked among them as if I could see Panfilo in their midst. How many times I knowingly deceived myself in this! But it was much to my benefit to see them, in spite of this deception. If their appearance did not fool me, I perceived them to be filled with the same compassion which I was feeling and did not seem as cheerful as usual, as if they were missing their friend. Oh, if reason had not held me back, how often I would have liked to ask what had happened to their friend! But sometimes Fortune was surely favorable to me in this matter, because wherever they talked about him, unaware that I was listening, they said that his return was imminent. How much this pleased me I would labor in vain to express. So in this manner, with these thoughts, and doing these kinds of things and many others such as these, I tried to spend the short but painful daytime wishing for the night to come, not because I felt that it was more beneficial to me, but because once it came, there was less time that still had to go by.

When the hours of daylight drew to an end, swallowed by the night, most often there would be new preoccupations coming my way. I had feared darkness since childhood, but now I felt secure in it since Love kept me company, and when I heard that everyone in my house was asleep, I climbed alone to the place where in the morning I had seen the sun rising, and like Aruns among the white rocks of the Lucanian mountains, I meditated on the heavenly bodies and their movements, spending in this manner the interminable hours of the night; and feeling that my worries were hostile to my sleep, I watched the sky from that angle and thought to myself that its fastest planetary motion was extremely slow.

Since my desire to see the moon's four phases completed was greater than her own speed, I sometimes fixed my eyes on the horned moon and judged that not only was she not running towards her fullest phase but each night she was more pointed than before.

Oh, how often, in spite of her frigid light, I admired her with pleasure for a long time, imagining my Panfilo's eyes fixed upon her just as mine were! I now have no doubt that having already forgotten me, not only was he not looking at the moon but neither had he a single thought about her and was probably in bed fast asleep.

I remember that as I was fretting about the slowness of her course, I helped her on her way (with various sounds, following ancient errors) so that she could reach her fullness, and when she reached it, as if she were pleased with her full light, she seemed to care little about becoming horned again but remained indolent in her roundness; but at times in my mind I forgave her for this, since she considered it more pleasant to stay with her mother than to return to her husband's dark domain.[1]

I remember well, however, that many times the words used in prayers to make things easy for her I turned into threats, saying:

"O Sister of Phoebus,[2] you poorly requite the favors done for you; I try to alleviate your toils with humble prayers, but you, with your lazy delays, do not care whether you make my own labors greater. So if you should need my help to become horned again, you will find me as indolent as I perceive you to be. Do

1. her husband's dark domain: Fiammetta appears to be subscribing here to the occasional late Classical identification of Diana with Proserpine (see Glossary).

2. Sister of Phoebus: Diana, or Phoebe (see Glossary).

you not realize that the faster you show yourself four times horned and as many times full, the sooner my Panfilo will return? And when he will have returned, you may be as slow or as fast as you please in completing your cycles."

Certainly the same insanity which led me to pray in this way made me so beside myself that I sometimes believed that (fearful of my threats) she hastened in her course to please me, but at other times she seemed to slow down more than usual, as if she took no notice of me. My frequent observations made me so knowledgeable about her course that whether her figure was full or thin, no matter which part of the sky she was in or which star she was in conjunction with, I could tell exactly how much of the night had gone by and how much more was left, and if the moon did not appear, the two Bears would also reassure me about it after I had made a lengthy scrutiny.[3] Dear me, who would believe that Love could teach me astrology, an art that occupies the greatest talents, not the minds which are prey to his furor?

When the sky was covered with very dark clouds and swept by high winds so as to prevent me from seeing her anywhere, sometimes (if I had no other obligations) I gathered my maids together in my chamber and recounted, or had them recount, all sorts of stories, and the further from the truth they were—as most of these people's tales are—the greater power they seemed to have in chasing my sorrows away and making me a cheerful listener; and there were many times when I laughed about them with great pleasure in spite of all this melancholy. And if for some legitimate reason this pastime was not possible, I looked in various books for other people's miseries, and by comparing them to mine, I felt as if I had company, and so the time passed less tediously. I do not know which I enjoyed more: watching the hours go by or, after having been occupied with something else, finding them gone.

When finally these and other activities had kept me occupied for a long while, I nearly forced myself to go to sleep—or rather to lie down in order to sleep, knowing all too well that it was impossible. As I was lying alone in my bed, not bothered by any noise, nearly all the thoughts of the day returned to my mind, and in spite of myself I had to go over them with many more ar-

3. the two Bears: Ursa Major and Ursa Minor.

guments for or against; and I often wanted to have other thoughts, but seldom was I able to do that, although a few other times I forced these thoughts out of my mind, and while I lay on that side of the bed where Panfilo used to lie, nearly smelling his presence, I seemed to be content, and I mentally called his name, begging him to come back soon, as if he were listening to me.

Then I imagined that he had returned, and by making believe that he was with me, I told him and asked him many things, answering myself in his place, and sometimes it happened that I fell asleep in the midst of these thoughts. Certainly sleep was kinder to me than waking, because what I had been falsely pretending while I was awake was given to me by sleep just as if it were real—if it had lasted. Sometimes I had the impression that he had returned and that I was with him wandering about together, as we had done before, in magnificent gardens adorned with all sorts of trees, fruits, and flowers, and there, walking hand in hand, I made him tell me everything that had happened to him, and frequently I seemed to interrupt what he was saying with a kiss, but because what I was seeing seemed hardly true to me, I said:

"Pray, is it true that you are back? Indeed it is, since I am holding you!" And then I kissed him again.

Another time I thought that I was with him at a merry gathering at the seashore, and it seemed so real that I confirmed it to myself by saying:

"I am not just dreaming that I am holding him in my arms!"

Oh, how painful it was to awaken while this was happening! When sleep went away, it always took with it what it had lent me without any effort on its part, and although I was left quite sad, for the entire day that followed I felt full of hope and contentment, wishing for the night to come quickly so that I might have while asleep what I could not have when I was awake. But even though sleep was kind to me from time to time, it could not bear that I should feel such sweetness without bitterness, so that there were many instances in which I seemed to see my lover dressed most miserably, entirely covered with some very dark blotches, pale and frightened, and calling out "Help me!" as if he were being pursued. On other occasions I seemed to hear people talking about his death; once I saw him dead and in many other situations distressing to me. Never was sleep stronger than pain; therefore, suddenly awakened and conscious of the futility of my dream, I was almost thankful that it had been a dream and thanked God for it, but I was nevertheless troubled, afraid not so much of what I had seen, but that not all but at least some of these things might have been in part the truth or images of the truth. Even though I told myself and heard other people say that dreams are useless, I was never glad when I had no news of him, for I had become a most astute and eager inquirer of such news.

As you have heard, this is how I spent nights and days waiting. It is true that, as the time of the promised return approached, I thought that it would be useful for me to live happily, since my good looks, which had faded considerably because of the pain I had been feeling, would come back to their proper place, so that on his return I would not disappoint him with my homeliness. And this was very easy to do, for I had already become accustomed to my troubles and could stand them with little effort, and besides this, the approaching hope of the promised return made me feel an unaccustomed joy more strongly with each passing day. I began to participate anew in the entertainments I had abandoned for some time under the pretext of foul weather, and my mind, which had been constrained by serious, bitter experiences, began to expand in this joyful life, so that I became more lovely than ever; and I refurbished my cherished garments and precious ornaments (not unlike the knight who repairs and polishes, where needed, his formidable weapons for the imminent battle) in order to appear more adorned on his return, for which I, deceived and in vain, was waiting.

So as the actions changed, so did my thoughts. I no longer had in mind the fact that I had not seen him leave, nor the evil omen of the stumbling foot, nor the hardships he was sustaining, nor the pain he experienced, nor the inimical jealousy; but about eight days before the promised one, I said to myself:

'Now Panfilo is sorry to have been away from me, and knowing that the date he promised is closer, he is preparing to come back, and perhaps he has left his old father and is on his way now."

Oh, how I enjoyed such thoughts, and how gladly I dwelled on them, often entertaining the idea of how graciously I would have to present myself to him again! Alas, how often I said:

"When he comes back, I will embrace him a million times, and my kisses will multiply so many times that they will not allow one entire word to come out of his mouth, and I will give him back twice as many kisses, without receiving any in return, as he gave my face while I lay unconscious."

In my own mind I doubted more than once whether I could restrain the burning desire to embrace him in front of others when I would first see him. But the gods took care of this in a way that was more painful to me. Furthermore, whenever I was in my room, as soon as someone came in, I believed that person had come to announce, "Panfilo has arrived." I did not hear a single voice anywhere that would not alert my ears to catch every word, thinking that his return was being discussed. I believe that I must have risen more than a hundred times from my seat to run to the window, as if I were attracted by something else, looking up and down after having first made myself foolishly believe this thought:

"It is possible that Panfilo has now arrived and is coming to see you."

But as I recognized the error in my thinking I went back inside, somewhat confused.

By explaining that on his return he had to bring back certain things for my husband, I often asked, or I had others ask, whether Panfilo had come back or when he was expected. But by these means I obtained no better answer than if I were asking about someone who was never supposed to return, as in fact was the case.

F O U R

In which this Lady tells of the thoughts she had and of the life she led when the date of Panfilo's return arrived without his coming back.

And so, compassionate ladies, as you have heard, not only did I reach the impatiently awaited date, but I saw many days go by after it, and uncertain within myself as to whether I should still blame him or not, with my hope greatly diminished, I abandoned my carefree thoughts, to which I may have returned too wholeheartedly, and new things I never considered before began to run through my head. Having set my mind on wanting to learn, if possible, what was or could be the reason for his absence, which was much longer than he had promised, I began to think about it, and before anything else I found as many ways to justify him as he could find himself if he were here, and perhaps more. At times I said:

"For pity's sake, Fiammetta, do you truly believe that Panfilo would stay away and not return to you unless he were unable to do so? Unforeseen business often weighs people down, and it is not possible, as some believe, to give such a definite limit to future things. But then who can doubt that devotion to someone present is far more binding than to someone far away? I am quite sure that he loves me very much and that now he thinks of my bitter life and feels compassion for it and that more than once he has wanted to come here out of love; but maybe his old father has somewhat prolonged his stay with tears and prayers and has detained him against his will. He will come when he can."

These kinds of arguments and excuses often compelled me to imagine more serious things, and sometimes I said:

"I wonder whether he may not have been unduly impatient to see me and to meet the promised deadline so that he put aside all pity for his father and abandoned all other business, leaving perhaps without waiting for the turbulent sea to be calm; and could it be that trusting false and foolhardy seamen eager for gain, he embarked on some vessel that aroused the wrath of wind and waters and perished thereby? For no other reason Hero lost Leander. Besides, who knows that he has not been pushed by fate onto some desolate rocky shore where, after having escaped death by water, he has met it from hunger or at the hands of wild beasts? Or could he have been inadvertently abandoned on some deserted rocks, like Achaemenides, and is awaiting someone to bring him here? After all who does not know that the sea is full of hidden dangers? Perhaps he has been caught by hostile hands or pirates and is confined in irons in some foreign prison. All these things are possible, and we have seen them happen many times before."

On the other hand, it occurred to me that his journey was no safer by land, and that thought made me envisage a thousand accidents that could similarly detain him. As always, my mind immediately rushed to think of the worst, and trying to find sounder excuses for him the more serious his case stood, at times I thought:

"Look, the sun is now hotter than usual and is melting the snow on the mountain tops, from where the muddy waters of turbulent torrents are rushing, and he must cross many of them. If impatient to cross one of these rivers, he ventured on it, fell in, and being dragged down and swallowed with his horse, gave up the ghost, how can he come then? It is not the first time that rivers have injured travelers or swallowed men. But if he has escaped even this danger, he may have run into an ambush set by robbers; he may have been robbed and is being held by them; or perhaps he was taken ill on his journey and is now staying somewhere and will certainly come back here once he has regained his health."

Alas, whenever I was in the grip of such fantasies, my whole body was covered by cold perspiration, and I became so fearful of them that I often implored God in my thoughts to make them stop, just as if Panfilo were present before my eyes in such dangers. I remember that sometimes I wept as if I were absolutely certain of seeing him in one of the perils I had imagined. But then I said to myself:

"Oh, what are these things that my mind is placing before me? May God not allow any of them to be true! He should stay as long as he wishes or not come back at all rather than risk any of these things happening in order to please me. Such fantasies are now truly deceiving me, because even if they were possible, they cannot be kept hidden, and it is impossible to believe that the death of such a young man may be kept concealed, especially from me, who had anxiously and continually made very subtle inquiries about him. Besides, if any one of the evil things which I considered were to turn out to be true, who can doubt that rumor, a very speedy messenger of bad news, would have brought it here already? And Fortune, now hardly my friend in such matters, would have opened wide the way to make me most miserable. Of course, I am inclined to believe that Panfilo is suffering as seriously as I am if he does not come, and that he is now forced to stay where he is, and will soon come, or apologizing for the delay, will comfort me by explaining the reason."

Although these ideas haunted me quite fiercely, certainly they were also easily overcome, and with all my might I was now holding on to Hope, which was trying hard to escape from me because the appointed time had gone by; and I placed before it the long-lasting love that I felt for him and he felt for me, the given word, the gods on whom he swore, and the unending tears; and I asserted that it was impossible that such things could hide any deception. However, I could not help it that Hope, which I held on to in such a manner, would give way to the abandoned thoughts that were slowly and quietly trying to reoccupy their former position by pushing Hope itself out of my heart little by little and bringing back to my mind evil presentiments and other such things; and at first I hardly realized that these feelings had become very powerful and that Hope had almost been chased away.

While several days passed by without my hearing anything about Panfilo's return, among the thoughts that lay heaviest on my mind was jealousy. This jealousy was goading me more than I wished—it invalidated all excuses I gave myself about him—and often proposing again to me the arguments I had previously rejected, it said:

"For goodness' sake, how can you be so foolish as to believe that pity for his father or any other pressing business or pleasure could keep Panfilo over there if he loved you as much as he claimed he did? Do you not know that Love conquers everything? He is surely in love with someone else and must have forgotten you, and the pleasure of this love, which is powerful because it is new, now keeps him there as yours kept him here. As you have already said, those women are in all ways ready to love, and he is in every respect just as naturally disposed toward and deserving of love as they; by complying with his pleasure and he with theirs, they must have made him fall in love again. Do you not believe that other women have eyes in their heads as you have and know as much as you do about such things? They certainly do! And do you not believe that he too can be attracted by more than one woman? I certainly believe that if he could see you, it would be difficult for him to love another, but he cannot see you now, nor has he seen you for many months.

"You must understand that no earthly condition[1] lasts forever; just as he fell in love with you and felt attracted to you, so it is just possible that he was attracted to another and now loves her after having forgotten your love. New things are more appealing than those one often sees, and men always desire more intensely what they do not possess than what they do possess, and nothing is so delightful that it does not become tiresome after prolonged use. And who would not more willingly love a new woman in his own home than one he already knows well who is in a foreign land? Moreover, he may not have loved you as fervently as he showed, and one should not believe that his or anyone else's tears are as precious a token as the love that you believed he was feeling for you.

"Besides, men at times grieve and weep when they part, even after having known one another for just a few days, and they also swear to one another and promise many things which they firmly intend to do, but then when something new happens, those oaths are forgotten. The tears, the oaths, and the promises of young men—are they not still a pledge of future deceit to women? Generally, they know how to engage in these things before they know how to love; their desire for adventure drives them to this; there is not one who would not rather have ten women each month than belong to only one for ten days. They never cease to believe that they can find new ways and new

1. earthly condition: *mondano accidente*. In speaking of love, Boccaccio, like Dante (*Vita Nuova* 25), sometimes makes use of the medieval scholastic distinction between substance and accident and identifies love as the latter, that is, a nonessential property or attribute of an entity. We have taken the liberty of translating *accidente* as "condition."

forms, and they boast about having obtained the love of many women. Then what are you hoping for? Why do you let yourself be led in vain to a futile illusion? You are not in a position where you can draw him away from this; stop loving him, and show how you deceived him with the same art he used to deceive you."

I kept repeating these and many other words to myself, and they enkindled in me a fierce anger that made my soul burn with such a violent heat that it almost led me to the most enraged behavior. And it was not before this self-born fury passed all bounds that my tears flowed so abundantly and lasted so long that this rage left my heart, taking the tears with it; to comfort myself, I rejected in my heart what my prophetic soul was telling me and I nearly forced the hope, which had already fled, to come back on the poorest of excuses. And thus having found again some of my lost cheerfulness, I remained hoping and despairing, sometimes for several days on end, always exceedingly anxious to learn discreetly what was happening to the one who was not returning.

FIVE

In which Fiammetta shows how she heard that Panfilo had taken a wife and then tells of the anguish in which she lived while despairing of his return.

Compassionate ladies, up to this moment my tears were slight and my sighs pleasant in comparison to those which my sorrowful pen (slower in writing than my heart in feeling) is about to show you. And indeed, if carefully considered, the pains experienced up to now may be said to be those of a wanton young woman more than those of a tormented one, while those still to come will seem written by a different hand. Therefore, take heart, do not let my promises frighten you so that past events may seem so grievous that you will not even want to look at the extremely serious ones ahead; and to tell the truth, I do not invite you to consider these sorrows so that you may feel pity for me but rather so that the more you become aware of the wickedness of the one who is causing this to happen to me, the more cautious you may become about entrusting yourself to any young man. In this way I may be indebted to you for listening to my reasoning, and you to me for my counsel, that is, for warning and advising you on the basis of what has happened to me.

So, ladies, I will say that while I was constantly occupied with various fantasies, as you could understand from what I said earlier, one day, more than a month after the promised date, I received news of my young lover. With an attitude of devotion I had gone to visit some nuns, perhaps to have them offer to God devout prayers on my behalf, so that He might return the serenity I had lost, either by giving me back Panfilo or by putting him out of my mind; and it so happened that while I was sitting with these ladies, who spoke quite discreetly and pleasantly and who were closely related to me by family ties and old friendship, a merchant arrived (just as Ulysses and Diomedes had appeared before Deidameia) and began showing the sisters various beautiful jewels suitable to ladies of their station.

I understood from his speech—and he admitted it himself when questioned about it by one of the nuns—that he came from my Panfilo's land. And after he had shown much of the merchandise, some of which was bought at an agreed-upon price and the rest of which was returned to him, he and the nuns cheerfully spoke about other things while he was waiting to be paid, and then one of them who was young, very beautiful in appearance, and noble in blood and manners (the same one who had questioned him earlier about his origins), asked whether he had ever met his countryman Panfilo. Imagine how this question suited my desire!

Of course I was delighted, and I listened carefully to the answer which the merchant gave without hesitation:

"And who would know him better than I do?"

To this the young woman replied as if she were pretending to know something about what had become of him:

"And how is he now?"

"Oh," the merchant said, "it has been a long time since he was called back home by his father, who had been left with no other sons."

Then the young woman asked again:

"When did you last have news of him?"

"Certainly not after I left him," he said, "which I believe may not be more than a fortnight."

And the lady continued:

"How was he then?"

To which the merchant replied:

"He was very well. In fact, I can tell you that on the same day I left I also saw an extremely beautiful young lady entering his house with great fanfare, and according to what I heard, she had just been married to him."

While the merchant was saying these things, although I listened to him in very bitter pain, I kept staring at the inquiring young woman and wondered why she was asking such detailed questions about a man I believed to be scarcely known to any other woman but me, and I noticed that as soon as she heard that Panfilo had taken a wife, she lowered her eyes and blushed while the next word died in her throat, and as far as I could tell, she had great trouble holding back the tears which had already filled her eyes. On hearing this, I was first seized by an extremely deep grief, and then, as I watched the scene, I was suddenly seized by another pain just as sharp, and I could hardly restrain myself from reproaching her very rudely for her display of emotion, for I was jealous of the open signs of love she was showing towards Panfilo, suspecting that, like me, she might have a legitimate reason to grieve at the words she had just heard. Nevertheless, with an effort that was painful and, I believe, unequaled by any other, I tried to hide the turmoil in my heart under an unchanged face, more willing to weep than to listen further.

However, by keeping her pain to herself, perhaps with as great an effort as my own, and acting as if she were not the person who was so troubled a moment earlier, the young woman asked him to vouch for the trustworthiness of those words, but the more questions she asked, the more she found the answers contrary to her wish and to mine too. Therefore, after having said goodbye to the merchant, who wished to leave, we remained talking of this and that longer than I wished, while she hid her sadness under false laughter.

When our conversation languished, we went our separate ways, and with my soul filled with sorrowful rage, as furious as a Lybian lion that discovers hunters on its tracks, now flushed and now pale, sometimes walking slowly and sometimes faster than feminine dignity allows, I returned home. Once I could behave as I wished, I walked into my room and began weeping bitterly, and when after a long time the abundant tears had relieved some of the deep sorrow and I felt more free to speak, I began in a very weak voice:

"Now, my unhappy Fiammetta, you know why your Panfilo is not coming back; now you have what you were trying to find. What more do you want, you miserable one? What more do you ask? This should suffice: Panfilo is no longer yours, let go of your desire to have him back, free yourself of your misplaced hope, forget this passion and abandon your insane thoughts, trust at last the omens and your intuitive soul, and start learning about the deceptions of young men. You have reached the point usually reached by women who trust too much."

And with these words my anger flared again; I wept harder, and I began again to speak words much too daring:

"Where are you, O gods? Where have you turned your eyes now? Where is your anger now? Why is it not falling upon the one who scorns your power? What are your lightning bolts doing, Jupiter, by whom false oaths were sworn? Where are you using them now? Who has deserved more to be struck by them for impiety? Why do they not descend upon the wicked young man so that others from now on may fear to swear by you in vain? O brilliant Phoebus, where are now the arrows that had the mischance to wound the Python instead of the one who falsely called you as witness to his deception? Deprive him of the splendor of your light, and turn against him no less fiercely than you turned against the wretched Oedipus. And you other gods and goddesses, whoever you are, and you, Love, whose power my love has scorned, why do you not show your strength and rightful anger now? Why do you not turn heaven and earth against the new bridegroom so that he will no longer remain in this world to mock you further—an example of deception and a destroyer of your power? Far smaller errors have moved your anger to a less just vengeance! Then why do you hesitate now? You could hardly be too cruel to him to punish him as much as he deserves.

"How miserable I am! Why is it not possible for you to feel the effect of his deceit as much as I do, so that the desire for punishment is aroused in you as it is in me? O gods, set loose on him some or all of those perils which I feared earlier; have him die any kind of death you prefer, so that I may feel fully and all at once the ultimate pain I should ever have to feel for him, and you would avenge yourselves and me at the same time.

"Do not allow me to be the only one who weeps for the effect of his sins, and do not let him happily enjoy his new bride after he mocked all of us, lest your sword should wound the wrong way."

Then, no less stirred by anger, but with more vehement tears, I remember addressing myself to Panfilo, and I began this way:

"O Panfilo, now I know the reason for your delay; now I am aware of your deceit; now I see what is keeping you and what kind of pity is holding you. Now you are celebrating the sacred rites of Hymen, and I, who am self-deceived and deceived by you and by your words, waste away weeping, and with my tears I make way for my own death, whose painful approach will rightly be attributable to your cruelty, and my life span, which I so desired to lengthen, will be shorter because of you. You are a wicked young man, quick to make me suffer! With what feelings have you taken your new bride? Do you intend to betray her as you have betrayed me? How did you look at her? With the same eyes which you unfortunately used to charm me, who was too credulous? What faith did you pledge to her? The same you had promised me? How could you? Do you not remember that something already pledged cannot be pledged again? By which gods did you swear? Those by whom you had sworn falsely?

"How miserable I am in that I do not know what perverse pleasure blinded your mind so that you gave yourself to someone else while feeling that you were mine! Alas, what did I do to deserve being taken so little to heart? Where has that flighty love gone so quickly? Alas, what a wicked destiny it is that constrains so miserably those who suffer! Now you have forgotten the gods by whom you perjured yourself when you promised so willingly to return, as well as the solemn word you gave to me with your right hand, and you no longer remember the enticing words you used in so great a number or the tears that moistened not only your face but mine too; you have taken all of this together and thrown it to the winds, and you mock me while you live happily with this new woman.

"Alas, who could ever have believed that your words were hiding such lies and that your tears were cunningly shed? I certainly could not! On the contrary, since I was speaking in good faith, I accepted words and tears in good faith. And let us even assume the opposite—that your tears were genuine and that the oaths and the vows were offered with a pure heart—what excuse will you give then for not having kept them as purely as you promised to? Will you say that the attractiveness of the new lady was the reason? It is certainly a weak one and a clear proof of a flighty spirit. And besides, will this give me any satisfaction? Certainly not! You wicked youth! Were you not aware of the burning love I felt and still feel for you even against my will? Certainly you were! So, You did not need to be so cunning in deceiving me. But then in order to show more subtlety in your discourse, you wanted to use all sorts of artful means but did not consider what little glory you would derive from cheating a young woman who trusted you. My naiveté deserved more faith than you had. But what is the use? I believed in you no less than I believed in the gods by whom you swore, and now I beg them that the greatest part of your fame will rest on your having deceived a young woman who loved you more than she loved herself.

"Ah, Panfilo, tell me now: had I done anything to deserve being betrayed so cleverly? Surely I never committed any offense against you other than falling in love with you unwisely, and then I trusted and loved you more than I should have, but this sin did not deserve to receive such penance, at least from you. To tell the truth, I do recognize having perpetrated a wicked deed by which I rightly provoked the gods' anger, and this consisted in receiving you, who are an evil and pitiless young man, in my bed, and in having allowed your body to touch mine, although in this regard, as the gods themselves know, you are the culprit, not I, because you took me in the quiet of the night with your bold cunning when I was safely asleep, and like someone who has done it before and is used to deceiving, you took me first in your arms and violated my chastity almost before I was entirely awake. What was I supposed to do when I saw this? Should I have screamed and brought endless shame on myself and death on you, whom I loved more than myself? As God knows, I resisted as much as I could, but as my strength was not equal to yours, you won and possessed what you were stealing. Alas, how I wish now that the day before that night had been my last, one in which I could have died virtuous!

"How many pains I feel and how harshly they will assail me now! And whenever you will be with the young woman you have led on, you will tell her of your old love affairs in order to be more pleasing to her and will belittle me by making me look guilty on many counts, vilifying my beauty and my ways, both of which you used to celebrate with the highest praise as being above those of other women, and you will praise hers to the fullest; and those things which I did for you, acting out of compassion and driven by love, you will say were prompted by a burning lust.

"But among the untruthful things you will talk about, remember to recount those true deceptions in which you can say that you left me tearful and miserable, and add to them the honors you have received, so that your ingratitude will be very clear to your listener. Do not forget to tell how many and what kind of young men tried to get my love, and of the different means they used to try to obtain it: the doors adorned with wreaths of love, the night brawls, and the daily acts of bravery they performed out of love; and never could they take me away from your deceiving love. And you, you also exchanged me right away for a young woman you hardly knew, but if she is not as naïve as I am, she will always consider your kisses suspicious and be on her guard against your deceptions, from which I could not protect myself. I pray that she will do to you what the wife of Atreus did to him, and what Danaus' daughters did to their grooms, or what Clytemnestra did to Agamemnon, or at least what because of your wickedness I did to my husband, who did not deserve such insult. May she bring you to such misery that just as I weep now and pity myself, you may make me shed tears for you, and I pray that this may happen soon, if the gods look with any pity on those who are miserable."

Although I felt hurt by these doleful lamentations and often returned to them, not just on that day but on many following ones, I was no less troubled by the agitation I had observed in the young woman mentioned earlier, and this sometimes led me to have very painful thoughts, and as I had done before, I said to myself:

"Oh, Panfilo, why do I suffer because you are far away and belong to another woman, since even when you were here you belonged to someone else? Oh, worst of all men, into how many parts was your love divided, or capable of being divided? I can assume that just as this young woman and I were your women (and now you have added a third one), you had many like us, while I believed that I was the only one, and so it happened that while I believed myself involved in my own affairs, I was invading someone else's territory. Could it not be possible that this was already known to some woman more deserving of the gods' favors than I and who prayed to be avenged for the insults received and to do me harm asked that I should be, as I am, full of anguish? But whoever she is, if there is someone, may she forgive me, for I sinned out of ignorance and my ignorance deserves forgiveness. But you, how could you pretend so skillfully? With what conscience did you do it? What kind of love or tenderness made you do this? I have often heard that it is impossible to love more than one person at a time, but this law does not seem to apply to you: you loved, or pretended to love, many.

"Ah, did you give to all of them or only to the one who could not hide what you concealed so well the same faith, promises, and tears you gave to me? If you did that, you can rest assured that you are obliged to none, since what is given indiscriminately to many is as if it were given to none. Really, how can it be that he who steals so many hearts should not have his own caught sometimes? Narcissus was loved by many, but because he was hard-hearted with all of them, he was ultimately fascinated by his own form; the inflexible and fast-running Atalanta surpassed her lovers, until Hippomenes overtook her with a masterful trick and defeated her, as she herself wished. But why do I give ancient examples? Even I, who could not be caught by anyone, was taken by you, so why have you not found among so many one who caught you?

"But I do not believe this to be the case; on the contrary, I am sure you were captured, and if you were, why don't you return to whoever may have been the one who captured you with such force? If you do not wish to come back to me, at least go back to the one who was unable to conceal your love affair; if it must be that luck is against me (and perhaps in your opinion I may have deserved it), my sins should not harm others. At least return to these women and keep first your word to them even before you keep it to me; do not, to spite me, hurt the many women whom I believe you may have left behind full of hope, nor let one over there be more powerful than many right here. That one is already yours and cannot be otherwise, even if she wanted to; so leave her confidently and come, so that those who cannot become yours you will keep as your own by virtue of your presence."

After these many useless words, which did not reach the ears of the gods or those of my ungrateful young man, it sometimes happened that I would suddenly change my mind and say:

"You miserable one, why do you wish Panfilo to come back here? Do you believe that you can endure what is close better than what is burdensome when far away? You seek your own harm. Since you now do not know whether he loves you or not, by his returning you might be made certain that he came back not for you but for someone else. Let him stay away and keep you in doubt of his love by remaining where he is rather than by coming close make you sure that he does not love you. At least rejoice that you are not alone in suffering such pain, and find the kind of comfort unhappy people usually find by sharing their miseries with others."

It would be difficult for me to show you, ladies, how vehement an anger, how many tears, and what a heartache would accompany these thoughts and arguments of mine nearly every day, but because everything that is hard ripens and softens in time, it happened that after several days of this kind of life my pain began to subside considerably, since I was unable to suffer more than I was suffering. As I became less mindful of my grief, passion and a faint hope were rekindled proportionately, and so, since the pain remained as well, my mind changed little by little, and the original desire to have my Panfilo back returned. And although everything was contrary to the hope of ever having him back, the greater my desire for it grew, just as flames grow into a greater blaze from being stirred by the wind, my love grew stronger by having gathered all its strength against hostile thoughts. Therefore, I suddenly regretted all the things I had said.

As I reflected on what my rage had driven me to say, I felt ashamed as if he had heard me, and I blamed this anger of ours which first assails and seizes the mind with such intensity that it does not allow it to discern any truth. Nevertheless, the heavier the assault of such fury is, the colder it becomes as time goes by, allowing us to discern clearly what evil it has made us perpetrate; thus, I regained clarity of mind, and I began by saying:

"What is your trouble, you silly young woman? Why do you get so angry without a sure reason? Even if we assume that what the merchant said is the truth (and perhaps it is not), namely, that Panfilo has taken a wife, is this such an important fact or novel thing that you should not have any hope? It is necessary that young men please their fathers in such matters. If it was his father's wish, with what pretext could he have denied it? You must not believe that all those who take or have a wife love her as they love other women; the excessive doting that wives practice on their husbands is cause of quick regret, even if at first they liked it very much; and you do not know how much he likes her. It may be that Panfilo was forced to take her, and because he loves you more than he loves her, he may find it tiresome to be with her, and even if he is attracted to her, you can hope that he might soon be tired of her. You surely have no reason to complain about his faith and his oaths, because if he should return to you and your bedchamber, he would keep both.

"So pray to God that Love, who has more power than any sacred vow or sworn faith, will make him return. Furthermore, why do you mistrust him because of the uneasiness of that young woman? Do you not know how many young men love you hopelessly and would certainly be very troubled if they knew that you belong to Panfilo? Thus, you must accept the possibility that he is loved by many women who also find it hard to hear it said about him what you too found painful, although it may bother each one for different reasons."

And in this manner, I contradicted myself, for instead of uttering numerous curses, I almost returned to my former hopeful state and implored with prayers for the opposite.

But Hope, having been recovered in such a way, was not strong enough to cheer me up; on the contrary, I always appeared troubled in my mind and in my appearance, and did not know what to do with myself. My earlier preoccupations had disappeared; under the first impulse of anger I had thrown away the stones which were reminders of bygone days; I had burned the letters I received from him and had destroyed many other things. I no longer enjoyed contemplating the sky, and I felt as unsure about his return then as I had seemed certain before. My inclination to invent tales had disappeared, for the season with its shorter nights did not allow it, and quite often I spent all or a good part of my nights sleepless, weeping, or thinking incessantly; and when by chance it happened that I slept, I had different kinds of dreams—sometimes cheerful and at other times extremely sad. I found social gatherings and religious services burdensome and participated in them very seldom, almost only when I had no choice. My face was once again pale, which made the entire house gloomy and caused people to gossip, and I kept waiting, sullen and melancholy, almost not knowing for what.

For the most part, my doubtful thoughts kept me wavering the entire day, uncertain about whether I should complain or be cheerful, but when the night came (the time most suitable to my woes) and I found myself alone in my bedchamber, I wept and spoke to myself at length, and then, as if moved by a better idea, I addressed my prayers to Venus, saying:

"Most extraordinary heavenly beauty! O most compassionate goddess! O holy Venus, whose image appeared to me in this room when my troubles first began, give some relief to my sorrow, and in the name of that true and venerable love you felt for Adonis, soften my misfortunes. See how much I endure for you, see how many times the terrible image of death has appeared before my eyes, and consider whether my innocent trust has deserved as much suffering as I bear. As a trusting young woman inexperienced in your arrows,[1] I submitted myself without questioning to your first wishes. You know how many good things you promised me, and I do not deny having received some, but if the troubles you give me are intended to be a part of your boon, may the heavens and the earth perish at once, and may laws such as these be remade in the world to come! Although it may be hurtful, as I seem to feel, may the good you promised come, my gracious goddess, so that your blessed lips cannot be said to have learned to lie as men's do.

"Send your son with his arrows and with your torches wherever Panfilo is, so far away from me, and if his love for me may have cooled because he has not seen me or because he is interested in someone else, rekindle his flame in such a way that by burning as I do, nothing can stop him from coming back, with the result that with renewed courage I will not perish under this burden. O most beautiful goddess, may my words reach your ears, but if you do not wish to rekindle his love, take your arrows out of my heart so that like him I too may spend my days free of anguish."

Although I saw such prayers turn out to be useless, I would find in hope relief to my torment because even then I believed them nearly granted, and beginning to murmur anew, I would say:

"Panfilo, where are you now? What are you doing? Have you spent this quiet night sleepless and shedding as many tears as I have, or were you perhaps in the arms of the young woman

---

1. trusting young woman: *lasciva giovane.* "Trusting" is only one of many meanings of *lascivo*: "lustful," "careless," and "compliant" are other possibilities.

about whom, unfortunately for me, I have just heard? Or are you sleeping most sweetly, with no thought of me? Ah, how can Love treat two lovers who are both deeply in love, as I am and you may be, by such different standards? I am not sure, but if it is true that we are both engaged in the same thoughts, what prison or chains hold you so that you do not break them to come back to me? I certainly do not know who could stop me from coming to you, if I were not held back by my own sex, which undoubtedly would be an obstacle and shame to me in many places. Whatever business or whatever other reason you may have had to stay must already be finished, and your father must be tired of you by now; as the gods know, I often pray for his death, firmly believing that he is responsible for your stay there, and if not so, he is at least responsible for taking you away from me. But I do not doubt that by praying for his death I may be prolonging his life, so much are the gods against me and unwilling to grant me anything.

"Ah, if your love is as it used to be, may its power prevail so that you might come. Do you not think of me lying alone throughout most of the night during which, if you were here, you would faithfully keep me company as you did before? How endless were those nights without you in my enormous bed this past winter! Ah, do remember the many pleasures we often took in various things; I am sure that if you remembered them no other woman could ever take you from me. And perhaps this belief, more than any other, assures me that the news I heard about a new wife is false, and even if it were true, I believe that she could take you away from me only temporarily. So do come back, and if those charming pleasures do not have the power to bring you here, may the wish to save from a horrible death the woman who loves you above all else bring you back here. Oh if you should return now, I believe that you would scarcely recognize me, since this anxiety has changed me so. But I am sure that whatever has been taken away from me by these endless tears would be restored by the brief joy of seeing your beautiful face, and I would surely become again the Fiammetta I used to be.

"Oh, come, come, my heart is calling you, do not destroy my youth, which is waiting for your pleasure. Oh, if you came back, I don't know how I could restrain my happiness so that it would not be evident to others, for I have reasons to believe that our love, which was most cleverly but painfully kept hidden for so long, would be discovered by everyone. Now you should come to see whether, for better or for worse, these crafty lies took hold. Oh if only you were here already, I believe I could find a remedy for everything, but if the case cannot be that much better, let everyone know who wants to know."

After having said this, I would immediately rise and run to the window, as if he had really heard me, and I would fool myself into believing that I had heard what I had not heard, namely, that he was knocking on our door as he used to do. Oh how often I could have been tricked had my eager suitors known this and if at such times a mischievous one had pretended to be Panfilo! But after I had opened the window and looked out of the door, my eyes made me more certain of what I knew already to be a deception; this futile joy turned into inner turmoil, and I became like a helpless, tottering ship with tangled sails, its mast shattered by strong winds, about to be swallowed by tempestuous waves. And I keep weeping miserably as I return to my usual tears, but then, in an effort to give my mind a rest, I close my eyes, inviting moist dreams,[2] and calling sleep to invade me, as follows:

"O Sleep, you are of all things the most pleasant rest and the true serenity of the mind, you who flee as an enemy from all cares, come to me and do what you can to banish most of my worries from my heart. You who give delight to bodies burdened by difficulties and restore new strength, why do you not come? Ah, you who give rest to everyone else, give me some because I need you more than anyone else! Run from the eyes of happy young women who reject and hate you while they embrace their lovers and exert themselves in Venus' arena; invade my eyes, since I am alone, abandoned, and overcome by tears and sighs. You who are the soother of all wounds and the best aspect of human life, comfort me and stay away only when Panfilo's pleasant talk will delight these ears so eager to listen to his voice. You who are the languid brother of harsh death, you who mix false things with true ones, come into my miserable eyes! You who invaded Argos's one hundred vigilant eyes, come now and invade

2. moist dreams: *umidi sonni*. A phrase which invites several interpretations.

my two eyes which so desire you! O gateway to life, light's rest and night's companion, you who are welcomed by most powerful kings and by humble servants alike, come into my wretched heart and restore my strength. O sweetest Sleep, you who oblige the human race, fearful of death, to become accustomed to its longest rest, seize me forcefully, and chase from me the mad emotions amidst which the mind struggles to no purpose."

Sleep, who is more compassionate than any other god to whom I pray, is slow in granting the grace for which I beg, but after a long while he comes lazily, as if he were forced rather than willing to serve me, and, without saying a word or giving me warning, creeps into my tired head, which out of need eagerly grabs on to him and entirely wraps itself up in him.

But while Sleep sometimes comes, the much desired Peace keeps away, and instead of thoughts and tears, a thousand visions full of countless fears frighten me. I believe that there is no other kind of Fury in the city of Dis who has not already appeared to me in various and terrible guises, threatening me with different misfortunes, and such Furies interrupted my sleep with their hideous appearance, and I was almost pleased when this happened, for it meant that I would no longer see them. In short, after I had received the inaccurate news about the acquired bride, there were few nights that afforded me any pleasure in my sleep as I often used to have when I saw my Panfilo in a happy state, and this hurt me immensely and still does.

I am speaking of all these matters—such as tears and pains—but not of their cause, of which my darling husband took no notice; but since he observed that my rosy cheeks had turned pale and that my eyes, which were once lovely and sparkling, had now purple rings around them and were so small as to nearly disappear into my forehead, he was often surprised and wondered about this. And because he also noticed that I had lost my appetite and was unable to rest, sometimes he asked the cause of this, and I answered by blaming my stomach, which for some unaccountable reason had gone bad, making me abnormally thin. Imagine! By fully trusting my words he believed me and ordered an infinite number of medicines, which I took in order to please him and not because I expected any relief from them. After all, what bodily relief could alleviate the passions of the soul? None, I believe, but it may be that once the passions of the soul are alleviated, the body may find relief. The medicine suitable to my illness was only one, but it was too far away to be beneficial to me.

Since my betrayed husband, who was more loving towards me than his duty required, noticed that I derived little or no benefit from these many remedies, he tried new and different ways to chase this melancholy away from me and restore the cheerfulness I had lost, but in vain did he try so many things. Once he addressed himself to me with these words:

"My lady, as you know, just on the other side of Mount Falerno, between the ancient ruins of Cumae and Pozzuoli, lies the rocky coast of Baia high above the seashore, and no sight under the sun is more beautiful or more pleasant than this. It is surrounded by the most lovely mountains thick with trees and vineyards; in the valleys any game that can be hunted is available; nearby lies a vast plain perfect for hunting birds of prey; and for amusements, not far away are the islands of Pithecusae and Nisida, which abound with rabbits, and there is the gravesite of the great Misenus, leading into the realm of Pluto; there are the oracles of the Cumaean Sibyl, the lake of Avernus, and Mount Barbaro, and the amphitheater where the ancient games convened, and the Pools, vain projects of the wicked Nero. These very ancient and new sights provide no small diversion to modern minds. In addition, there is an infinite number of healthy baths which cure all illnesses, and the extremely mild weather of this season gives us occasion for visiting them. In the company of knights and noble ladies one is never without entertainment and great merriment. So I want you, who, from what I can tell, have an unhealthy stomach and a mind troubled by bothersome melancholy, to come with me to cure the one and the other; I am sure our visit will not be useless."

After having listened to these words, I hesitated for a long time to give an answer, for I feared I might miss seeing my darling lover if he were to come back in the middle of our stay there, but then, as I observed my husband's pleasure, imagining that if my lover came he would join me wherever I might be, I answered that I was ready to do as he wished, and so we went there.

Oh what an ill-suited medicine my husband was using for my pains! Granted that physical ailments can be readily healed there, seldom or never did anyone go to that place with a healthy mind and return with a mind still healthy, nor did sick minds regain their health there. Indeed, this is not surprising: I do not know whether it is because that place is close to where Venus was born or because the time when it is most frequented (that is, springtime) is more conducive to certain things, but, as it has often seemed to me, there more than anywhere else even the most chaste women forget their feminine modesty and seem to take more liberties on all occasions; and I am not alone in holding this opinion, for almost all people familiar with it agree. There, for the most part, time is spent in idleness, and when it *is* spent more actively, women, either alone or in the company of young men, speak of love; there people consume nothing but delicacies, and the finest old vintage wines strong enough not only to excite the sleeping Venus but also, if she were dead, to bring her back to life inside every man, and those who have tried the power of the baths know to what extent their beneficial effects also contribute to this. There the beaches, the lovely gardens, and every other place always resound with festivities, novel games, most graceful dances, music, and love songs composed, sung, and played by young men and by young women as well. Therefore, in this place those who can should be on guard against Cupid, who, insofar as I know, in that very place, which seems to be his choice domain, exercises his powers with little effort.

To such a place, compassionate ladies, my husband wished to take me to cure my love fever, and when we arrived there, Love did not treat me differently from other women; but while my soul could no longer be seized because it already had been taken, and since it had somewhat cooled (though in fact very slightly) because of Panfilo's long absence and all the tears shed and the pains sustained, Love rekindled in it the hottest flame which I seemed to have ever experienced. This was not only for the reasons I just mentioned but also because I remembered having been there before, escorted by Panfilo; therefore, when I found myself there without him I certainly loved and suffered more than anyone else. I did not see a mountain or a valley around me which had not witnessed our happiness when with him and other people we carried nets, led hounds, set traps, and caught wild animals. I could scarcely see beach, rock, or little island without saying:

"I was here with Panfilo, and here he said this, and here we did that."

In the same way, wherever I looked, there was nothing that could not make me first remember him more vividly and then send me back into the past with greater desire to see him again here or elsewhere.

According to my husband's wishes, we began amusing ourselves in various ways. At times we mounted our horses before dawn, and with hounds or falcons or both we rode fast on the nearby lands rich with game, through shady woods and open fields, but while everyone else was heartened by the variety of prey they saw, I felt my pain only slightly diminished. Whenever I noticed a good flight or a particularly interesting run, I would repeat: "O Panfilo, if only you too could be here to see this, as you were then!" Alas, up to that moment I had been able to bear watching and doing things with little annoyance, but as I remembered this I let everything go, nearly overwhelmed by my hidden grief. Oh, how many times I remember dropping my bow and arrow on such occasions, as if I had never been one of the best trained of Diana's followers when it came to spreading nets or letting hounds loose! And not once but many times, in the thick of the bird hunt, when any bird could easily be caught, as if I were completely absent-minded, I would unwittingly let the bird fly out of my hands, and while in the past I had been very diligent in such a thing, now I cared little about it. After we had searched each valley, mountain, and vast plain, my friends and I, laden with the spoils of the hunt, returned home, which most of the time we found animated and festive in various ways.

After we had placed our banquet on the sand, we sometimes had our meals in the company of young men and women, in the refreshing shade of the high rocks that extend themselves over the sea. No sooner did we leave the tables than the young people began dancing to the sound of various instruments, and at times I too was almost forced to join them, but perhaps because my mind was reluctant to participate or my body weak, I soon withdrew and sat on the spread mats with the other women. There I listened to the sweet notes that filled my mind, and at the same time I thought of Panfilo, mixing joy and sorrow in a state of turmoil, because as I listened to the pleasant sounds, every little flickering flame of love dormant in my heart was revived, and I remembered the happy moments in which I used to dance with great skill and grace in the presence of my Panfilo; but because I did not see him there, I would have been willing to weep over him sadly and with doleful sighs if it had seemed possible to me. Moreover, the same effect was usually elicited in me by the songs many ladies were singing, and if one of the songs referred to troubles similar to mine, I listened attentively, wishing to learn it so that by repeating it to myself I would and could sometime lament in public in a more orderly and covert language, and especially about that aspect of my miseries treated by the song itself.

When the young women were exhausted by the repeated whirling of the dances, they all sat with us, and it often happened that as the handsome young men crowded around us they formed a crown-like shape so unusual that I have never seen one like it either here or anywhere else, and it reminded me of the first time I had seen Panfilo and how he charmed me, standing apart from everyone else, so that I often raised my eyes searching in vain among them, still hoping to see my Panfilo in a similar position. So, as I looked among them, I sometimes noticed that some stared very intensely at the object of their desire, and because I had been very clever in such matters in the past, I observed everything with a perplexed eye,[3] and I knew who was loving and who was mocking; sometimes I praised this one and sometimes that one, and at other times I said to myself that it would have been better for me to have done what they were doing, to keep the soul free by cheating as they did, but then I condemned such a thought, glad (if one can be happy to be in pain) to have loved faithfully. Then my eyes and thoughts turned to the games these young lovers played, and as if I were deriving some consolation from watching those who loved passionately, I praised them more within myself because of this, and after having admired them wholeheartedly, I began saying silently to myself:

3. perplexed eye: *occhio perplesso*. The phrase appears to conflict directly with the rest of this passage, in which Fiammetta claims discernment in matters of love and flirtation.

"Happy you to whom the view of yourselves is not denied as it is to me! What a pity that you are doing what I used to do! May your happiness endure so that I alone could be an example of misery to the world! If at least Love made me dissatisfied with the thing I adore and made my days on earth fewer, it would follow that, like Dido, I would become renowned forever for my sorrow."

After I said this, I silently kept watching how differently various people behaved. Oh, how many of them I also saw in such places who after having searched for their lady without finding her, considered the festivities less attractive and sadly left! And I smiled (although faintly) in the midst of my woes, as I perceived that I had company in my suffering and understood other people's misfortunes through my own.

So, dearest ladies, as my words demonstrate, these were my inclinations after the delicate baths, the fatiguing hunts, and the beaches full of festivities, and because my pale face, my continual sighing, and the loss of appetite and sleep proved to my deceived husband and the doctors that my ailment was incurable, we returned to the city we had left, where entertainments permitted by the good season were being prepared but which were to cause me all sorts of torments.

It happened not once but many times that when fresh brides were given to their grooms, I was the first to be invited to the new season's weddings of relatives, friends, or neighbors, which my husband often forced me to attend, believing that by these means my obvious melancholy would be alleviated. Therefore, on such occasions I was obliged to wear once again the ornaments I had abandoned and to tend as well as I could to my neglected hair, which was once considered golden, but had become almost ashen. As I did this I fully remembered the one who used to admire it as my greatest charm, and my mind, already in turmoil, was even more perturbed; and at times oblivious of myself, I remembered that my maidservants recalled me as if from a deep sleep and would then pick up the comb I had dropped and resume the forgotten task. Afterwards, I wished to consult with my mirror about which ornaments to wear, as young women usually do, but as I saw myself in it as horrible as I was and recalled my lost image, I would look around, not certain whether the face I saw in the mirror was my own or that of some infernal fury. But once bedecked and in a frame of mind not unlike that of the other women, I went with them to the cheerful gatherings, and I mean cheerful for the others, because—as the one from whom nothing can be hidden well knows—there was never a single such gathering after my Panfilo's departure that did not cause me grief.

Although there were several weddings occurring at different times, whenever we arrived at where they were arranged to take place, I was perceived in only one way, namely, with a face feigning cheerfulness as much as possible, and with a heart entirely prone to lamentations since it found reasons for its pain in both joyful and sad events. After we were received with many honors by the other ladies, my eyes turned all around wishing not to rest on the ornaments that were shining everywhere but deceiving themselves with the idea that here they could see Panfilo as they had seen him before in a similar place; but when I did not see him, I felt almost exhausted, as if I had become more certain of what I was already quite certain, and sat with the other ladies, rejecting the homage that was offered, since I could not see the one for whom I used to cherish them. Then after the bride had arrived, the grand display of the ceremonial banquet had been removed, and the dances had begun, led by a singer's voice or directed by the sounds of musical instruments, the house in which the wedding festivities were held became full of cheerful sounds; to appear courteous rather than impolite, I danced awhile but then sat down again with new thoughts in mind.

I also remember how solemn had been a similar reception given for me when innocent, free, and without melancholy, I was myself honored, and as I compared in my mind those moments with these and observed how different they were, I felt an immense desire to weep, and I would have, had the place allowed it. As I looked at the young men and young women having an equally good time, my mind went back in a flash to a time I had entertained my Panfilo in similar places when he looked at me doing the same things skillfully in various ways, and I suffered less for not being merry than for being deprived of the cause for merriment. Then as I listened to the songs, both words and music, and remembered the past ones, I sighed and showed false pleasure, for I felt discontented with having to wait so anxiously for the end of these festivities. I was nevertheless observing everything, and since the many young men had gathered around to look at the young women who were resting, I clearly perceived that many if not all of them sometimes stared at me and wondered silently to themselves about one aspect or another of my appearance, but in such a way that much of their hidden talk would reach my ears either through imagination or hearsay.

And some would say to others:

"Oh look at that young woman; her beauty was without equal in our city; look what she has become now! Don't you see how bewildered she looks; what could be the reason?"

Having said this, they looked at me in a very humble way as if they had been moved to compassion by my misfortunes, and when they departed they left me feeling more sorry for myself than usual. Others asked themselves:

"For goodness' sake, has this woman been ill?"

And then they answered themselves:

"It seems so, since she has become so thin and emaciated, and it is a great shame, considering her lost beauty!"

There were others with keener intuition who, unfortunately for me, after lengthy conversations said:

"This young woman's pallor is a sign of a heart in love. What illness makes one so extremely thin except too passionate a love? She must really be in love, and if it is so, the one who causes her the kind of trouble that makes her so thin is cruel."

When this happened I must say that I could not restrain myself from sighing as I observed more pity for me in others than in the one who should have reasonably felt it, and after giving way to my sighing I humbly and silently prayed to the gods for those people's well-being. And certainly this reminds me that my virtue so impressed those who reasoned in this way that some of them justified me by saying:

"God forbid that anyone should believe this woman has love troubles; she is more virtuous than any other; she never showed signs, nor was any rumor ever heard among lovers about a love affair of hers, and certainly this is not the kind of passion that can be kept hidden for very long."

"Alas," I said then to myself, "how far from the truth these people are if they believe that I am not in love only because I do not place my love affairs, like a fool, before the eyes and on the lips of young people as many other women do!"

In this place I was often faced with noble, handsome, and pleasant young men who in the past had more than once tried to catch my eye in various ways and by different means in an attempt to attract my glances to their wishes. But after having looked at my ugliness for a long while, they went away, perhaps glad that I had not loved them, saying: "This lady's beauty is spoiled."

Why will I conceal from you, ladies, what not only I but also women in general do not like to hear? What I am saying is that although my Panfilo was not nearby, my heart ached deeply when I heard that I had lost the beauty I so greatly cherished for his sake.

Moreover, I also remember that at such gatherings it sometimes happened that I found myself in a circle of ladies speaking of love, and there, by listening with a curiosity about other people's love affairs, I easily understood that no other love has been as passionate, as secretive, and as burdened with anxieties as mine, although there are a great many happier and less virtuous. In this manner, therefore, sometimes looking and sometimes listening to what was happening in the places where I was, I pensively whiled away the fleeting time.

So, after the ladies had rested by sitting for a while, it sometimes happened that when they rose to go dancing after inviting me to do the same, but to no avail, I watched these young women and their partners so intent in their dancing that their hearts seemed empty of all other intentions; and while some of these ladies seemed to wish to demonstrate their dancing skills, others were spurred by Venus' ardor, and I remained seated almost all alone watching with a scornful mind the unusual movements and the qualities of many of these women. And it certainly happened that I criticized some of them, although I desired immensely to do what they were doing, if it had been possible and had my Panfilo been there; and each time I thought and think of him, I became and still become melancholy, because, as God knows, he does not deserve the great love I feel and have felt for him.

But sometimes, after watching for hours those dances with marked displeasure—for they became tedious because of my other thoughts—I would leave the public place as if I had to do something else, because I wished to give vent to the pain I was holding inside, and if I could easily do it, I went to some solitary corner where I let my tears flow at will to reward my foolish eyes for the vanities they had seen. And the tears did not flow unaccompanied by words inflamed with anger; on the contrary, aware of my wretched Fortune, I remember speaking to her in this manner:

"O Fortune, you are a dreadful enemy of anyone happy and the only hope of those who are very unhappy; you are a barterer of kingdoms and a bestower of human destinies; with your hands you raise and you quash as your rash judgment moves you, and when you are not satisfied to belong entirely to someone, you exalt him in one way or humiliate him in another, or after offering happiness you add new worries to the mind so that by remaining in a continual state of need (as they define it) human beings may always plead with you and adore your blind divinity. Blind and deaf, you ignore the weeping of the miserable and rejoice, smiling and beguiling, with the exalted, who embrace you with all their might but unexpectedly find themselves cast down by you and wretchedly learn that you have changed face. And I find myself among such miserable ones, not knowing what hostility induced you to do this nor what wrong I have done you that has led you to do me such harm in this matter.

"Alas, whoever trusts in great things and is a powerful master in high places and credulously inclined to believe what is pleasing should look at me, who, after having been a great lady, have become the meanest servant, and even worse, since I am scorned and rejected by my lord! If one looks at this with a clear mind, it will be perceived that you, O Fortune, have never given a more instructive example of mutability than me. I was welcomed into the world by you, O fickle Fortune, with a great abundance of your gifts (if, as I believe, nobility and riches are among them), and besides this, I grew up among them, and you never withdrew your generous hand. Of course, always magnanimous, I owned these things and treated them as temporary, and contrary to feminine nature, I used them most liberally.

"But I was still inexperienced and did not know that as the bestower of the soul's passions, you played such an important role in the domain of Love, and as was your wish, I fell in love and loved that young man and no other, whom you alone, and no one else, placed before my eyes when I believed myself to be the furthest from falling in love. When you felt that my heart was tied with an indissoluble knot to the pleasure I derived from him, you have tried several times to transform it into vexation, and sometimes you have troubled the intimacy of our minds with inane and beguiling tricks, and at other times you did the same with our eyes, so that our love would have been harmed by being revealed. More than once, according to your wishes, odious rumors about my beloved reached my ears, and I am sure you caused the same kind of words about me to reach him, which I am sure could have generated hatred if they were believed; however, such gossip never furthered your intentions because if you, O goddess, steer external events as you please, the qualities of the soul are not subject to your power, and our good sense has always had the better of you in this. But what is the use of opposing you? You have a thousand ways to hurt your enemies, and what you cannot do by right, you achieve with underhanded means. Since you could not generate enmity in our minds, you ingeniously tried to place in them something like it and added to it extremely deep pain and anxiety.

"Your schemes were foiled in the past by our wit but they had their revenge in a different way, and you who are his enemy and mine too provided the reason for my beloved young man to be separated from me by a long distance.

"Alas, when could I have thought that the cause of my miseries would, by your intervention, be born in a place so far away from here, separated from this by so great a sea, by so many mountains, valleys, and rivers? Certainly never, and yet it is so; but in spite of all this, and even though he may be far from me and I from him, I have no doubts that he loves me as I love him, and I love him above all else. But is this love in effect worth more than if we were enemies? Certainly not, so our wit had no power at all against you. With him you took away all my pleasure, all my riches, and all my joy, and with them the merriment, the clothing, the beautiful things, and the happy life, leaving in their stead tears, sadness, and unbearable anguish, but certainly you did not and can never take away the fact that I love him.

"For pity's sake, if I offended your divinity in something because I was still young, the innocence of my age should be forgiven. But even if you wished to take revenge on me, why didn't you do it in your own sphere of things? You have unjustly meddled with the affairs of others. What have you to do with matters of love? I own beautiful and mighty houses, vast fields, and numerous livestock, all treasures bestowed upon me by your own hand. Why did your wrath not extend itself to these things with fire, or water, or theft, or death? You left me things that cannot have any comforting value for me except what Bacchus gave to Midas to satisfy his hunger, and you have taken away the only one whom I cherished above all other things.

"Oh cursed be the amorous arrows that dared to take vengeance upon Phoebus and that carry so many of your insults! Oh if only they had pierced you as they pierce me now, you would perhaps think more carefully before hurting lovers! But you have hurt me anyhow and driven me to the point where I, who was once rich, noble, and powerful, am now the meanest thing in my land, as you clearly see. Every man rejoices and makes merry, while I alone weep, and this has not begun just now but has lasted for so long that your fury should be appeased.

"But I would forgive you anything if it pleased you to rejoin my Panfilo and me as you have separated him from me, but if your anger should persist, give vent to it on the rest of my belongings. For goodness' sake, have pity on me, O cruel one! You see that I have become such that I am on everyone's mouth like a popular fable, while my beauty used to be praised for its lofty reputation! Begin to have pity on me so that I, who wish to praise you, may honor your majesty with pleasing words, and I swear on it that from this very moment if you should grant me the favor I have asked, the gods be my witnesses that I would honor you by placing my image, as suitably adorned as possible, in any temple most dear to you, and on it these lines would be inscribed for all to see: *This is Fiammetta, by Fortune raised from the most dejected misery to supreme joy.*"

Oh, it would be too long and tedious to recount how many other things I repeated over and over! But I can say briefly that all ended in bitter tears, from which it sometimes happened that I was lifted with comforting words by the ladies who happened

to hear me and who took me back against my will to the cheerful dancing.

Who would believe, loving ladies, that a young woman's
heart could contain so much gloom that not only did everything
fail to cheer me up but neither could anything continue to cause
her greater grief? Everyone finds this incredible, but since I am
the one who experiences it, I feel and know that it is true. It often happened that because of the very hot weather brought by
the season many other women and I took to the sea on a very
swift galley in order to pass the time more pleasantly; we plowed
through the waves, singing and playing musical instruments,
searching for remote rocks and caverns naturally carved into the
mountains and most inviting with their shade and fresh air. Alas,
while these were certainly the most wonderful remedies offered
for my physical comfort, from all of this I derived no relief to my
burning soul, because when the external heat (undoubtedly annoying to our delicate bodies) ceased, immediately more room
was provided for thoughts of love, which, if one considers this
carefully, are the substance that not only nourishes Venus' flames
but also makes them greater.

When we reached the place we were seeking and occupied a
broad stretch for our amusement, following our own desires, we
went to look around, now at one group of young men and
young women and then at another, because every little rock or
beach even slightly protected from the sun by the mountain's
shadow was full of them. Oh, what a great delight this is for
healthy minds! In many places around there one would see the
whitest of tables spread so beautifully and so preciously decorated that the mere sight of them could arouse appetite even in
the most indifferent person, and elsewhere people could be seen
having their morning meal, since it was already that time, and
we or anyone else passing by were cheerfully invited to join
their pleasure.

When like the rest we too had finished our festive meals, the
tables were cleared, and as usual we whirled around in joyful
dancing; then we boarded our boats and swiftly sailed around.
In some places an extremely desirable sight appeared before the
young men's eyes: beautiful women covered by sheer, silky tu-
nics, barefooted, and with bare arms, walking in the water, picking sea shells from the hard rock, and as they bent in their task

they revealed the hidden delights of their ripe bosoms. Elsewhere more resourceful people, some with nets and some with other novel devices, were seen luring the hidden fish.

But what is the use of recounting each particular pleasure one has in this place? There would be no end to them. Those with enough imagination may picture for themselves how many and of what sort they must be, since the only ones who go there are young and gay, and if others go there they are not seen. There the minds are open and free, and so many and so varied are the reasons for this that in such a place one can hardly refuse anything that is asked. I must confess that in these places I falsely showed a happy face not to upset my women friends, but I did not take my mind away from its grief, and only those who have experienced this can tell how difficult it is to do so. How could I be lighthearted when I remembered having seen my dear Panfilo amusing himself in the same way, with or without me, since I now felt that he was very far from me and I had no hope of seeing him again?

Not only was I plagued by other troubles, but my mental anxiety was so great that it kept me continually in doubt about many things; and what would one think of the eagerness to see him which deprived me of judgment to the extent that, knowing for certain that he was not in those places, I would argue that he could be, and then, as if it were absolutely true that he was there, I would proceed to see if I could find him? There was no boat left among those swiftly darting about which I did not search out first with my eyes and then in person, and that inlet of the sea was as filled with them as the sky is with stars when it appears at its brightest and clearest. I did not hear the sound of any musical instrument, even though I knew that Panfilo was trained in only one, without becoming all ears in an attempt to discover who the player was, always imagining that it might be the one I was looking for. No beach, no rock, no grotto, no squad of youth did I neglect to explore. Of course I must confess that this sometimes futile and sometimes false hope drew many sighs out of me almost as if they had gathered within the hollow of my brain; after this hope had left me, those sighs which needed to depart breathed out through my sorrowful eyes, having been turned into the most bitter tears.

More than all other Italian cities, ours offers a great number of festivities and not only entertains its citizens with weddings, or bathing, or beaches, but it abounds in many diversions and frequently entertains its people, now with one and now with another. But among other things, it appears especially splendid during its frequent jousting tourneys. So when the rainy winter days are over and spring has restored its lost beauty to the world with flowers and green grass, it is an ancient tradition on the most important holidays to gather together the noble ladies at the knights' quarters, where they all come wearing their most precious jewels, because youthful minds are excited by the character of the season and more than ever ready to express their desires.

And I do not believe that it was a nobler or richer experience to look at Priam's daughters-in-law with the other Trojan women whenever they gathered before their father-in-law all bedecked with jewels for a celebration than to watch the local ladies in several parts of our city; and when they are seen assembled in large numbers at the theaters, each one displaying herself as beautifully as she possibly can, I have no doubt that if any discerning stranger were to arrive and take into account the proud manners, the remarkable costumes, the ornaments more fitting for queens than for other women, he would think us not modern women but some of those magnificent ancient ones returned into the world. One, he would say, resembles Semiramis for her haughty bearing; another would be believed to be Cleopatra, to judge from her jewels; another could be seen as Helen, for her beauty; and still another be said to be in no way different from Dido, if one carefully observed her demeanor. But why should I continue comparing all of them? Each one by herself appeared to be a creature filled with divine as well as human majesty. And to think that I, poor wretch, before I lost my Panfilo, often heard young men asking one another whether I resembled more the virgin Polixena or the Venus of Cyprus, since some of them said that it was an exaggeration to compare me to a goddess, while others retorted that it was not enough to compare me to a mortal woman.

Here, among such a large and noble company, one does not sit or keep silent or whisper for long; rather, as the older men look on, the bright young men take the ladies by their delicate hands an sing aloud of their feelings of love as they dance, and in this manner and in as many joyful ways as can be imagined, they spend the hot part of the day. When the sun's rays begin to grow cool, one can see the honorable princes of our Ausonian kingdom arrive, clad as magnificently as their rank requires, and after having admired the charms of the ladies as well as their dances, they leave with nearly all their young men, knights as well as pages, and return shortly thereafter with a very large following, wearing costumes entirely different from what they had worn before.

What language is either so splendidly eloquent or so rich with wonderful words that it can completely and entirely describe the noble attires and their full range? Neither Homer the Greek nor Virgil the Latin, who have already described many Greek, Trojan, and Italian rites in their verses, could do so. In a lighthearted manner, therefore, as an imitation of reality, I will try my best to share them in some small way with those ladies who have not seen them firsthand. And may this not be an irrelevant demonstration in the present account; on the contrary, with the help of ladies who are wise one will understand that my wretchedness is unceasing and beyond that of any other women past and present, since the dignity of the many lofty things seen has not been able to destroy it with any happy means.

To return to my task, I will then say that our princes arrive on horses which run not only faster than any other animal but so fast that in running they would leave behind even those very winds believed to be the fastest; and the princes' youth, their remarkable beauty, and their notable excellence makes them exceedingly pretty to those who look at them. They appear on caparisoned horses, dressed in crimson or in garments woven by native hands with designs of different colors and interwoven threads of gold and also garnished with pearls and precious stones; their long blond hair falling onto their extremely white shoulders is tied onto their head with a gold ringlet or held by a small garland of fresh branches. Furthermore, their left hand is armed with a very light shield and their right one with a lance, and at the sound of the summoning trumpets, one after the other and followed by many others all wearing the same costume, they begin their jousting before the ladies, who praise most the one who in such a game gallops on his horse, keeping the tip of his lance closest to the ground and holding himself most tightly under his shield without any awkward movements.

Although I am so wretched, I am still invited to such festivities and pleasant games, as I used to be, but this does not happen without arousing great resentment in me, because when I see these things I remember having already seen sitting as a spectator among our oldest and most revered knights my dear Panfilo, whose competence earned him such a place at a very young age. And it sometimes happened that standing among those knights in their ceremonial garbs, he looked like none other than Daniel among the ancient priests, judging the accused woman[4]; and one of them resembled Scaevola in his authoritative demeanor; another could have been either Cato the Censor or Cato of Utica for his seriousness, and others appeared so dignified, judging from their faces, that one could have believed them to be none other than Pompey the Great and still others more robust resembled Scipio Africanus or Cincinnatus. These elders also watched all the riders, thrilled as if they were recalling to themselves their own younger years, praising now this one and now that one, and Panfilo agreed with what they were saying, and at times, as he was talking with them, I heard him compare young and valiant old riders to the ones of antiquity.

Oh, how glad I was to hear this, and I rejoiced for the one who was saying it, also for those who intently listened to it and for my fellow citizens about whom this was said. I was so glad that I still enjoy remembering it. He used to say that one of the young princes, all of whom revealed in their appearance their royal minds at their best, looked like the Arcadian Parthenopaeus, who was believed to have been the most beautiful youth who went to the siege of Thebes, where he was sent by his mother when he was still a child; he asserted that another next to this one resembled the charming Ascanius, a youth whom Virgil's high testimonial described in many verses; a third he compared to Deiphobus, and a fourth, for his beauty, to Ganymede.

Then, as he came to the more mature throng of men who followed them, he made other comparisons no less felicitous.

4. accused woman: Susannah (see Glossary).

There came one with a ruddy complexion, red beard, and blond hair flowing over his white shoulders, and just as Hercules may have worn it, it was tied back by a very fine small garland of green leaves[5]; he was dressed in garments of the finest sheer silk which covered no more than the bulk of his body, adorned with various articles handcrafted by a master, and with a mantle fastened by a golden buckle and draped over his right shoulder; a shield covered his left side, and in his right hand he carried a light lance suitable for the appointed games; and for his bearing he compared him to the great Hector. After him one came adorned in the same clothes, with a face no less bold, who had thrown both sides of his mantle over his shoulders; he masterfully led his horse with his left hand, and Panfilo judged him to be almost like another Achilles; another followed tossing his lance about and carrying a shield on his back; his blond hair was tied with a fine veil, perhaps a gift from his lady, and Panfilo was heard calling him Protesilaus; then came one wearing a pretty little cap on his head; he had a dark complexion, a thick beard, and ferocious looks, and Panfilo named him Pyrrhus; another with a more gentle face, very blond, beardless, and more adorned than all the others; he said that he could have been Menelaus or the Trojan Paris.[6] There is no need to prolong my story with this; in the endless troop he showed Agamemnon, Ajax, Ulysses, Diomedes, and every other Greek, Trojan, and Latin who was worthy of praise. Nor would Panfilo name them casually, but sustained his argument, giving acceptable reasons about the manners of those named and would show that they were properly compared; thus, listening to his arguments was no less entertaining than watching those of whom he was speaking.

After having paraded at a slow canter two or three times in front of the surrounding crowd, the cheerful company began their competition; straight in their stirrups, tightly protected by their shields, but still with the points of their light lances nearly touching the ground, they ride their horses faster than the fast-

---

5. garland of green leaves. As a sign of his strength, Hercules is said to have worn a garland of oak leaves.

6. Trojan: *frigio,* i.e., an inhabitant of Phrygia, where Troy was located.

est winds; the atmosphere resounding with the cheering voices of the surrounding crowd, with the ringing of bells, with the sounds of all kinds of instruments, and with the flapping of mantles that covered horses and men, encourages them to ride better and more vigorously. And so under everyone's eyes, not once but many times, they make themselves deservedly praiseworthy in the hearts of the spectators. Oh, how many ladies I often saw greatly rejoicing to see either their husband or lover or close relative among the jousters! Certainly there were not only many of these, but strangers as well. Although I may have seen and still see my husband and relatives there, I alone looked at the jousters and since I did not see Panfilo there, remembered that he was far away.

For goodness' sake, is it not astounding, ladies, that what I see is a matter of complaint for me and that nothing can make me cheerful? Pray tell, what soul is condemned in hell to such a pain that at perceiving these things would not feel cheer? Certainly none, I believe. Fascinated by the sweetness of Orpheus' lyre, even they forgot their sorrows for awhile, but I, with a thousand means at my disposal, among an infinite number of diversions and numerous festivities of all sorts, am unable not only to forget my pain but to alleviate it slightly.

Even though sometimes at gatherings such as this one I hide my grief under a false appearance and give a halt to my sighing, when the night comes or whenever I find myself alone and give myself the opportunity, I am not spared any tears; on the contrary, they are sometimes more numerous than the sighs I have held back during the day. And since these festivities gave me several ideas and led me to consider especially their vanity, which can be more harmful than beneficial—as I well know from having experienced it—sometimes, when the festivities ended and I was leaving them, justly vexed by worldly spectacle, I said:

"Happy is the innocent one who makes of the solitary countryside his home under the open sky! Since he knows only how to prepare cruel traps for wild animals and snares for innocent birds, he cannot be troubled by any mental anxiety, and if by chance he sustains heavy physical labors, he immediately restores his strength by resting on the fresh grass and by moving his dwelling now to the banks of a running brook, now to the shade of a thick forest, where he hears the plaintive birds fluttering with their sweet songs and where the trembling branches moved by a gentle wind hold still as the birds continue to sing. O injurious Fortune, if you had only granted me such a life, to which your highly coveted generosity brings a great deal of trouble! Oh, of what use are the great palaces to me, the fancy beds, and the large retinue if my mind is full of anxiety, wandering in foreign places searching for Panfilo and allowing no rest to my weary limbs?

"Ah, how delightful and charming it is to step with a free and tranquil mind onto the banks of running rivers and sleep lightly on the naked earth with our dreams nurtured without fear by the running waters with their murmuring sweet sounds! This kind of sleep is granted without envy to the poor country dweller and is far more desirable than the kind which is coaxed and often broken by the pressing tension of city living or by the noise of a tumultuous household. If sometimes he is spurred by hunger, the rustic man satiates it by picking apples in the safest of woods, and the new tender grass sprouting naturally from the ground of the hillsides also gives him tasty nourishment. Ah, how sweet for him is the water of the spring and of the river, scooped up in the palm of his hand to quench his thirst!

"Oh, what troubled anxieties mortals have, although nature demands and offers the lightest of things for their sustenance! We believe that we can fully satiate our bodies with an infinite variety of food, unaware that in them are often the hidden causes that corrupt more than nourish the order of our humors; and as we prepare elaborate beverages in gold and jeweled vessels, we often find that we are tasting the most chilling of poisons; and if that is not the case, at least we are swallowing Venus; and sometimes this leads us to arrogance, by which in words or deeds we acquire a miserable life or a shameful death. And frequently it also happens that after having taken many of these drinks, the drinker becomes worse than a senseless body. The rustic man has Satyrs, Fauns, Dryads, Naiads, and Nymphs as innocent companions; he cannot distinguish whether it is Venus or her biform son, and even if he can, he experiences this presence in a very crude form and does not do much loving.

"Oh, if only it had been God's pleasure that I too should never have known her, but had lived crudely and received the visits of simple companions! I would be far from the incurable anxieties I am facing, and for the good of neither my soul nor my fame, both most sacred, would I care to watch worldly festivities as fleeting as the winds, nor would I derive from watching them the anguish I feel. The rustic man feels no burning concern for high towers, fortified dwellings, large households, soft beds, marvelous clothing, fast-running horses, or for a million other things that steal away the best part of life. He lives free of the fear of evil men, who do not seek out remote and obscure places for their robberies; and without looking for insecure rest in the noble homes, he asks for air and light, and the sky is a witness to his life.

"Oh how little known and rejected by everyone as inimical is this kind of life today, when it should be sought and cherished by all! I certainly choose to think that life in the first age, which produced both men and gods, was like this. Oh, no other life is without vices or more free or better than the life lived by primitive people or by the person who still today abandons the city to live in the forest. How happy the world would be if Jupiter had never chased Saturn away and the golden age still lived on under pure laws! We would all then be living like these early people. Alas, whoever follows the rites of the ancients does not burn as I do, with the blind fury of the corrupt Venus, nor is the man who chooses to live in some neck of the mountainous woods a subject of any kingdom; he is not subject to whims of the populace, nor to the untrustworthy mob, nor to pestilential envy, and not even to the fragile favor of Fortune, for now I, from having trusted it too greatly, perish from too much thirst while in the midst of water. As if it were a tremendously great accomplishment to be able to go on living without great things, we attribute great quietude to small things. He who is superior or wishes to be superior in the greatest matters pursues the vain honors of transient riches, and certainly most of the time false men like important connections, but he who lives isolated in the countryside is free from fear and hope and does not know the dark wrath of that devouring envy that bites with vile teeth, nor does he have various sorts of hatred or incurable love affairs, nor does he sin as do the people who mingle in the city, nor fear any turmoil—being well acquainted with it—nor care to put together fictitious words, whose traps ensnare men of pure faith; but the other one, while he stands almighty, is never free of fear and is afraid of the very same knife he carries at his side.

"Oh, what a wonderful thing it is not to have to resist anyone, and take one's food in safety while reclining on the ground. Seldom or never do the greatest sins enter small homes. In early times there was no yearning for gold; there were no stones placed by law to divide the fields of primitive people; they did not cleave through the waves in bold ships, so they knew only their own shores; their cities were not surrounded by sturdy palisades, deep moats, and high walls with many towers; the knights did not maintain and make use of merciless weapons; no war machines battered down bolted doors with heavy stones; and if minor warfare broke out among these early men, they fought with their bare hands, and rough tree branches and stones became their weapons. The thin and light cornel-wood lance reinforced with a sharp iron point did not yet exist, and no one carried a sharp sword at his side, nor did the flowing crest adorn the shiny helmet; but the best and greatest advantage for these people was that Cupid had not yet been born; thus their pure hearts, which were later guarded by the winged god who flies all over the world, could then live securely.

"Oh, if God had only let me live in the kind of world in which people were satisfied with little, feared nothing, and knew only animal urges! And even if I had not been given as many privileges as they had but were free from such troublesome love as I have felt and do feel and from so many sighs, I could be considered happier than I am in these times filled with innumerable delights and so many frills and entertainment. Alas, the first sacred covenants bestowed by nature upon her people, so easy to keep, were broken by an ungodly desire for gain, by excessive anger, and by those minds that burn with itching appetites. Then appeared the thirst for domination, that bloody sin, and the weaker became prey of the stronger and force became law; and then came Sardanapalus, who refined the ways of Venus, which had already been made dissolute by Semiramis, by giving to Ceres and to Bacchus forms still unknown to them; then came the belligerent Mars, who found new artful ways to give a thousand forms to death, and from that moment on all lands were blood-stained, and even the sea turned red with blood.

"Without a doubt it was then that the greatest sins entered all homes, and soon no serious wickedness was without example: brother killed brother, father killed son, son killed father, and the husband fell under the blows of the wife, and the impious mothers more than once killed their offspring; and I say nothing about stepmothers' cruelty toward their step-children, since that is a daily occurrence. So wealth brought with it avarice, pride, envy, lust, and every other vice; and with all these things there also came into the world dissolute Love, lord and maker of all evil and creator of sins, whose assaults on human minds made numberless fallen and burnt cities smolder, and people endlessly fought and still fight bloody battles because of him, and a great number of people in kingdoms that have been overwhelmed are still oppressed. Oh, let us not talk of his other very terrible effects; may just those he has caused in me be the only examples of his evil doing and that cruelty of his which grips me so harshly that I am unable to turn my mind to anything else."

At times, after reflecting on such matters, I believe that what I am doing is a very serious thing in God's eyes and that my incomparably troublesome pains have some power to alleviate my anxiety (insofar as the much greater evils perpetrated by others make me appear nearly innocent), so I am becoming more able to bear these pains, and although I do not believe the sufferings of others to be as serious as my own, I can see that I am not the first nor the only one to suffer; so I often pray to God that He should end this suffering either by granting me death or by allowing Panfilo to return.

As you can hear, in such a life, and even worse, Fortune left me a very small consolation, but do not interpret consolation to mean my being without pain, as it usually means for other women; while she does not grant me any additional favors, she allows me, though only occasionally, to stop weeping. Continuing in my task, I will then add that in the past, with other young ladies of my wonderfully resplendent city, I seldom missed any of the celebrations held in its divine temples, and the townspeople did not consider any of them lovely without my presence; as the time for such ceremonies was approaching, my maidservants were urging me to participate in them, and still observing the ancient tradition, they also prepared my beautiful clothes, and sometimes said:

"Make yourself attractive, Lady; the celebration in that temple has come upon us and awaits only you to be more complete."

Oh, I remember that sometimes I angrily turned against them just like a wild boar caught by a pack of dogs, and I answered irritably with a voice empty of all sweetness:

"Away, you most vile members of this household, take away from me these frills; a rag is enough to cover my wretched limbs, and do not remind me of any temple or celebration, if you care to be in my good graces."

Oh, how many times I heard that these places were visited by many noble people who went there not so much out of devotion, but more in order to see me, and when they did not see me, they were troubled and turned away saying that these celebrations were worthless without me! But even though I scorn these festivities, sometimes I am nonetheless obliged to participate in them in the company of my noble women friends, but I go there dressed simply, in everyday clothes, and once there, I no longer seek the most prominent seats, but refuse the honors I had previously sought and sit humbly among the women in the more lowly places; and here, listening to whatever is said by one or the other of the ladies, with my sorrow kept hidden as much as possible, I while away whatever time I spend there. Oh, how many times I have heard it said nearby about me:

"My goodness, what a surprise is this! This lady, who was such a unique ornament of our city, has become so modest and humble! What divine spirit has inspired her? Where are her noble garments and her proud demeanor? Where have her admirable charms gone?"

Were it possible, I would gladly answer these words as follows:

"When he left, Panfilo took all these things with him, and many others even more precious."

Still surrounded by the ladies and besieged with various questions, I find it necessary to please everyone with a sham face. One goads me with these words:

"O Fiammetta, you infinitely surprise me and the other ladies, since we do not know what made you suddenly abandon your precious robes, the jewels you enjoyed wearing, and all the other things suitable to your young age; you are still a girl and should not go around in such a garb. Do you not think that if you were to take it off now, you would be able to put it on later? Use the time according to its quality. You will not lack time later to wear the garb you are wearing now with such modesty. Look at any of us: we are older than you are, but we are skillfully adorned and dressed in sophisticated and elegant clothes, and you too should be as elegantly embellished."

To her and the others waiting for some words from me, I give with a humble voice this answer:

"Ladies, one comes to these temples to please either God or men. If one comes to please God, the soul adorned with virtue is sufficient, and it makes no difference if the body is covered with a hairshirt. If one comes here to please men, I must confess that the frills used by you, and by me too in the past, are necessary, since most people are misled by false advice and judge inward things by those which are outward. But now I do not care about this; on the contrary, I am sorry about my former vanity, and wishing to make amends before God, I make myself as annoying in your eyes as I possibly can."

At this point, tears, forced out by the intrinsic truth of this, stream down my sad face, and I silently say to myself:

"O God, you who see into our hearts, do not condemn as sinful the untruthful words I have pronounced. As you see, not the wish to deceive but the need to hide my feelings of anguish compel me to lie, so you should rather reward me for it if you consider that by leaving out the bad example, I give a good one to your creatures. It is very distressing for me to lie, and I bear it with a heavy heart, but I can do nothing else."

How many times, ladies, I have received compassionate praise for this wickedness, since the ladies around me said that after having been inordinately vain, I had become again a very devoted young woman! Of course, I often heard that many of them were of the opinion that I was tied to Almighty God by such a bond of friendship that He would not deny me any grace I might ask of Him, and more than once I was also visited by saintly people as if I were a saint, since they were ignorant of what my wretched face was hiding inside my mind and how far my desires were from my words. Oh, deceptive world, if deeds are kept hidden, how much more powerful false faces are than righteous minds! I, who am more sinful than any other woman and afflicted by my dishonest feelings of love, am considered a saint because I conceal them under virtuous words, but God knows that if it could be done without danger, I would disabuse each person I have deceived by telling the truth, and I would not conceal the reason that keeps me wretched, but this is not possible.

As soon as I finished answering the lady who had questioned me first, another one next to me, seeing that my tears were drying, said:

"O Fiammetta, what has happened to the charming beauty of your face? Where is your rosy complexion? Why are you so pale? Your eyes, which were like morning stars, now have a purple ring around them and can barely be discerned in your forehead? And why is your golden hair, which in the past was always masterfully groomed, now disheveled, covered, and hardly visible? Tell us, for you surprise us to no end."

I freed myself from this one with a few words, and said:

"It is well known that human beauty is a short-lived flower which fades from one day to the next, and if some women should derive confidence from it, in the long run they find themselves wretchedly cast down by it. He who gave it to me but who underhandedly subjected me to the trials that chased it away has reclaimed it, and he is capable of giving it back to me whenever it pleases him."

After having said this, unable to repress my tears, I wept profusely, wrapped inside my cloak, lamenting to myself with these words:

"O Beauty, you are mortals' dubious possession, a temporary gift that arrives and disappears faster than the fields radiant with the many flowers of sweet springtime and those lofty trees laden with many leafy boughs adorned by the power of Aries which are marred by the summer heat and discarded, none of which is saved in the autumn even if some of them survive the heat; so it is for you, O Beauty, who most of the time are destroyed in the middle of your best years, being hurt by many accidents, and even if youth should spare you, mature age takes you away by force, though you resist. O Beauty, you are a fleeting thing, similar to the waves that never return to their origins, and no one who is wise must rely on your fragile gift. Oh, how I loved you, how dear you were to me, who am now so wretched, and with what care I looked after you! But now I curse you and with good reason.

"You, who are the main cause of my losses and foremost captor of my dear lover's mind, lacked the strength to hold him here and to recall him once he was gone. Had you not existed, I would not have pleased Panfilo's charming eyes; had I not been pleasing to him, he would not have attempted to attract my own eyes; and had he not attracted me as he did, I would not be suffering now. Therefore, you alone are the reason and origin of all my woe. Blessed are those women who without you withstand the stigma of their coarse looks! In chastity they observe the sacred laws and are able to live without anxiety, their souls free from the cruel tyranny of Love; but you cause us to be harried by whoever sets eyes on us and forces us to destroy that which must be most carefully guarded. Oh, happy Spurinna, worthy of eternal fame, who aware of your effect chased you away from him with a harsh hand in the flower of his youth, choosing to be loved by the wise for a virtuous deed, rather than for his sensual beauty by wanton young women. Alas, had I done the same, all these woes, thoughts, and tears would be far away and my life, which was subsequently corrupted, would still be in its first, praiseworthy stage."

The ladies recall me hence and scold me for my excessive tears by saying:

"O Fiammetta, what kind of behavior is this? Do you despair of God's mercy? Do you not believe that He is compassionate enough to forgive your small digressions without your shedding so many tears? What you are doing is to seek death instead of forgiveness. Rise, dry your face, and take part in the sacrifice offered to almighty Jupiter by our priests."

As I hear these voices I hold back my tears and raise my head, but I do not turn around as I used to do, perfectly aware that my Panfilo is not here to be seen, nor do I wish to see whether anyone is looking at me, or who is doing so, or to know how I appear in the eyes of the people around me; instead, by concentrating on the one who sacrificed himself for the salvation of all,[7] I offer pious prayers for my Panfilo and for his return, trying out on him these words:

"Greatest ruler of the highest heavens, universal judge of the entire world, henceforth put a limit on my burdensome labor and an end to my anxieties. You see that there is no certainty in any of my days; for me the end of one misfortune is invariably the beginning of another. I, who considered myself already happy when I was unaware of my miseries, unconsciously offended you at first by my vain concerns with embellishing my youth, already over-endowed by nature, and you made me subject to the unbounded passion that spurs me now, and then through it you filled my mind, unaccustomed to such terrible anxieties, with new preoccupations, and finally you separated from me the one I love more than myself, thus adding an infinite number of dangers to my life, one after another. For pity's sake, if sometimes you pay attention to the wretched, lend your merciful ears to my prayers, and by overlooking the many sins I have committed against you, kindly consider my few good deeds, if I ever did any, and give them due reward by hearing my speeches and supplications, which may hold matters of little concern to you but are supremely important to me; I do not ask you anything else but that Panfilo should be given back to me. Alas, I know all too well that this prayer is unfair in your view, most fair judge!

"But according to your very own kind of justice, one must wish a lesser evil to prevail over a greater one. You, from whom nothing can be hidden, know that in no way will I forget my charming lover nor the events of the past, and the memory of him and of them puts me into such a state of dreadful pain that in order to run away from them I have sought a thousand ways to die, all of which were taken from my hands by the little hope I have left in you. Therefore, if the lesser evil is to keep my lover as I already had him and not to kill the body together with the wicked soul, as is my belief, then let him come, and give him back to me. You should prefer keeping sinners alive and allowing them to know you instead of having them dead, without

---

7. the one who sacrificed himself for the salvation of all: *colui che per la salute di tutti diede se medesimo.* Christ. One of the few explicit Christian references in the work.

hope of redemption, and you should want above all to lose a part, rather than the whole, of the creatures you have created.

"And if it is difficult to grant me this, at least do grant me that which is the ultimate end of all suffering lest constrained by a very great grief, I seize it by myself with determination. May my words reach your presence, and if they cannot touch you, may any other god who inhabits the celestial regions accept them—given that there is one among you who has ever felt the burning flames I feel while living down here—and offer them for me to the one who does not take them from me, so that I may first be allowed to live happily down here and then, at the end of my days, up there with you; and if he is taken before the sinners, imploring grace from me, this would demonstrate how fitting it is for one sinner to forgive and give help to another."

After having pronounced these words, I place on the divine altars perfumed incenses and worthy offerings in order to make the gods well-disposed towards my prayers and Panfilo's well-being; then, as the sacred ceremonies end, I leave with the other ladies and return to my gloomy home.

SIX

*In which Lady Fiammetta tells how she came
to extreme desperation and wanted to kill herself
when she heard that Panfilo was unmarried but
was not returning because he was in love
with another woman.*

As you may have understood by what has been said so far, most
compassionate ladies, my life was spent in conflicts of love and
made still the worse for it, but if we think carefully, it may not
be wrong to call it pleasant in comparison to what was still to
come. Remembering with fear that to which love ultimately
brought me and toward which I am still nearly driven, I have
written of less severe things with a sluggish hand and with long
digressions in order to delay reaching that point, either because
I feel ashamed of my madness or because by writing of it I will
feel as if I were reentering it; but now, no longer able to avoid
such matters, I will get to them, drawn by my argument and in
spite of my fear. But you, most blessed Pity, who dwell in the
gentle hearts of tender young women, keep a tighter rein on
those hearts than you have done so far, lest, that by outdoing
and giving more of yourself than suitable, you change into the
opposite of what I am looking for and thereby deprive my
women readers' lap of my weeping head.

Since the time of Panfilo's departure, the Sun had returned
once again to that place in the sky which had been scorched
when his carriage was recklessly driven by his presumptuous
son,[1] and I, who was long accustomed to my wretchedness, had
learned to bear my pains and lamented more moderately than
usual; I did not believe that one could endure more pain than I
was already experiencing, when Fortune, not satisfied with my

---

1. his presumptuous son: Phaeton (see Glossary). The sun is now in the zodiacal sign of Scorpio (October 24—November 22), which means that Panfilo
has been gone for nearly a year.

troubles, wished to show me that she had more bitter poisons to give me. Thus it happened that one of our dearest servants returned from Panfilo's land to our city and was received very graciously by everyone and by me in particular. As he was recounting what had happened to him and what he had seen, mixing the good with the bad, he was by chance reminded of Panfilo, whom he profusely praised, remembering how honorably the former had received him, and as I listened I felt so glad that my reason could hardly hold back my desire to run and embrace him and inquire about my Panfilo with the affection I was feeling. But although I restrained myself (while others asked how he was), after he replied to all of them that Panfilo was well, I alone questioned him, with a cheerful face, about what Panfilo was doing and whether it was his intention to return to us. He answered my questions this way:

"My Lady, what would Panfilo return here for? From what someone told me, in his land (which has more splendid women than any other) there is no lady more beautiful than the one who loves him above all else; and he, I believe, loves her too; if otherwise, I would consider him insane, while in the past I thought him very discerning."

At these words my heart skipped a beat, as it must have happened to Oenone while waiting on the high mountains of Ida when she saw the Greek lady approach with her lover in the Trojan ship[2]; and I could hardly prevent fear from showing in my face (if I succeeded at all), so I said with a false smile:

"I am sure you are telling the truth: this land of ours was unkind to him and could not offer him a lover suitable to his virtue, so if he found one there, he is wise to stay with her. But tell me, how does his young bride bear this?"

He then answered:

"He has no bride: the one who not long ago was said to have come into his home was really his father's bride, not his own."

As I was listening to him pronounce these words, I was freed from one anguish and plunged into another much greater; pricked by sudden anger and pain, my poor heart began to beat as loud as the swift wings of Procne flapping at her own white

---

2. Greek lady: Helen of Troy (see Glossary).

sides as she flew faster; similarly frightened in my spirits I began to tremble all over, as does the sea surface rippled by a gentle wind or as pliant reeds softly moved by the air, and I began to feel my strength leaving me. For this reason I excused myself as politely as I could and retired to my room.

I left everyone, and as soon as I found myself there alone I began shedding so many bitter tears that I was like a full spring gushing into damp valleys, and I held back my loud wailing with difficulty as I threw myself—or, should I say, I fell face down—onto the sad bed that had witnessed our loving, wishing to say, "Panfilo, why did you betray me?" But my tongue and all my limbs lost their strength so suddenly that these words were caught in my throat, and for a very long time I was considered nearly dead (and believed dead by some women), and no physician's remedy could restore my wandering spirits to their proper place.

After my wretched soul, which was about to depart, had more than once bidden farewell to my unhappy spirits but still remained in my tormented body and gathered its dispersed energies, the lost light returned to my eyes, and when I raised my head, I saw several women bent over me who as they wept had done me a compassionate service by bathing me with precious liquids. I also saw next to me various instruments of diverse uses, and I was rather astonished by the women's tears and by these things, so that when I was able to speak again, I asked why they were there, and one of them answered my question by saying:

"These things were brought here to recall your lost soul."

Then, after a long sigh, I said with difficulty:

"Alas, out of great pity what a cruel task you performed against my will! Thinking to help me you were hindering me, and as I see it, you forced my soul, inclined to abandon the more miserable body, to stay with me, so that I live. Oh, there is nothing that I or anyone else desired with more yearning than what you have denied me! I was already free from these tribulations and about to reach my desire but you have taken it away."

After these words the women comforted me in several ways, but their ministrations were in vain. I pretended to feel better and gave different reasons for the unfortunate incident so that they would leave and let me be alone to grieve. When some of them had left and others had been dismissed because I looked almost cheerful once again, I remained alone with my old nurse and with the one maid who was aware of my troubles, and to my true infirmity both of them applied soothing ointments which would have cured it had it not been fatal. But because my mind focused only on the words I had heard, I suddenly became hostile towards one of you—I do not even know which one, my ladies—and I began having some very dark thoughts, so I blurted out with an enraged voice the pain that could no longer be kept entirely inside, and this is what came out of my wretched bosom:

"O wicked young man, you are the enemy of compassion; you are worse than anyone else, Panfilo, you who are now with another woman after having forgotten me, who am so miserable; cursed be the day and hour I first saw you and the place where I first liked you! Cursed be that goddess who by appearing before me dissuaded me with her words from pursuing my good intentions while I was strongly resisting my love for you! I certainly do not believe that she was Venus, but an infernal fury in disguise who infused me with insanity as she did to the wretched Athamas. O most cruel young man, whom I most ill-advisedly chose as the best among a large number of noble, handsome, and valiant ones, where are the prayers now which you offered in tears so that your life might be saved, asserting that your life and death rested in my hands? Where are those pitiful eyes now with which you wept at will when you were miserable? Where is the love you showed me, and the sweet words? Where is the grave concern you proffered to my service? Have you forgotten all of them? Or have you used them again to ensnare the woman you have caught?

"Ah, cursed be this pity of mine that freed your life from death so that by making another woman happy you condemned my own life to an obscure end! Those eyes that wept in my presence now laugh before this new woman, and your changed heart has addressed sweet words and promises to her. Alas, where are the gods to whom you perjured yourself, O Panfilo? Where is the promised faith? Where are those false tears, many of which I swallowed so miserably believing them shed for compassion when they were full of deceit? You have deprived me and yourself as well of all these things, and have placed them in the bosom of this new woman.

"Oh how devastating it already was to hear that by Juno's laws you had given yourself to another! But since I felt that your vows to me were not to be preferred to those, I withstood it with less anguish but with no less difficulty, although overcome by a rightful sorrow. But now it is an unbearable torture to hear that after drawing away from me you have given yourself to another woman by the same laws that bind us. Now I understand your delay and also the naiveté with which I have always believed that you would return if you could. O Panfilo, did you need so much cunning to deceive me? Why did you make such solemn oaths and offer me such absolute faith if you intended to betray me like this? Why did you not just go away without taking leave or without any promise to return? As you know, I loved you with my whole heart, but I did not imprison you, so you could have left whenever you wished, without false tears. Had you done so, I would undoubtedly have despaired over you, immediately aware of your deception, and either death or oblivion would have put an end to my torments, but by making them last longer and making me hope in vain, you deliberately nourished them, and this I did not deserve.

"Oh how sweet your tears were to me! But because now I know their effect, they have again become very bitter. Alas, if Love rules over you as fiercely as he does over me, was it not enough for you to be taken once, if you did not want to be caught a second time? But what am I saying? You never loved. On the contrary, you only enjoyed mocking young women. Had you loved as I believed you did, you would still be mine. And could you ever belong to anyone who loved you more than I do? Oh, whoever you are, O woman, who have stolen him from me, although you are my enemy, I am forced to pity you since I feel my own anxiety. Beware of his deceit, for those who have deceived once have already lost all honest shame and are no longer conscious of deceiving. O most vile man, how many prayers and gifts I have offered to the gods for your salvation, and you betrayed me and gave yourself to another!

"O gods, my prayers are fulfilled but to another woman's advantage; I have had the grief, and someone else has the pleasure.

For pity's sake, most wicked young man, did not my appearance suit your desires, and was my nobility not befitting yours? It was much greater! Were my riches ever denied to you, or did I ever take yours? Certainly not. Did I ever show love to any other young man than you by my attitude, my actions, or my looks? You must admit I did not, unless this new love has kept you from seeing the truth. Then what error of mine, and what right reason of yours, what greater beauty or stronger love than mine snatched you from me and gave you to another? Certainly none! And may the gods be my witnesses that I never did anything against you, except love you beyond all reasonable limits. Whether this deserves the betrayal you have perpetrated against me, only you know.

"O gods, just avengers of our failures, I demand vengeance, and not unjustly. I do not wish nor seek the death of the one whom I saved but who wants my own death, nor do I demand for him any other disgrace than (if he loves this new woman as I love him) that she will abandon him to give herself to another, as he did me, leaving him in the same state he left me."

Then, flailing around with uncontrolled movements, I threw myself violently on my bed and tossed about.

I spent that whole day talking about such things as I have just mentioned, or similar ones, but when the night came (which is much worse than the daytime when it comes to pain, since darkness is more akin to miseries than light), it happened that as I lay in bed at my dear husband's side, quiet but kept awake by my painful thoughts, with nothing to stop me from remembering the past, both sad and happy memories freely came into my mind; and in particular the pain for having lost Panfilo's love to another increased to such an extent that unable to contain it, I gave vent to it by wailing and crying loudly but always remaining silent about the love that was its source.

My sobbing was so loud that my husband, who had been sleeping soundly for a long time, was forced by it to awaken; he turned toward me, who was covered with tears, took me in his arms, and said in a tender and compassionate voice:

"O my sweet soul, why are you crying and so full of grief in the silence of the night? What has made you for some time so continually melancholy and afflicted? Nothing that displeases you must be kept concealed from me. Is there anything your heart desires that I would not give you if I could, if you only asked for it? Are you not my only good and comfort? Do you not know that I love you more than anything else in the whole world? And not one but many proofs of this can let you live in certainty. Why do you cry then? Why do you distress yourself with sorrow? Do I not seem a young man worthy of your nobility? Or do you believe me guilty of something for which I could make amends? Say it, speak, reveal your wish; there is nothing that will be left undone, if it is only possible. In your demeanor, looks, and acts, you have again become so sorrowful that you are making my life wretched, and never before have I seen you as full of pain as you appear to me today. I thought that your pallor was due to a physical ailment, but now I know well that it is a spiritual malaise which brought you to the state in which I see you; therefore I beg you to reveal to me the reason for it."

At this, with a woman's presence of mind, I decided to lie—an art I never exercised before—and replied:

"Husband, more dear to me than anyone else in the world, I lack nothing that you could provide, and I know that you are undoubtedly more worthy than I am; only my dear brother's death, of which you are aware, has brought me and to this day brings me such sadness. It obliges me to weep every time I think of it, and I certainly do not deplore death itself, to which I know we all must come, but the manner of his death, which, as you know, was unfortunate and foul; and aside from this, the sad happenings that followed his death constrain me even more painfully. No sooner do I close my aching eyes to sleep than he appears before me pale, dreary, and covered with blood, showing me his fresh wounds. A moment ago when you heard me weep, he had just appeared in my dreams as a horrible image, tired, frightened, and panting as if he could hardly speak, but with the greatest of efforts he said: 'Dear sister, dispel the shame that makes me walk with furrowed brow and downcast eyes, wailing among other spirits.' Although I felt somewhat comforted in seeing him, I was overwhelmed with pity by his looks and words; I suddenly shook myself and sleep fled, just as my tears (which you are now consoling) followed, paying the price for the pity I had felt; and as the gods know, I would have avenged him already if I could bear arms, thereby allowing him to hold his head high among the other spirits, but I cannot do so. Therefore, my dear husband, not without reason do I grieve so miserably."

How many loving words he offered me, doctoring the wound that had healed long before and attempting to calm my weeping with authentic reasons suitable to my lies! But when he fell asleep believing that I was comforted, I began to weep again silently, and aching even more sorely as I thought of his compassion, I resumed the interrupted grieving by saying:

"O most cruel caverns inhabited by furious beasts! O hell, O eternal prison to which the guilty crowd is condemned, O whatever other greater place of confinement may be hidden down below: take me in and give me well-deserved tortures for my guilt. Supreme Jupiter, you who are justly angry with me, send your thunder and with a swift hand strike me with your lightning. O blessed Juno, whose most godly laws I have disgracefully corrupted, take revenge. O Caspian rocks, dismember my wretched body. Fast-flying birds and ferocious animals, devour it. O most cruel horses that tore apart the body of that innocent Hippolytus, tear me apart, I am the guilty one.

"O dear husband, full of compassion, plunge your sword into my heart in justified anger, and in a torrent of blood cast out of it the vile soul that deceived you. Have no pity nor mercy for me, since I preferred a stranger's love to the fidelity of the sacred bed. O most contemptible female, who are deserving of these and of any other greater torture, what fury appeared before your pure eyes the day you first fell for Panfilo? Where did you leave the devotion due to the sacred laws of matrimony? What did you do with your chastity, which is a woman's highest virtue, when you abandoned your husband for Panfilo? What happened to your beloved's devotion to you, and where is the consolation he offered you in your misery? He merrily spends the fleeting time in the arms of another woman without a thought for you, and it is right and reasonable that this has happened to you and to any other woman who places legitimate feelings of love after lustful ones. Your husband, who more than anyone else would have the right to hurt you, tries to comfort you, but the one who should comfort you does not care if he hurts you.

"Oh, was he not just as handsome as Panfilo? He certainly was. His virtues, his nobility, and anything else: were they not superior to those of Panfilo? Who doubts it? Then why did you abandon him for another? What blindness, what arrogance, what sin, and what iniquity induced you to it? Alas, I do not know myself! Usually only things which one easily possesses are demeaned, though they may be of great worth, while those hard to obtain are considered very precious, even if they are of very little value. The excessive generosity of my husband (which I should have appreciated) misled me, and I, capable of resisting, deeply regret not having done it; rather, I am sure I would have been able to do it, had I wanted to, by thinking of what the gods showed me in my sleep at night or when awake on the morning that preceded my downfall.

"Now that I cannot leave off loving even if I wanted to, I know what kind of snake pierced my left breast and slithered off full of my blood, and I am also aware of what the crown fallen from my wretched head was meant to signify, but these insights come too late. Perhaps the gods, to purge some inborn anger which they felt against me, regretted their warning signs, but unable to withdraw them they made it impossible for me to understand them, just as Apollo took away from his beloved Cassandra her credibility after he had given her the gift of prophecy; therefore, I waste my life away, made miserable without a reasonable pretext."

Thus lamenting, I spent almost the entire night turning and tossing in my bed without being able to go to sleep, and even when sleep entered my wretched heart, it dwelt in there so precariously that any slight change disrupted it; because it was still feeble it did not enter into any fierce conflict with my mind nor did it remain with me. This happened not only on the night I just mentioned, but many times before, and it has happened almost continually ever since, yet for that reason my soul is and has been in the same tempestuous turmoil whether awake or asleep.

The nightly struggles did not prevent the daily ones; on the contrary, having found an excuse for my lamentations in the lies told to my husband, from that night on I did not hesitate to weep and lament in public quite often.

When the morning arrived so did my faithful nurse, from whom none of my troubles was hidden, since she was the first to recognize on my face the stirrings of love and also to foresee in it future events by observing me when I was told that Panfilo had another woman; so, apprehensive and most attentive to my needs, as soon as my husband left my room, she immediately came in, and when she saw me still lying there, only half-alive because of the previous night's turmoil, she tried to relieve my horrible pains with various words, and she took me into her arms, wiping my wretched face with her trembling hand, and pronounced these words haltingly:

"Young woman, your troubles grieve me beyond measure, and they would distress me even more had I not warned you beforehand; but because you are more willful than wise, you ignored my advice and listened to your own desires, and I see from your doleful face that you have reached the inevitable conclusion of such mistakes. But because as long as one wishes, one can, while still alive, depart from an evil path and return to a right one, I should like it if you were at last to clear your mind by removing the veil from your eyes, which are invaded by the darkness of this wicked tyrant and to recover for them the clarity of truth. The very brief pleasures and the lengthy suffering you have experienced and are still experiencing for his sake can make manifest to you what he is. Because you are young and followed your wishes more than your reason, you have loved, and by loving you have attained that objective which one can desire from love, and as it has been said before, you learned how brief this pleasure is, and one can never have or wish to have more than you have had. And even if it should happen that Panfilo were to return to your embraces, you would not feel any pleasure other than what you have already felt.

"Usually the most fervent desires are aroused by new things in which we often hope to find some hidden treasure that may not be there, and these desires annoy us by feeding an eager yearning for them, while familiar things usually are only moderately desired; but having spent too much of your time in wantonness and having set your mind wholly on destruction, you are doing just the opposite. Discerning people normally draw back when they find themselves full of doubts and in difficult places, preferring, once they have wasted the energy they spent in arriving where they think they are, to return safely rather than proceed further and risk death. Follow such an example then while you still can, and now that you are more self-restrained than usual, be wise and pull yourself out of the dangers and anxieties into which you have foolishly let yourself be drawn. If you look from a healthy perspective, you will see that Fortune is benign towards you and has not blocked the way back nor obstructed it, so that by still discerning clearly your footsteps you would be able to return to where you began and be again the Fiammetta you used to be. Your reputation is intact and untarnished in people's minds by any misdeed you committed; once a young woman's reputation has been corrupted, it has caused many of them to fall into the basest of evils. Do not wish to be so forward if you do not want to ruin what destiny has kept in reserve for you; take courage and pretend to yourself that you have never seen Panfilo or that he is your husband. Imagination adapts itself to everything, and good fantasies can bear being handled playfully. Only this path can give you joy, and this is what you ought to long for if you are as distressed as your actions and words demonstrate."

I listened dejectedly to these or similar words several times without answering, and while I was exceedingly perturbed, I nevertheless knew that they were true, but my yet ill-disposed nature made me receive them without profit; rather it happened at one point that as I was tossing back and forth, moved by a tremendous anger, mindless of the presence of my nurse, with a voice enraged beyond ladylike dignity and wailing beyond any other wailing, I said:

"O Tisiphone, you infernal fury! O Megaera! O Alecto! You who are the tormentors of doleful souls, straighten your fierce manes, inflame the frightening Hydras with rage toward new horrors, swiftly penetrate the wicked bedchamber of the evil woman, and, as she joins with the lover she has stolen, light your wretched little torches and carry them around the sumptuous bed as a sign of a fatal omen to the most ignoble lovers. O you, whoever you are, dwellers in the dark houses of Dis, and you gods of the immortal kingdom of Styx, come forth and frighten the unfaithful couple with your ugly lamentations! O mournful owl, sing on the unhappy roof! And you, Harpies, give a sign of future harm! O infernal shadows, eternal Chaos, and you, darkness, so inimical to light, invade the adulterous homes so that wicked eyes will enjoy no light, and as avengers of vicious deeds, let your hateful feelings occupy those minds inclined towards fickleness and cause violent strife among them!"

Right after this, I gave out an ardent sigh and added to my broken speech:

"You most vicious woman, I do not know you, but whoever you are, you now possess the lover for whom I have long waited, and I am languishing in misery far away from him. You enjoy the rewards of my labor, and I remain empty-handed, reaping no fruit for what I sowed in prayer. I have offered incense and prayers to the gods for the prosperity of the man you had to steal secretly, and those prayers were heard to your advantage. Look here, I do not know with what art or in what manner you replaced me in his heart, and yet I know that it is so; may you derive from it contentment as brief as you allowed me. And if it is difficult for him to fall in love for the third time, may the gods divide your love as they did the love between the Greek lady and the judge of Ida,[3] or that of the young man from Abydos from his woeful Hero,[4] or that of the unhappy children of Aeolus, by turning the harsh verdict against you and leaving him unscathed. O most odious female, by looking at his face you should have known that he was not without a woman, and if you thought of that (and I know you did), with what kind of attitude did you proceed to steal what belonged to another? Certainly with an inimical one, I assure you. So, as long as I live I will always haunt you as I would an enemy and invader of my territory; I will always live on this earth nourishing myself with the hope of your death, which I pray will not be just like any other: rather you should be catapulted,[5] in place of heavy lead or stone, into the midst of the enemy; may your lacerated body, instead of being burned or buried, be split and torn apart to appease rapacious hounds, which, I pray, after having consumed the soft flesh may fight fiercely over your bones so that by gnawing on them ravenously they may demonstrate how you took pleasure in robbery when you were alive.

"There will be no day, night, nor hour in which my tongue will not curse you, and my cursing will have no end. First, the

3. judge of Ida: Paris (see Glossary).
4. young man from Abydos: Leander (see Glossary).
5. catapulted: *nella concava fionda gittata*, literally, "thrown in a hollow sling."

Great Bear would have to dive into the Ocean,[6] the voracious wave of the Sicilian Charybdis be still, and the dogs of Scylla be silent; crops would have to grow in the Ionian sea and the dark night glow with light, water agree with fire in supreme trust, life with death, and the sea with the winds. Instead, I will fight you as long as the Ganges remains warm and the Danube cold, and as long as the mountains bear oaks and the fields gentle pastures. Nor will this anger end with death: by following you among the dead, I will do my best to torment you with all the harmful means used there. And if you should survive me, whatever the manner of my death and wherever my unhappy spirit will go, I will use all my strength to free it from there, and by taking possession of you, I will make you as raving mad as the virgins after they have received the god Apollo, or I will appear to you in all my horror when you are awake, and in the quiet of the night I will awaken you with terrifying dreams; in brief, whatever you are doing, I will continually spring into view before your eyes, lamenting this insult to myself, and nowhere will I leave you in peace, and because of me you will be haunted by this fury as long as you live, and when you are dead I will be the cause of even worse things.

"Oh, unhappy that I am, how far do my words go? I threaten you and you harm me by keeping my lover and showing as much concern for my menacing injuries as the mightiest kings show for the least powerful of men. Oh, if only I had Daedalus' ingenuity or Medea's chariots, so that by adding wings to my shoulders or by being carried through the air I would immediately find myself where you hide the amorous booty! Oh, how many and what words I would utter with troubled and menacing looks against that lying young man and against you, who rob other people's goods! With how much abuse I would reproach you for your transgressions! And after having shamed you, I would proceed to take revenge without restraint or hesitation; I would grab your hair and pull it hard with my very own hands, pulling you here and there by holding on to it; I would satisfy my angry feelings before your perfidious lover and make shreds of all your clothes. Nor would this be enough: on the

6. Great Bear: Ursa Major, a constellation which throughout the year remains visible above the horizon when viewed from the latitude of Italy.

contrary, with my sharp fingernails I would plow deeply all over that face which so pleased his treacherous eyes, leaving on it eternal signs of my vengeance; with my hungry teeth I would tear your whole wretched body apart, and then I would let it be treated by the one who now deludes you, and I would cheerfully find my way back to my sad home."

As I pronounced these words with my eyes glaring, my teeth tightly closed, and my fists clenched as if ready to do such things, it seemed to give me partial revenge, but the old nurse said to me, on the verge of tears:

"My daughter, since you know the fierce tyranny of the god who is tormenting you, contain yourself; hold your tears back, and if the compassion you owe to yourself does not allow you to do that, consider your honor, which could easily be stained by a new shame born from a past sin; or at least be silent so that your husband may not hear these vile things and have double reason for blaming you deservedly for what you have done."

At that moment I remembered my husband, and moved by a new pity, I cried louder, and turning over in my mind the broken word and the laws I so badly observed, I said this to my nurse:

"O most devoted companion of my labors, my husband has little to lament. The one who has been the cause of our sin has also been its harshest chastiser, and I have been reaping and still reap what I deserve according to my merits. My husband could not harm me more than my lover already has; if death is as painful as they say, only with death can he increase my suffering. Let it come then, and give it to me; it does not frighten me, but gives me pleasure because I desire it, and it would be more welcome if it were from his hands than from my own. If he does not give it to me or if it does not come on its own, my quick wit will find it, since through it I hope to put an end to all my tribulations.

"Even in the most sizzling corner of hell, with its most terrible tortures for those who are damned, there is no punishment like mine. Tityus is cited as an example of excruciating pain by ancient authors who say that vultures continually peck at his ever-renewing liver, and I certainly do not consider this a meagre punishment, but it is nothing in comparison with mine, because while the vultures peck at his liver, a thousand fears, stronger than any bird's beak, continually tear my heart apart.

Similarly, they say that Tantalus is dying of hunger and thirst while surrounded by waters and fruit, but placed in the middle of worldly pleasures, affectionately hungry for my lover and unable to have him, I certainly suffer as much as he does, or more, since the proximity of the waves and the nearby fruit give him some hope that sometime he will be able to satisfy himself fully, but I now completely despair of anything in which I had hoped to find my consolation, and since I love more than ever the one who by his own free will is kept in someone else's power, I have been deprived of all hope. And even the unfortunate Ixion, rotating on that fiery wheel, does not suffer the kind of pain that can compare with mine; continuously whirled about in a mad rage by my adverse destiny, I suffer more than he does. And if the daughters of Danaus with useless labor keep pouring water into perforated water jars believing they are filling them, through my eyes I keep shedding tears which are drawn from my wretched heart.

"Why do I labor recounting one by one all these infernal pains? The truth is that there resides in me an altogether greater pain than there is in those souls who are scattered and disconnected. And even if I were not suffering more than they do, I must keep my pains hidden (or at least their cause) while they can show theirs with loud screams or in other ways suitable to their grief, so my woes should be deemed greater than theirs.

"Oh, how much more fiercely does the contained fire burn than the one which spreads its flames broadly! And what a difficult and miserable thing it is when one cannot give voice to one's pains or speak of their pernicious cause, all the time keeping them in the heart and hiding them behind a cheerful face! Death would therefore not be grievous to me, but a relief from grief. So let my dear husband come and take revenge for himself and at the same time free me from suffering; let his knife slit open my miserable bosom and let him take out my aching soul, my love, and my sorrow all at the same time with much blood; may he tear apart my heart, the holder of these things, as the principal deceiver and as the one who shelters his enemies, just as the perpetrated inequity deserves."

When my old nurse saw that I had ceased speaking and was deep in tears, she began talking softly to me:

"My dear girl, what are you saying? Your words are useless and your intentions terrible. I am very old and have seen many things in this world, and I have certainly been familiar with the love affairs of many ladies, and even though I am not to be counted among you, I have nevertheless been well acquainted with the poisonous love which weighs just as heavily on humble people as on more powerful ones, and more so at times, since the poor have fewer ways open to satisfy their desire than do those people who with their riches find them in their leisure; besides, I have never felt (or heard it said) that which you speak of as being so painful to you and nearly impossible, is as hard as you indicate. And even if such grief were extremely great, you should not let it consume you, as you are doing, to the point that you seek death, which you are asking for more out of anger than reason.[7] I well know that rage spurred by vehement ire is blind; it does not bother being hidden, does not accept limits, and does not fear death; on the contrary, driven by its own impetuosity, it throws itself upon the fatal tips of piercing swords; but if such rage were allowed to cool down a good deal, I do not doubt that this burning madness would be clear to the one who has cooled down. So, my girl, bear well its dangerous force; make room for this fury, pay close attention to my words, and keep your mind on the examples I have given you.

"If I have understood your words accurately, your grievous and tormented lamentations are due to the departure of your beloved young man, to a broken promise, to Love, and to a new woman; and in this sorrow of yours, you consider no other pain equal to yours; of course, if you will be as wise as I wish you to be, by fruitfully concentrating on what I have said about all these things, you will be taking a useful remedy. According to the laws of love, the young man you love must undoubtedly love you as much as you love him, and if he does not, he is doing wrong, but nothing can force him to do so. Each one can use the privilege of freedom as one wishes. If you love him so deeply as to bear intolerable pain for it, he is not to be blamed for that, and you cannot justifiably complain about him, since you alone

7. more out of anger than reason: *piu adirata che consigliata domandi.* The context of the passage implies that a state of grief can lead to an act of anger.

are the main cause of it. Although Love is a very powerful lord and his strength unequalled, he could not have forced this young man into your mind against your will; your judgment and idle thoughts were the beginning of this love; if you had opposed it forcefully, all of this would not have happened, but being free you could have mocked him and anyone else, just as you say he mocks you by not caring about you. But because you yielded your freedom to him, you must then behave according to his pleasure, and since it is his pleasure to stay away from you, it is also fitting that you must like this without complaining. If in tears he gave you his very own word and promised to return, he used not a new but a very ancient lovers' trick, since these are the customs used at the court of your god.

"But if he has not kept his word, no judge is ever to be found who would hold him responsible, and the only thing that can be done about this is to say, "He did wrong" and then to rest in peace, knowing what could be done to him if fate should give you the same chance it gave him in regard to you. He is also not the first to do such a thing, nor are you the first to whom this has happened. Jason abandoned Hypsipyle in Lemnos to return to Medea in Thessaly; Paris left Oenone in the forest of Ida and went back to Helen in Troy; and Theseus left Ariadne in Crete to join Phaedra in Athens; but neither Hypsipyle nor Oenone nor Ariadne killed themselves, rather, by putting aside their futile thoughts, they forgot their false lovers. As I said before, Love is not harming you nor has he harmed you more than you wanted to be harmed. He uses his bow and arrows indiscriminately, as we see happen every day, and his ways must be obvious to you through innumerable clear examples, so that no matter what happens to anyone on account of him, one should feel sorry not for him but for oneself. He is a lascivious, naked, blind child who flies around and shoots his arrows any which way, and there is no satisfaction in complaining about him, nor in dissuading him from his ways because it is mostly a waste of words.

"This new woman, who was charmed by or who may have charmed your lover, and whom you threaten with so many insults, may have conquered him through no fault of her own; rather, he may have become hers through his own forwardness, and like you, who could not resist his entreaties, she too (just as soft-hearted as you) could not resist them without feeling sorry for him. If, as you say, he knows how to weep whenever he likes, you should know that beauty and tears combined have a tremendous power. Moreover, let us even assume that this noble woman ensnared him with her words and behavior; this is customary in the world today, where each person seeks his own interest and on finding it takes advantage of it as much as possible, without taking anybody else into consideration. The good lady, perhaps no less wise than you in these matters and aware of his abilities in Venus' army, attracted him to herself. And who prevents you from doing the same to someone else? I do not praise such a thing, but if nothing else is possible and if you are obliged to be Love's follower, whenever you wish to regain your freedom from him (which you can do), there are, as far as I know, many young men more deserving than he is who would serve you willingly, and the pleasure they will give you will make you forget him, as this new lady may have made him forget you.

"Jupiter laughs when the promised vows and oaths of lovers are broken, and he who treats others the way he is treated may not make such a big mistake but uses the world according to the ways of others. To keep one's word with those who break it is today considered insane, and to return deception for deception is seen as the highest wisdom. When Medea was abandoned by Jason, she took Aegeus, and when Theseus left Ariadne, she acquired Bacchus as a husband, and thus their weeping turned to joy. Therefore, face your sorrows with more patience, since you have more reason to complain about yourself than about others; and many ways can be found to forget these sorrows when you have the will to, especially if you consider that other women felt them just as deeply as you do and have got past them. What can you say of Deianeira, who was abandoned by Hercules for Iole, and of Phyllis, who was left by Demophon, and of Penelope, whom Ulysses betrayed with Circe? Their afflictions were more serious than yours in that their love was just as passionate or more so, and if one considers the manner in which things were done and the notable position of these men and women, they withstood them well. Therefore, you are not alone nor the first in this situation, and cases in which a person is not alone can hardly be as unbearable or severe as you are showing.[8]

"So rejoice and chase your useless worries away, and be careful of your husband; supposing this matter should reach his ears and he should, as you say, impart to you no greater punishment than death, keep in mind that since we die no more than once, when man has a choice, he must choose the best way to die. Think how much infamy and endless shame would stain your memory if death were to pursue you as you in your rage are asking it to. It is necessary to learn to treat worldly things as changeable, and above all, neither you nor anyone else should trust too much in things when they are flourishing, nor should you when prostrate in adversity despair of better things. Clotho mixes one thing with another, forbids fate to be stable, and turns each destiny upside down; no one ever had the favor of the gods such that he could hold them accountable for the future; moved by our sins, God overturns our affairs. It is equally true that Fortune fears the mighty and humiliates the timid.

"Now is the time to see whether there is any virtue in you, because even though prosperity can never entirely dislodge virtue, it very often hides it. Furthermore, in the midst of affliction, hope has this way of not showing any way out; therefore one who cannot hope for anything should not despair of anything. We are moved by the fates, and believe me, things established by them cannot be easily changed. What we mortals do and bear comes for the most part from the heavens; Lachesis enforces the decreed law with her spinning wheel and leads everything along a restricted path; our first day has determined our last, and it is not permitted to change the course of what has happened.

"Many have already been harmed for having wanted to believe that the order was alterable, and many others for having feared it, because while they were afraid of their destiny they had already fulfilled it. So forget the sorrows you have chosen of your own free will, live joyfully hoping in the gods, and do good deeds, for it has often happened that when a man believes happiness to be far away, he steps into it unwittingly. Countless ships sailing happily on the high seas foundered as they entered

8. person: *uomo,* i.e., man, but a literal translation would be awkward here since the remark is directed at Fiammetta.

safe harbors, while others that utterly despaired of safety ultimately found themselves secure in port. I have also seen a number of trees that had been struck by Jupiter's fiery thunderbolt
soon afterwards covered with green branches, while others, tenderly cared for, withered away through some unknown chance.
Fortune offers you a choice of ways, and in the same manner
that she caused you grief, she will also give you joy, if you nourish your life with hope."

Not once but many times my wise nurse spoke to me in this
fashion, believing that she could chase my sufferings away and
restrict my worries to those about dying, but few or none of her
words touched my preoccupied mind fruitfully; most of them
were lost to the four winds; each day my disease invaded my
aching soul more and more, and so I lay on my sumptuous bed
with my face down and hidden by my arms, turning over in my
mind a variety of grand things.

I am now going to tell about some very brutal things, things
considered almost unthinkable in a woman had not such
things—or worse—been seen to happen in the past.

Feeling desperately far away from my lover and with my
heart overwhelmed by an unbearable pain, I began saying to
myself:

"Here it is! Panfilo has given me the same reason—and an
even worse one—which was given to Elissa the Sidonian for
leaving the world. It is his wish that I abandon these regions to
seek new ones, and because I am his slave, I will do what he
wants; and all at once I will make appropriate amends for my
love, for the evil I perpetrated, and for the injury done to my
husband; if in the next world there is any freedom for the spirits
separated from the prison of the flesh, I will undoubtedly be reunited with my lover, and where my body cannot be, my soul
will be in its place.

"So I will then die, and because I wish to flee this harsh suffering, I must inflict this cruelty upon my very own self, since no
other hand could be cruel enough to do properly what I deserve
having done to me. So I will embrace death without hesitation
because while death is mysteriously dark when one thinks about
it, I expect it will be more gentle than a painful life."

Since I had finally come to a decision about this resolution,
in my own mind I began searching among the numerous means

to die for the one most suitable for taking my life; at first I thought of sharp metal weapons, which have caused the death of many, when I recalled that Elissa, whom I have already mentioned, died that way. Then, I pictured to myself the death of Byblis and Amata, whose methods of dying suggested themselves as a means to end my life; but because I was more concerned with my reputation than with myself and more fearful of how to die than of dying itself, and because I was under the impression that one method was infamous and the other excessively cruel in the eyes of people, I had reasons to reject both. Then I imagined doing what the Saguntans did for fear of Hannibal the Carthaginian and what, for fear of Philip the Macedonian, the citizens of Abydos did by committing their belongings and themselves to the flames; but, seeing that this would cause great injury to my beloved husband, who was not responsible for my troubles, I discarded this manner of dying as I had the preceding ones.

Then I thought of poisonous drinks which in the past had brought an end to the days of Socrates, Sophonisba, Hannibal, and of many other princes, and these means suited my taste well, but because I realized that it was necessary to have time to obtain them, and believing that in the meantime my resolution might waver as I was searching, I tried to devise another way, and it occurred to me that I could give up the wretched ghost between my knees,[9] as many have done before, but fearing some obstacle—and I could foresee one—I went on to consider another kind of idea.

For the same reason I eliminated the live coals Portia used, but then I thought of the death of Ino and Melicerte and that of Erysichthon too, but because one required going somewhere, and the other a long wait, I abandoned these means, calling to mind that, in regard to the latter, pain would nourish the body for a long time. However, among all these ways of dying, I thought of the death of Perdix, who fell from the highest rock of

9. between my knees. The Segre edition has "e pensato mi venne di volere . . . come molti gìa fecero, rendere il tristo spirito," indicating what is apparently a deliberate omission. The Einardi-Ricciardi and Maier editions have "venne di volere intra le ginocchia, come molti gìa fecero," that is, "I could give up the wretched ghost between my knees." It is not clear what manner of suicide Fiammetta is referring to.

Crete, and it pleased me to choose this kind of sure death free from all infamy, and I said to myself:

"If I throw myself from the highest part of my house, my body, shattering into hundreds of pieces, will release my unhappy, stained, and broken soul through each piece to the fiendish gods; thus, no one will be able to think that I was so cruel or insane to seek death, but by attributing my death to an unfortunate accident one will curse Fortune and shed tears of pity for me!"

This decision was made in my mind, and I was extremely pleased to pursue it, thinking that I would be exercising great self-pity if I were to become pitiless toward myself.

My intention was already fixed, and all I needed was the opportune moment, when a sudden chill pierced my bones, making me tremble all over and brought with it these words:

"O wretched one, what are you planning to do? Do you wish to annihilate yourself because of anger and discontent? If at this moment you were compelled to die from a serious illness, would you not attempt to live in order to see your Panfilo at least once again before dying? Do you not realize that if you die you will not see him anymore and that his compassion for you will be useless? What advantage did the impatient Phyllis derive from the belated arrival of Demophon? Had she been able to endure, she would have welcomed him as a woman, and not as a tree; in bloom, she felt no pleasure by his coming.

"Live then, because he will certainly return some time, either as a lover or as an enemy, and no matter in what mind he will come back, you will love him anyhow, and you will perhaps be able to see him and arouse his compassion for your situation; after all, he did not burst out from an oak, or a cave, or hard rock, nor did he drink the milk of a tiger or some other fierce animal, and his heart is not made of diamond or steel such that he should not feel compassion and understanding for you, but even if he should not be overcome by pity, by staying alive you will then have more of a right to die. You have borne this wretched life for more than one year without him; you certainly can continue to do so for another. Death never fails those who want it; since it is so quick, much better later than now; you can certainly hope that he will shed some tears at your death no matter how hostile and ruthless he may be. Therefore, take back the decision you have made too quickly, because those who decide in a hurry are doing their utmost to regret it. What you wish to do is something that cannot be followed by repentance, and even if it were, you cannot reverse it."

With my soul filled with such matters, my sudden resolution was kept suspended for a long time, but because Megaera was spurring me with harsh pains, I decided to follow my resolution, and I quietly considered how to bring it about; with kind words I showed my nurse, who was already silent, a feigned calm on my wretched face, and to convince her to leave I said:

"There, there, my dearest mother, your truthful words have found a fertile place in my heart, but to let this blind madness out of my mad soul leave this place and let me sleep, as I wish to do."

But being very shrewd and nearly guessing my intentions, she praised my wish to sleep but lingered about me, taking her time about the order she had received, and in no way did she want to leave the room. So, not to arouse her suspicion about my intention, I endured her presence beyond my wish, imagining that after a while, seeing me calm, she would leave. So I disguised the deceitful plan by resting quietly, and although nothing showed outwardly, I lamented to myself in these moments which I thought had to be my last, by saying these words:

"O unhappy Fiammetta, most sorrowful of all women, finally your day has come! Today, after you have thrown yourself onto the ground from the top of the mansion, and after your soul has left your shattered body, your tears, sighs, anxieties, and desires will end, and you will have freed yourself and your Panfilo all at once from the pledged faith. Today you will receive his well-deserved embraces; today the banners of Love's army will cover your body with shameful destruction; today your spirit will see him; today you will know for whom he has abandoned you; today you will force him to become compassionate; and today you will begin to take revenge on your female foe. But if there is some pity in you, O gods, listen to my last prayer: let my death be known among people without infamy. If by inflicting death on oneself a sin is committed, such sin carries its own reparation, namely, that I die without daring to reveal the reason; if I believed that by telling the reason I would not be blamed, this would be of no small consolation to me. Also, allow my dear husband to bear my death with patience, because if I had properly cared about his love, I would still be happy and ask to live instead of offering you these prayers. But because I am a female, heedless of the goods I have received and, like other women, always choosing the worse, I now give myself this reward.

"O Atropos, in the name of the infallible blow you deal to all humanity, I humbly beg you to guide my falling body in your power, and with little torment release my soul from the threads of your sister Lachesis; and to you, O Mercury, who receives it, I pray that in the name of that love whose flames already burned you and in the name of my own blood, which I am offering to you from now on, you may kindly guide my soul to wherever your discretion has decided to place it, and may that place not be prepared for it with such severity that it would regard as slight the ills it has already experienced."

As I said these things to myself, Tisiphone stood before my eyes, and with an incomprehensible whisper and a threatening aspect, made me fearful of a life worse than the past one. But then, speaking more clearly, she said: "Nothing experienced only once can be severe," and she inflamed my troubled mind with a more fervid desire for death. Therefore, seeing that my old nurse was not yet leaving, and believing that too long a delay might make me, who was ready to die, hold back on my decision, or thinking that some accident would deprive me of it, I said weeping, with my arms stretched as if I were embracing my bed:

"Rest with God, my bed, may He make you more gracious to the next woman than He has made you to me."

Then, as I looked around that room which I had no hope of seeing again, I was seized by a sudden pain and I lost my sight; shaken by a mysterious trembling, and feeling my way around, I tried to rise, but my limbs, overcome by terror, did not support me; rather, I fell on my face not once but three times, and I felt a fierce conflict raging inside of me between my irate soul and my frightened spirits, the one forcefully holding back the other that wished to flee. But although my soul won and chased the cold fear away, it made me burn with fiery pain, and I regained my strength. With the pallor of death already painted on my face I rose violently and did what a mortally wounded bull does, furiously jumping about and kicking itself; in like manner Tisiphone wavered before my eyes; unconscious of my impulses I threw myself from the bed to the floor as if possessed by a bacchic madness, and running after the Fury I started out towards the stairs leading to the highest part of my lodgings; and having already broken out of my bedchamber and crying loudly, I looked wildly around all of the house and said in a weak, broken voice:

"O home that was so hostile to me when I was happy, stand eternal and let my lover know of my fall if he returns; and you, my dear husband, comfort yourself and look right away for a wiser Fiammetta. Dear sisters, relatives, any other women companions and friends, faithful maidservants, live on in the good graces of the gods."

With these words I was angrily pushing myself along a disgraceful course, but my old nurse, like someone aroused from sleep by a frenzy, left her spinning, amazed at seeing this, suddenly lifted her very heavy limbs and began screaming and following me as fast as she could. With a voice I found hard to believe, she said:

"My girl, where are you running? What madness is driving you? Is this the result of my words in which you said you had taken comfort? Where are you going? Wait for me!"

Then, even more loudly she screamed:

"Maids, come and stop this insane woman and calm her madness."

Her shouting served no purpose, and her laborious running even less: I seemed to have grown wings, and I was running towards my death faster than any wind. But unexpected circumstances, contrary to good as well as to evil intentions, saved my life, because while my very long garments could have been a hindrance to my purpose for their length, they did not impede my running, but somehow, as I was hurrying, they tangled themselves around a sharp piece of wood and halted my impetuous flight, and no matter how hard I pulled, not a piece of them came free. Because of this my heavy nurse reached me as I was trying to untangle them; red in the face and screaming, I remember saying to her:

"You wretched old woman, if you care for your life, go away. You think you are helping me, but you are harming me; let me die now while I am disposed toward it with the greatest will, because he who stops from dying the one who wishes to die does not do anything else but kill him; you are killing me, in the belief that you are saving me from death, and like an enemy you try to prolong my suffering."

My tongue was shouting, my heart was ablaze with ire, and my frantic hands, intending to untangle, were entangling myself, and no sooner did I think of the alternative of disrobing than my screeching nurse reached me and hindered me as much as she could; but once I became free, all of her strength would have been inadequate, if at her screams the young maids had not rushed in from everywhere and held me fast. Several times I believed that I could free myself from their hands with sudden jerks and superior strength, but finally exhausted, I was overcome and escorted to my room, which I had thought I would never see again. Oh, how many times I told them in a plaintive voice:

"Most vile servants, what kind of audacity is this that allows you to seize your mistress with such violence? Which fury has inspired you, O miserable ones? And you, wicked nurse of this miserable body that will be a future symbol of all pains, why did you oppose my final desire? Do you not realize that you would do me a greater favor by ordering me to die than by protecting me from death? If you love me, as I believe you do, let me fulfill my sad task, and let me decide on my own what to do with myself; and if you are as compassionate as you seem to be, use your pity in the service of the uncertain fame that will survive me, for your efforts to stop me now in this matter might be useless. Do you believe that you can take away the sharp weapons on whose points rests my own desire, or the painful nooses, the poisonous herbs, or the fire? What is the use of this cure of yours? It slightly prolongs this mournful life, and by postponing my death it may add shame to it, while it would have come to me now without any shame. Miserable one, you will not be able to deprive me of it by keeping guard over me, because death is everywhere and resides in all things, and it has been found even in the most life-saving remedies; so let me die before I become more afflicted than I am and seek it out with a fiercer mind."

As I was wretchedly pronouncing these words, I did not keep my hands at rest, but by angrily grabbing now one and now another of my maidservants, I pulled one's braids, leaving her bald and thrust my fingernails into the face of another, scratching her wickedly and making her bleed, and I even remember tearing all the humble clothing off one of them. But alas, neither my old nurse nor the wounded servants responded in kind to this treatment; instead they compassionately and tearfully cared for me. So, I tried even harder to overcome them with words, but to no avail; hence I began shouting loudly:

"O wicked hands, capable of all evil, you adorned my beauty so that I became more desirable to the one I loved most, and since evil has come to me from your actions, make amends by using your impious cruelty on your own flesh; tear it apart, open it up and take out my mean and invincible soul with an outpouring of blood. Rip out this heart, wounded by blind Love, and because you have been deprived of weapons, tear it to pieces pitilessly with your nails, because it is the main cause of all your troubles."

Alas, my own words threatened me with these evil things which I desired and gave the order to my willing hands to carry them out, but my alert maids hindered me by holding them against my will.

Then my wretched and importunate nurse began saying sorrowfully:

"My dear girl, in the name of this unhappy bosom from which you took your first nourishment, I beg you, that you listen with a humble mind to a few of my words. With them I will not try to dissuade you from your lamentations, nor do I want to convince you to chase away or perhaps to overcome through habit the well-founded anger that burns in you so furiously, nor do I wish that you be resigned and bear it pleasantly, but I will bring back to your lost memory what is life-giving and honorable for you. It is necessary that you, a well-known young lady of great virtue as you are, not remain subject to pain or turn your back on troubles as if you were defeated. It is not brave to ask for death as if one were afraid of life, as you are doing, but it is extremely courageous to face intervening misfortunes and not run before them. I do not know what need those people have to seek out death and why they demand it, who, humiliated by fate, have scattered and wasted the gifts of life (as you have done), since they are both cowardly wishes. Consequently, if you wish to put yourself in a state of utter misery, do not seek this through death because death is the ultimate destroyer of misery. Chase from your mind this madness through which, as it seems to me, you are seeking both to have a lover and to lose him at the same time. Do you believe that you will get him by vanishing?"

I did not answer anything, but in the meantime the noise spread through the large house and into the nearby neighborhood, and as it happens when a wolf howls, everyone around gathers together in one place, so all the servants hurried from everywhere, and all of them sadly inquired about what had happened. But I had already forbidden those who knew about it to say anything, so by their covering up the horrible accident with a lie, the others were satisfied. My dear husband came running, and so did my sisters, beloved parents, and friends, and they were all equally deceived, so that instead of being seen as wicked, I was considered most pitiful, and after many tears, each one felt sorry for my sorrowful life and then tried to comfort me. Oh, but at this point it also happened that some believed me driven by some kind of fury, and looked at me as if I were nearly mad. However, others, more compassionate, by observing my meekness and regarding it as sorrow, which it truly was, made fun of what the others were saying, and pitied me. Visited like this by many people, I remained in a stupor for several days, and I was kept under silent and discreet surveillance by my clever nurse.

There is no anger that burns so fiercely that it does not become very cold with the passing of time. I saw myself for several days in the state I am depicting and clearly recognized the truth in my wise nurse's words, and I bitterly regretted my past folly. But even though my madness consumed itself in time and vanished, my love did not change at all because of it; on the contrary, I was left with the melancholy I used to feel at other such incidents, and I could hardly bear the idea that I had been abandoned for another woman.

I often sought the advice of my discreet nurse on this matter, wishing to find a way to get my lover back. Sometimes we planned to write letters full of lamentations, informing him of my sorrowful circumstances; other times we thought it would be better to send a wise messenger who by word-of-mouth would tell him of my suffering, and although my nurse was old and the journey was long and arduous, she was ready to go for me. But after weighing everything, we concluded that letters, no matter how pitiful, would not be effective in light of his new and

present love affairs, so we judged them useless; in spite of all this, I wrote some, with the results we had foreseen. I clearly perceived that if I sent my nurse, she would not live to reach him, and I did not believe that anyone else could be trusted; therefore, these first attempts were futile, and in my mind there was only one way left to have him back: for none other than I to go after him myself; and to this end several means occurred to me, but they were all ultimately rejected by my nurse for legitimate reasons.

At times I thought of searching him out in his land, dressed as a pilgrim in the company of a trustworthy woman companion; and although this idea seemed possible, I recognized it nevertheless as very dangerous to my virtue, knowing how female travellers with some visible shapeliness were often treated by scoundrels during their journey; besides this, I felt obliged toward my husband and did not see how I could go without him or his permission, which I had no hope of obtaining. For this reason I abandoned the idea as unfeasible, and I immediately considered another, quite crafty one, which I believed could be carried out and it will be if no accident should happen, and I hope it will not fail in the future, as long as I am alive. I pretended I had made a vow to God for having helped me out of the adversities I have spoken of, and by wanting to fulfill it I could have had and still could have a sound reason for insisting on passing through the midst of my lover's land; and if I did go through it, I would not lack a reason for wanting and having to see him: namely, to remind him why I went there.

And of course I revealed this, as I say, to my beloved husband, who to bring this about cheerfully offered himself, but said that he wanted me to wait for a more—as they say—convenient time. But waiting was very difficult for me, and fearing that it would also be harmful, it forced me to consider some alternatives, but they all fell short, except for Hecate's marvels, which (in order to entrust myself to the frightening spirits) I often discussed with various people who boasted of knowing how to use them; and some of them assured me that I would be swept off immediately; others claimed that Panfilo's mind would be freed from any other love and be returned to me; others said that I would recover my previous freedom; but when I wished to see the effects of these things, I found that they were more full of words than deeds, so that not once but many times I remained baffled by them in my hope; as a better solution, I no longer thought of such things and gave myself over to waiting for the more suitable time that my dear husband had promised for the fulfillment of my fictitious vow.

SEVEN

*In which Lady Fiammetta shows how she rejoiced
in vain when she was told that a certain Panfilo had
returned to the place where she was, and how she
eventually fell back into her earlier melancholy
when she discovered that it was another
Panfilo, not her own.*

In spite of the hope I had placed in the future journey, my anguish continued, and as the sun traversed the sky with ceaseless motion, drawing day after day with it without interruption, I was kept in vain hope for much longer than I wished, anxious and as much in love as ever. And Phoebus with his light was already in Taurus,[1] which had captured Europa; the days took time away from the nights, and from being very short they became very long; Zephyrus arrived bedecked with flowers, quieted Boreas' violent blows with his mellow and tranquil breath, and chased the mist from the cold air and the white snow from the high peaks; having dried the rain-soaked fields, he adorned anew every place with grass and flowers, replacing the cold winter's lingering whiteness with a green garb that covered the trees all over. In all places it was already that time in which joyful Spring graciously spreads around its riches everywhere and when the earth, a virtual constellation of violets, roses, and flowers of all sorts, competes in beauty with the eighth heaven.[2] Narcissus was in every pasture, and Bacchus' mother, already showing signs of her pregnancy,[3] leaned more heavily on her companion elm, which had itself now become more heavily laden with its acquired garb. Dryope and Phaeton's unhappy sis-

---

1. Taurus. The sun is now in the zodiacal sign of Taurus (April 20—May 21), which means that it is spring again and two years have passed since Fiammetta met Panfilo and sixteen months since he left.

2. eighth heaven: In Dante's *Paradiso* the realm of the fixed stars.

3. pregnancy. In this naturalization of myth, Jupiter's impregnation of Semele (see Glossary) and her giving birth to Bacchus become the fertilization and ripening of the grapevines through the effect of air and sun.

ters rejoiced too, after having shed the mean garments of hoary winter; everywhere the joyous birds filled the air with their delightful songs, and Ceres was gaily covering anew the open fields with her fruit. But beyond all this, my cruel master made his arrows burn more fiercely in longing minds, so that young men and charming maidens, all adorned according to their natures, sought to attract the object of their love.

Each corner of our city reveled in festivities even more lavish than those which took place in kindly Rome; the theaters resounded with songs and music and invited each lover to that kind of gaiety. Sometimes the young men jousted on their fast-running horses with their fierce weapons: at other times they skirmished with one another, surrounded by a jingle of resounding bells; at still other times, they gladly showed how expertly they could handle their spirited horses that were foaming at the bit. Enchanted with these things and decked with fresh garlands, the maidens gave joyful glances to their lovers, sometimes from high windows and sometimes from the doors below; and each one assured her lover of her amorous feelings, one with a new gift, another with a gesture, and still another with words.

I kept by myself, nearly removed from everyone in a solitary place, and disconsolate because of my disappointed hope, I was annoyed by that gaiety. Nothing pleased me, no festivity could give me any joy, and no thought or word could give me comfort; my hands did not touch a single green branch or flower or anything that gives delight, nor did I look upon them with a happy eye. I had become envious of other people's joys and most intensely craved that each woman should be treated by Love and Fortune as I was. Oh, what great consolation I often remember feeling as I listened to the miseries and misadventures of lovers happening anew!

But while the gods kept me in such a spiteful disposition, Fortune gave relief to my pains, but only because she is deceptive and because sometimes, in order to hurt more deeply the afflicted who are steeped in adversity, she shows herself with a happy face as if she were transformed, with the result that by abandoning themselves to her, the wretched fall with a greater crash, giving an end to her cheerful aspect; if the people who trust Fortune are then so foolish as to count on her, they find themselves knocked down like that unlucky Icarus, who mid-way in his journey placed too great a confidence in his wings and reached great heights but fell from up there into the waters that still bear his name. Aware that I was one of these people, and not satisfied with the troubles she had already caused me, Fortune prepared something worse for me, and with false gaiety drew back her anger and hostile measures so that by giving herself more space to move back she might hurt me all the more, just as the African rams do to impart a harder blow; and it was with empty merriment that she gave pause to my pains in the following manner.

My unfaithful lover had been away more than four times the number of months he had promised, and one day, as I was steeped in tears as usual, my old nurse, with her wrinkled face soaked in perspiration, came into the room where I was, walking faster than her age allowed her, and she sat down because her heart was pounding, and with a joyful glint in her eyes started more than once to speak, but each time her anxious panting broke her words in half. Full of surprise, I asked her:

"My dear nurse, what kind of fatigue is this that has seized you? What do you wish to say so quickly that you cannot first let your agitated mind rest? Is it happy or sorrowful? Should I prepare myself to flee or to die, or what must I do? I don't know how nor why, but your face greatly revives my hope; however, because things have been so unfavorable for so long, I fear the worse, which is usually what unhappy people feel. So, tell me quickly, and do not keep me in suspense. Why are you in such a hurry? Tell me if it is a joyful God or an infernal fury who has impelled you to come here."

Then the old woman, who had nearly caught her breath, interrupted my words and said much more cheerfully:

"Cheer up, my sweet girl: there is no cause for fear in what I am going to say; throw away all sorrow and recapture the joy you have lost: your lover is coming back."

As they reached my mind these words aroused in it a sudden happiness, as clearly showed in my eyes, but my usual wretchedness soon took it away: I no longer believed in it; on the contrary, I said in tears:

"Dear nurse, in the name of your old age and ancient limbs, which by now demand eternal rest, do not make fun of miserable me, whose pains should be in part your own. The rivers will flow back to their sources first, Hesperus will announce the light of day, and Phoebe will illuminate the night with her brother's rays before my ungrateful lover returns. Is there anyone who does not know that he enjoys more than ever being in love and is now having a good time with another lady? Wherever he may be now, he would turn to her and would certainly not leave her to come here."

But she immediately persisted:

"Fiammetta, if the gods are to receive the happy soul of this old body, your nurse isn't lying at all. Besides, it is not appropriate at my age to go around fooling anyone in such matters, and especially you, whom I love above all else."

"Then," said I, "how did this reach your ears and whence do you know it? Tell me quickly, so that if it seems possible to me, I may rejoice for such happy news."

I rose from where I was, and already more cheerful, I drew closer to the old woman, who said:

"This morning while I was walking slowly along the seashore with my mind fixed on taking care of household matters, and intent on them, keeping my back turned to the sea, a young man jumped from a boat (as I realized afterwards) and propelled by the vehemence of his careless jump, gave me a strong push, so invoking the gods against him I turned around in anger to complain about the blow I had received, but he immediately and humbly asked my forgiveness. I looked at him, and by his face and the way he was dressed, I judged that he was from Panfilo's land, and I asked him whether that was so: 'May God bless you, young man. Tell me, do you come from a faraway land?' 'Yes, woman,' he answered. Then I said: 'Tell me where from, if possible.' And he: 'I come from Etruria, from its most noble city; that is where I am from.'

"As soon as I heard this I knew that he and Panfilo came from the same land, and I asked him whether he knew Panfilo and how he was, and he said he did and recounted many good things about him, and added that Panfilo would have come with him had he not been detained by some small difficulty, and that he would be here without fail in a few days. In the meantime, while we were talking, the young man's friends had come to shore with their gear, and he left with them. I forgot all other business and ran as fast as I could, hardly believing that I would live long enough to tell you this, and I came here panting, as you have seen; so be happy and chase away your sadness."

I grabbed her then, and with a most joyful heart I kissed her old forehead, but because my mind was uncertain, I begged her several times and asked her over and over again whether this news was true, hoping that she would not deny it and having some doubts about whether she was telling me the truth, but then she affirmed several times with more oaths that she was telling the truth, and although my mind wavered back and forth, by believing it I was happy and thanked the gods with these words:

"O almighty Jupiter, most solemn ruler of the heavens! O brilliant Apollo, from whom nothing is hidden! O gracious Venus, full of compassion for your subjects! O blessed child, carrier of the beloved arrows, may all of you be praised! Truly those who persevere in hoping in you cannot in the long run perish. Here we see that it is by your grace and not by my own merits that my Panfilo is coming back, but I will not see him until your altars (at which in the past I have urged you with prayers, and which I have moistened with bitter tears) are honored with appropriate incense which I will offer you. And to you, O Fortune, once again full of pity for my troubles, I will immediately offer the image I had promised as testimony to your favors. Therefore, with the kind of humility and devotion that can make you more receptive I pray to you that you confound or prevent all incidents which could hinder the possible return of my Panfilo and that you bring him forth right here as healthy and as free as he ever was."

After I finished this prayer, as pleased with myself as the falcon that has escaped the hood can be, I began saying:

"My loving heart, weakened for so long by suffering, free yourself at last from bothersome worries, since our darling lover is remembering us and is on his way, as he had promised. May the pain, fear, and the deep shame that abounds in affliction take flight; don't let it cross your mind how Fortune has guided you in the past, but chase away all the clouds of cruel fate, and may all images of miserable moments leave you; turn your happy face towards the present good, and may the old Fiammetta, with a soul renewed, divest herself of everything."

As I gaily talked to myself in this manner, my heart became doubtful, and I know not from where nor how, but a sudden lukewarmness took hold of me entirely and removed all my eagerness to rejoice, and I halted in the middle of my discourse as if I were lost. Alas, this vice that haunts unhappy people is the incapacity to believe in happy things; and even if it should happen that good fortune returns, the afflicted resent rejoicing, and since they may believe themselves to be dreaming, they make sluggish use of it as if it were not real; almost stunned therefore, within myself I began:

"Who is hindering me or calling me away from this joy that has just begun? Is my Panfilo not returning? He certainly is, so who is ordering me to weep? No cause for sadness has overtaken me now. Who is then forbidding me to adorn myself with fresh flowers and rich robes? Oh, I do not know why or by whom, but it is nevertheless forbidden to me."

And so I remained nearly beside myself in the midst of my misconceptions, as tears fell from my eyes against my will, and as usual I wept as I spoke, such was my long afflicted heart's attachment to its customary weeping. As if my mind were predicting the future, it sent forth clear signs with tears of what had to happen, and through them, I now truly know that when tranquil waters swell without a wind, a great storm is in the making for sailors; but still desirous of overcoming what the soul did not want, I said:

"O wretched one, what presages and what impulses are you needlessly inventing ahead of time? Set your trusting mind on the good things that have happened, because whatever it may be that you foresee for yourself, you are fearing it too late and without profit."

So, from this reasoning I gave myself over to newfound joy, chased gloomy ideas away from me as much as I could, and after having encouraged my dear nurse to keep on the alert for the return of this lover of ours, I converted my mournful garments into colorful ones and began again to take care of myself so that I would not be rejected by him when he returned because of my sorrowful face. My pale face then began to recover its lost color; my lost weight began to come back; as they completely vanished, my tears took with them the purple circles that had formed around my eyes; and my eyes recovered their proper focus and regained their full light; my cheeks, which had become rough from weeping recovered their original softness; and although my hair did not turn blond immediately, it nevertheless resumed its usual neatness, and the cherished and precious garments which had been for so long neglected adorned me again.

What else? I renewed myself, along with everything else, and almost entirely turned myself back into my former condition and beauty so that my women friends, my relatives, and my dear husband felt admiration, and each one said to himself or herself: "What inspiration has taken this woman away from her abiding sadness and melancholy, which in the past neither prayers nor comforting words could ever chase away from her? This is no less than a major event." And with all these wonders they were very happy. Our house, which for so long had been dreary because of my tribulations, began to be lively again, along with myself, and as my heart changed, it seemed that everything changed from sad to happy.

Because I had taken hope in Panfilo's imminent return, the days, which seemed to me longer than usual, were proceeding at a slow pace and I did not count them any less often than I did those previous ones in which I was wrapped up in myself; and as I thought of those past sorrows and of the ideas I then had, I condemned them altogether, saying to myself:

"How many evil thoughts I have had about my dear lover, how wickedly I cursed him for his absence, and how foolishly I believed those who told me once that he belonged to another woman, and not to me! Cursed be their lies! O God, how can men lie with such a bold face? On my part I should have done all these things more advisedly than I did. Not only the faith which my lover often promised affectionately and tearfully but also the love he felt and still feels for me I should have weighed against the words of those people who spoke under no oath and who did not care to investigate further what they were saying but had only a first and superficial impression to go on; one thing seems very clear: because someone saw a new bride entering Panfilo's house and did not know that there was no other young man living there, and because he did not take into consideration the reprehensible lechery of old men, he believed that she was Panfilo's and said so, something which makes it quite clear how little this person cared about us; someone else, having perhaps seen Panfilo looking at or joking with a beautiful woman, who may have been perhaps a relative or a domestic genuinely believed that she belonged to him and affirmed it in such simple words that I believed it. Oh if I only had fully considered these matters, how many tears and sighs and how much pain I would have avoided!

"What can people in love do right? Our minds move according to impulses. Lovers believe everything because love is something worrisome and full of fear. Out of prolonged habit they always adapt themselves to harmful incidents because in their longing they believe that everything can be an obstacle to their desires, and they pay little heed to favorable things. But I must be forgiven because I have always asked the gods to make me a liar about my own desires. Behold, my prayers have finally been heard: my lover will not get to know about these things again, and if he should get to know them, what else could he say to himself about them but, 'She loved me passionately'? He will be obliged to appreciate the knowledge of my distress and of the dangers I have faced, because they are the truest proofs of my faith, and I have the vague suspicion that his prolonged absence may be due to no other reason than to prove that I could wait for him with a strong heart and without changing my mind.

"Well, I have waited for him courageously; therefore, by hearing with what labor, tears, and thoughts I have waited for him, nothing but love will be born from this. O God, when will he come so that he sees me and I him? O God, who sees all things, will I be able to control my urge to embrace him in front of everyone when I first see him? I scarcely believe so, to be sure. O God, when, holding him tightly in my arms, will I give him back the kisses he gave to my unconscious face without receiving any in return? Certainly the omen which came from my not having been able to bid him farewell has come true, and by it the gods showed me correctly that he would eventually return. O God, when will I be able to tell him of my tears and anguish and listen to the reasons for his long absence? Will I live that long? I scarcely believe it. Oh may that day come soon, because Death, whom formerly I not only invoked but eagerly sought, now frightens me; if it is possible that a prayer may reach Death's ears, I beg her to keep away from me and let me spend my youth happily with my Panfilo."

I was eager to have no day go by without hearing some reliable news of Panfilo's arrival, and I more than once urged my dear nurse to find again the young man who had brought the good message, in order to be more firmly reassured on what she had told me, and she did so not once but several times, and as time passed by, she kept announcing all along that his return was getting closer. Not only did I anticipate the promised date, but rushing ahead I often imagined the possibility that he had arrived, and innumerable times each day I ran to the windows and to the door, searching up and down the long street to see whether he was coming; no sooner did I see a man coming in the distance whom I imagined might be Panfilo than I eagerly waited for him until he was close enough for me to be certain that it was not him. This would disturb me so that I waited for others, if any were coming, and whenever this one or that one came by, I was kept in suspense; and if I was called indoors or if for some other reason I went in on my own, as if my soul were bitten by innumerable dogs, a million thoughts tormented me by saying: "Oh, perhaps he is passing by now, or he has gone by while you were not there to look. Go back!" And so I would return and get up and leave, and then return again to watch, going from window to door and from door to window, leaving very little time for anything else in between. Unhappy me! How much effort I put into waiting hour after hour for what was never to be!

When the day came that my nurse had been told Panfilo would arrive and which she had foretold more than once, I embellished myself just as Alcmene did at the news of Amphytrion's coming, and with a very skillful hand I left no part of myself lacking its own essential beauty, and could hardly stop myself from going to the seashore in order to see him sooner, since those ships were arriving on which my nurse had been assured he was to come, but I thought to myself, "The first thing he is going to do is to come to me," so I controlled my burning desire. However, he was not coming as I had imagined, and I began to feel very astonished, and various doubts arose in my mind in the midst of my mirth, which were not easily dispelled by happy thoughts. So, after a while I sent the old woman back to inquire about what had happened to him, and about whether he had come or not; she went then, but, it seemed to me, more lazily than ever, for which I repeatedly cursed her sluggish old age. But after a long time she returned to me with a sorrowful face, and at a slow pace. Alas, when I saw her, almost all life drained out of my heart, and I immediately thought that he had died during the journey, or that he had arrived ill. My face changed color many times in a moment, and as I walked towards the lazy old woman, I said:

"Tell me immediately; what news do you bring? Is my lover alive?"

She did not change her step or answer anything but immediately sat down and stared into my face, and I was trembling like a wind-shaken leaf and hardly able to restrain my tears; I said with my hands on my heart:

"If you do not tell me immediately the meaning of the wretched face which you are carrying around, I will tear to shreds every bit of our clothes. What kind of reason, if not an evil one, keeps you silent? Do not hide it any longer, reveal it while I believe the worst. Is our Panfilo alive?"

Prodded by my words, with downcast eyes she murmured:

"He is alive."

"So," I said then, "why do you not tell me immediately what sort of accident has detained him? Why do you keep me on tenterhooks? Is he kept away by illness? What accident holds him that he has not come to see me after coming ashore?"

And she said:

"I do not know whether it is an illness or some other matter that is keeping him."

"So," I replied, "have you not seen him, or perhaps he has not come?"

Then she said:

"To tell the truth, I have seen him, and he has arrived, but he is not the one we were waiting for."

Then I said:

"What makes you sure that he is not the one who has come? Had you seen him on another occasion, or have you gazed on him with a clear eye only now?"

"As a matter of fact," she replied, "to my knowledge I have never seen him before, but now I approached him, accompanied by the young man who first told me of his arrival, and upon being told that I had frequently inquired about him, he asked me what I wanted, and I answered that I wished his well-being; but when I asked him how his father was, and how his other affairs were, and why he stayed away so long after his departure, he answered that he had never known his father because he was born posthumously, that his affairs—by the grace of the gods—were all prospering, that he had never stayed here before, and that he intended to remain here briefly. These things surprised me, and believing that I was being fooled, I asked him his name, which he frankly told me and which I had never heard before, and I realized that you and I had been deluded by the similarity of names."[4]

As I heard these things, my eyes lost their sight, and each sensory function left me for fear of death, and as I fell onto the step where I had been standing, I hardly had enough strength left in my entire body to say, "Alas!" Crying miserably, the old woman called the other maids of the house, who carried me to my wretched bedchamber as if I were dead and put me on my bed, where they kept me for a long time in an attempt to revive my lost senses with cold water, believing and doubting that I was alive; but when after many sighs and tears, my lost strength returned, I asked my plaintive nurse once again if it was as she had said.

In addition to this, remembering how cautious Panfilo used to be, and believing he may have concealed himself from my nurse with whom he had never spoken before, I ordered her to describe the features of the Panfilo with whom she had spoken. After having first sworn that it was as she had said, she described meticulously his height, the shape of his features, and especially his face and clothing as well, and this made me fully trust that what the old woman had said was true. For this reason I chased all hope away, returned to my former woes, rose up in a sort of fury, took off my colorful clothes, put away the ornaments I liked so much, and with angry hands disheveled my tidy hair; completely discouraged, I began to weep harshly and to censure with bitter words the fruitless hope and the erroneous

4. the similarity of names: Although the nurse does address the narrator and protagonist a few pages earlier as "Fiammetta," we know from chapter 1 that this name and "Panfilo" are fictitious names which her lover has invented as part of their ruse to avoid detection, and for that reason it is difficult to identify the specific source of the confusion.

thoughts I had had about my wicked lover, and in short returned completely to my former miseries, and then I felt more excessively than ever a fervent desire for death, and I would not have run away from it as I did before, but the hope of a future journey held me back from it with no small force.

E I G H T

In which Lady Fiammetta, comparing her pains to those of many ancient ladies, demonstrates that hers are greater and then finally concludes her lamentation.

As you most compassionate ladies can presume from what you have heard, I am still living such a life, and the more my ungrateful master acts in an extraordinary way against me and the more he sees hope fleeing from me,[1] the more he blows onto his flames of desire and makes them greater; and as the flames grow, my tribulations increase, and since they are never soothed by a proper ointment, each becomes ever more violent, and the more violent they are, the more they torture my miserable mind. I do not doubt that if I had followed them in their course, they would have opened the way to death, which in the past I have desired so much to reach in a suitable manner; but because, as I have already said, I have firmly placed my hope on seeing, during my future journey, the one who causes me all of this, I do not try to mitigate my sorrows but to bear them. To do this, I have found that among other means only one is possible, namely, to compare my own misfortunes with those of other people who have lived in pain, and from this I derive two advantages: one is that I do not see myself as the first and only one in my miseries, as my nurse had already told me while she was comforting me, and the other is that, in my opinion, and after weighing carefully all aspects of other people's anguish, I judge my own misery to be much greater than that of everyone else; and this has brought me no small glory, since I can say that I alone am the one who has sustained more cruel pains while alive than any other woman. And with this glory, which everyone (including myself, if I could) flees as a supreme misery, I now spend time in melancholy, in such a manner as you will hear.

I am saying then that by anxiously seeking the sorrows of

1. my ungrateful master: *il mio ingrato signore.* Love.

others in my own, I immediately think of the love affairs of Ina-chus' daughter,[2] whom I first imagine as a soft and beguiling maiden, and then I think to myself how happy she must have been, feeling that she was loved by Jupiter, something which should undoubtedly suffice as the greatest gift for any woman, and then, as I see her transformed at Juno's wish into a cow guarded by Argos, I believe that she suffered beyond measure the greatest of anxieties. I certainly would judge her sorrows much greater than mine, if she had not continually had the protection of her lover-god. Who would doubt that if I had had my lover as a helper in my plight, or even if he felt pity for me, no pain would be burdensome for me? Besides this, this woman's end renders her earlier trials extremely light, because once Argos was dead, her heavy body was lightly transported to Egypt, where she regained her own form, married Osiris, and was seen to be a very happy queen. Certainly, if I could hope to see my Panfilo again as my own, even in my old age, I would say that my pains are not to be confused with those of this lady; but only God knows if this must be, since I deceive myself on this matter with false hope.

After this one, an image comes before me of the love of the unfortunate Byblis, whom I imagine leaving all her possessions to follow the inflexible Caunus. Together with her I consider the wretched Myrrha, who, after the evil pleasures of her love, ran miserably into death as she was fleeing the anger of her father, since he was threatening to kill her. I also see that sorrowful Canace, who had no other choice but death, after her wretched and ill-conceived childbirth; and as I carefully consider within myself the anguish of each one of these ladies, I unquestionably perceive it as immense, although their love affairs were abominable. But, if I consider it carefully, I see these sorrows as having ended or as about to end in a short time, because as she was quickly fleeing, Myrrha was transformed into the tree that bears her name, since the gods had complied with her wish, and she no longer feels any of her pains, given that the tree may continually weep as she did when her shape changed; so, as the cause of her suffering came to her, so was she reached by that which took her grief away. According to what some people say, Byblis also

2. Inachus' daughter: Ino (see Glossary).

ended her grief at once with the noose, although others believe that, helped by the nymphs who felt compassion for her troubles, she was changed into a fountain that still preserves her name, and this happened when she realized that Caunus refused altogether to pleasure her. What more can I say to demonstrate that my grief is much greater than theirs, except that the brevity of this sorrow of theirs is greatly surpassed by my own, which is longer lasting?

After having reflected upon these ladies, I am filled with pity for the unlucky Pyramus and his Thisbe, and I feel no little compassion for them, since I imagine them losing each other when very young and after having painfully loved for a long time and being on the verge of fulfilling their desires. What a piercingly bitter pain, believe me, must the young man have felt on that quiet night, when he found his Thisbe's garments, blood-stained and shredded by a wild beast, near the foot of the oak tree, and justifiably took those as signs that she had been devoured! Certainly his having killed himself shows it. Then, as I turn over in my mind the thought of that poor Thisbe when she saw her lover before her, drenched in blood and pulsing with little life, I feel her thoughts and her tears, and I know them to be so scorchingly hot that it is hard for me to believe any others could burn as much as hers, except my own, because for these two lovers, as it was for those mentioned earlier, grief ended when it had just begun. Oh happy were their souls, if one can love in the other world as in this one! No pain inflicted there can compare to the pleasure of their eternal companionship.

Much more forcefully than any other, the grief of the abandoned Dido comes next to mind, perhaps because I know it to be more like mine than any other. I imagine her presiding over the building of Carthage, most solemnly imparting laws to her people in the temple of Juno, kindly receiving the shipwrecked foreigner Aeneas there, and enchanted with his appearance, placing herself and her possessions at the mercy of the Trojan leader, who, after having used the regal delights for his own pleasure and having inflamed her love more warmly day by day, abandons her and departs. How incomparably miserable she appears to me, as I see her looking at the sea crowded with the ships of her fleeing lover! But as I reflect on her death, I finally consider her to be more impatient than woeful. In my opinion, when Panfilo first left, I too of course experienced the same grief she did when Aeneas left; if only the gods had then willed me to kill myself immediately, when I was suffering little! At least, just like her, I would have been freed of my sorrows, which have since continually grown greater.

In addition to these wretched thoughts, I imagine the melancholy of that doleful Hero of Sestos, and I seem to see her descending from the high tower to the seashore where she used to welcome her weary Leander with open arms; and here I seem to perceive her weeping grievously while looking at her dead lover pushed ashore by a dolphin and lying naked on the sand; and then with her gown she wipes the salty water from his dead face and drenches it with innumerable tears. Oh, what deep compassion binds me mentally to this lady! To be truthful, I felt for her so much more deeply than for any of the ladies already mentioned that sometimes I forgot my own grief and wept for her. And ultimately I do not find any other mode of consolation for her but one of these two: to die or to forget him, as we do with other dead people. Whichever of these one chooses, the pain will end; nothing lost and impossible to have back can cause pain for a long time. But may God not let that happen to me, yet even if it should I would make no other choice than death. However, while my Panfilo is alive—and may the gods make his life very long, as he himself wishes—such a thing cannot happen to me, because seeing that human affairs are continually changing always leads me to believe that sometime he will again be mine, as he was at another time; but such hope, having no fulfillment, continually makes my life very onerous, and I consider myself burdened by a greater sorrow.

At times I remember reading French romances in which, if they can be trusted, Tristan and Iseult loved one another more than any other lovers did and spent their earliest youth in pleasure mixed with innumerable adversities, but because they reached the same end together while loving each other most profoundly, it does not seem believable that either of them abandoned worldly pleasures without extreme grief; this is easily understandable if they left the world believing that the same delights could not be had anywhere else, but if they were convinced that they could live in the other world as they did in this one, one must believe that in dying they found more happiness than sadness, for I do not believe that a welcome death is as cruel and hard as many people think. What certainty about suffering can one provide by testifying to something he never experienced? Certainly none. Tristan's death and that of his lady were in his own hands; if it had been painful when he tightened its grip, he would have loosened it, and the pain would have ceased. Moreover, let us reasonably say that doing it may be extremely difficult: how serious—we will ask—can something be that happens only once and takes up very little time? Certainly not serious at all. So Tristan and Iseult ended pleasures and pains at once, but the lengthy period of my incomprehensible grief surpasses the pleasures I have had.

In my thinking I add the unhappy Phaedra to the number of ladies already mentioned, because with her ill-advised passion she caused a most cruel death to the one she loved more than herself. Of course I do not know what happened to her after such an error, but I am sure that if that should ever happen to me, nothing but a violent death would atone for it; yet if, as I already said, she kept on living, she easily forgot it, as dead things are usually forgotten.

Besides this, I compare Phaedra's pain to that of Laodameia and Deipyle and Argeia and Evadne and Deianeira, and many others who found comfort either in death or in necessary oblivion. How much can the fire, or the hot iron, or the molten metals sear the flesh of anyone who places a finger into them and quickly retracts it? Undoubtedly a great deal, I believe, but it is nothing compared to the pain of the one who is completely immersed in it for a long time, and this can be said of the state I have been in and am in continually, to which the pains I have described above show a likeness.

Those of which I have spoken were troubles of love, but besides these, if it is true that having been happy leads to extreme misfortune, I see before me tears no less wretched that have been provoked by the mean and untimely assaults of Fortune. These are the tears of Jocasta, of Hecuba, of Sophonisba, of Cornelia, and of Cleopatra. Oh, how much misery we will perceive if we look carefully into what happened to Jocasta: everything capable of upsetting any strong mind happened to her in her lifetime! While she was a young woman married to the Theban king Laius, it was necessary that she should send her first-born to be devoured by wild beasts in the belief that by doing so the unlucky father could escape what the heavens with unerring course were prescribing for him. Think what a great sorrow this must have been, and even more so, considering the close kinship of her who sent him away. Having been assured of what they had done by those who took her wretched son away, she believed him dead; sometime later her husband was miserably killed by the same one to whom she had given life, and she became the wife of the son she did not recognize and to whom she gave four children. So, she found herself mother and wife at once of the parricide, and recognized him when he made his offense known by depriving himself at one and the same time of realm and eyes.

In what an extreme pain her mind must have been steeped, when already full of years she wished rest more than anguish, but her still unforgiving fate added more troubles to her misery. After she saw the two sons divide the time of rule of the kingdom according to the pact, she witnessed most of Greece led by seven kings besieging the rebellious brother who was locked inside the city, and finally, after many battles and burnings, she witnessed the two sons killing each other; then after her husband-son was deposed, she saw her city's ancient walls, built at the sound of Amphion's lyre, fall under another ruler and her kingdom perish; and when she hanged herself,[3] she left her daughters in danger of a shameful life. What more could the gods, the world, and fate have perpetrated against this woman? Certainly nothing, it seems to me; one can hardly search all of hell and find so much misery. She also experienced every kind of anguish and guilt. No woman would say that my own pain could match this, and neither would I, if it were not a pain of love. Who can doubt that she considered her misadventures to be deserved, knowing that she, her husband, and her house had merited the wrath of the gods? Certainly no one who thinks that she was discerning would doubt it. If she was insane, she was far less conscious of

3. when she hanged herself. Boccaccio (or Fiammetta) either is confused or is following an otherwise unknown version of the story of Oedipus and Jocasta in which the latter does not commit suicide until after the destruction of Thebes and the death of her sons Eteocles and Polyneices.

her misfortunes, which by her not knowing them would not have brought her suffering. And those who are aware of deserving the grief they bear withstand it with little or no annoyance.

But I never did anything that could or would justifiably turn the gods against me; I always honored them and continually sought their favor with offerings; and I have never despised them as the Thebans did. One of you ladies may well ask:

"How can you say that you do not deserve any punishment, or that you have never made a mistake? Have you not broken the sacred laws and violated the matrimonial bed with an adulterous young man?"

Certainly. But if we look carefully this is my only fault, and it does not deserve such punishments because it must be taken into account that I am an immature young woman, unable to resist what the gods and lusty men could not resist. And I am not the first, the last, or the only one in this; on the contrary, I have the company of nearly all the women in the world, and the laws I have transgressed usually are applied leniently to the multitude. My fault is also well hidden, which must greatly reduce the vengeance. And besides all of this, given that the gods may have been rightfully angry at me and may have sought vengeance for my error, the right to impart punishment should not be given to the one who has been the cause of my sin. I do not know who drove me to break the sacred laws, whether it was Love or Panfilo's looks;[4] whoever it was, the one as well as the other had great powers to torment me harshly, so that what happened to me is not due to the error I have committed but is a different and special kind of pain which more harshly than anyone else torments the one who upholds it; moreover, if the gods have punished me for the sin I committed, they would be acting against their right judgment and customary ways, since they do not fit the punishment to the sin; in fact, if Jocasta's sins and the punishment given to her are compared with my own sin and the punishment I am bearing, she will be known for having been punished lightly and I too heavily.

---

4. Panfilo's looks: *la forma di Panfilo*. *Forma* can mean, among other things, "figure," "face," "appearance," "manner," "deportment," "essence," "soul," "image," and "likeness."

Do not any of you ladies argue with me by saying that, while I was deprived only of my lover, she was deprived of her kingdom, sons, husband, and ultimately of her own person. Of course I admit this, but with this lover Fortune took away all happiness, and what was left to me may appear happiness in the eyes of men, but is the opposite, because husband, possessions, relatives, and everything else are a heavy burden and contrary to my desire. If fate, instead of robbing me of my lover, had taken all these things, I would have been left with a wide-open path towards the fulfillment of my desire, a path which I would have used; had I not been able to fulfill it, I would have had at my disposal a thousand useful modes of death to end my troubles. Therefore, I correctly judge my own pains more severe than any of those already mentioned.

Hecuba, who comes next to mind, seems to me exceedingly sorrowful since she was left alone in her old age to contemplate the woeful remains of such a great kingdom, of a marvellous city, of a noble husband, and of many sons and lovely daughters and daughters-in-law and nephews and nieces, and of great wealth, of such preeminence, and of so many slaughtered kings and savage deeds, and of the dispersed people of Troy, of its fallen temples, and of the gods who fled, as she called to mind who the powerful Hector was, who Troilus, who Deiphoebus, who Polydorus, and who the others were whom she saw die so miserably; and can we imagine what sadness she must have felt as she remembered the blood of her husband, who not long before had been revered and feared by everyone, seeping onto her wretched lap, and when she saw Troy with all its majestic palaces and noble people burning in the Greek fire and entirely destroyed, and in addition to this, when she looked upon the dreadful sacrifice that Pyrrhus had made of her Polyxena? Certainly a great deal. But her grief was short-lived since her old and feeble mind, unable to bear all of this, went astray and she was driven insane, as her barking through the fields clearly demonstrated.

But with a memory more constant and firm than I need, to my own detriment I still have all my wretched wits and perceive more clearly the reasons for my grief, because by persevering in this ill for a longer time, as I am doing, I value it so that—

although it may in fact be slight—it appears to be more serious, as I have repeatedly said before, than the most severe one which is terminated by coming to a quick end.

Then Sophonisba appears before me, caught between the adversity of widowhood and the joys of marriage, sorrowful and cheerful at the same moment, prisoner and bride, stripped of a kingdom and given it back again, and ultimately, in the midst of these rapid changes, drinking poison, thoroughly tormented by anguish. She found herself as the very powerful queen of the Numidians, but when her family fortune suffered a reverse, she saw her husband Syphax taken prisoner by king Masinissa, and all at once she was dethroned and became captive of the enemy in the middle of a battle, and because Masinissa made her his wife, she was returned to her throne. Oh with what disdain she must have looked upon these changes, and doubtful of flighty Fortune, with what a sad heart she must have celebrated her new marriage! Her courageous death very clearly demonstrates this because she had endured not even one natural day after her wedding when, scarcely believing herself to be back in power, and struggling within herself about it (since her spirit was not yet attuned to Masinissa's new love as it had been to Syphax's old love) she received with a steady hand the poisoned solution from the servant sent by her new husband, and after pronouncing some scornful words, she fearlessly drank and gave up the ghost soon thereafter. Imagine how bitter her life would have been had she had time to think! But she must be placed among those who suffered mildly, considering that death nearly preceded her wretchedness, while death, to make my misery greater, has lent me much time, is still lending it to me, and will lend me more of it than I want.

After Sophonisba the sad Cornelia appears before me, whom Fortune had so elevated that she first became the wife of Crassus and then of the great Pompey, whose valor had nearly earned him the highest power in Rome; but since Fortune turned things around, she first left Rome and then Italy altogether with her husband, who was pursued by Caesar, and, after numerous adventures, left her in Lesbos, where she received him after he had been defeated in Thessaly and his army vanquished by his enemy. And besides all this she still followed her husband, who in the hope of regaining his power in the conquered Orient, crossed the sea and reached the kingdom of Egypt, which he himself had given to a young king, and here she saw his beheaded body knocked about by the waves of the sea. We ought to think that all these things, considered together and separately, afflicted her mind with incomparable pain, but the good counsels of Cato of Utica and the hopelessness of her getting Pompey back quickly diminished her grief, whereas I, hoping in vain and unable to drive this hope away, remain tearful and without counsel or comfort, except from my old nurse, who is aware of my troubles and in whom I perceive more faith than wisdom, because by believing that she gives relief to my grief she often gives me more pain.

There are also many people who would believe that the afflictions of Cleopatra, queen of Egypt, were intolerable and that her suffering was much greater than mine. Because she first saw herself riding along with her brother and abounding in riches and then was made a prisoner by him, it is thought that she was extremely unhappy, but the future hope in what in fact happened helped her to withstand such a grief. But after she left prison she became Caesar's mistress and was then abandoned by him, and there are people who think that she experienced this with the most serious anxieties, since they do not take into consideration that love's woes are short-lived in men and women who can at will leave someone to give themselves to another, as she showed that she could often do. But may God never allow me to find this kind of consolation! There never was and there may never be anyone besides Panfilo who could have said or could say that I have ever been or may be his own, except the one to whom I should rightfully belong; and as his own I live and will live; and I hope that no other love will ever be strong enough to extinguish his in my mind.

There may also be people who not knowing the truth might believe that being left disconsolate at Caesar's departure was painful to her, but it was not so, because, while she may have regretted his departure, she was nevertheless consoled by a joy more intense than any sadness: having been left with a son by him and a kingdom restored. Such joy has the power to overcome the greatest pains, which are not felt by people who love mildly, as she did, as I have already said. What must be added as her heaviest and most extreme sorrow is having been the wife of

Antony, whom she drove with her lascivious enticements to civil war against his brother,[5] perhaps hoping that by winning she would reach the height of the Roman empire, but from this she derived a double loss at one and the same time: the death of her husband, and her ruined hope; and so she is believed to have remained the most woeful of women. Of course, if we take into consideration that such high ambitions as the empress of the whole wide world must have had fell short because of an un-lucky battle, and if we add to this the loss of such a beloved hus-band, we must believe that her experience was extremely pain-ful; however, she immediately found the only medicine available to kill her pain, that is to say, death; but while her death was harsh, it did not take a long time since two snakes can quickly suck from the breasts the blood and life of one body. How many times, feeling no less pain than she did, albeit, in many people's opinion, for a lesser reason, I would have gladly done the same thing, if I had been allowed to or if fear of future infamy had not held me back from doing it!

Along with this lady and with the others already mentioned, I remember the greatness of Cyrus, killed bloodily by Thamyris; the fire and water of Croesus; the wealthy kingdom of Perseus; the grandeur of Pyrrhus; the power of Darius, the cruelty of Jugurtha; the tyranny of Dionysius; the eminence of Agamem-non; and countless others. All of them either experienced or in-flicted pains like those already described, but they were also helped by quick remedies, and since they did not dwell for long in their grief, they did not feel their burden as fully as I do.

As I go searching around in my mind for ancient misfortunes in the manner you have seen above, to find tears or tribulations truly similar to my own so that by having companions it might hurt me less, I see before me those of Thyestes and Tereus, both of whom were their sons' miserable tombs. And certainly I do not know what self-restraint stopped them from cutting them-selves open with sharp knives to let out of their paternal bowels their struggling sons, who were loathe to return to the place where they had entered, still fearful of cruel bites and with no other way out. But these two men, as if they found comfort in

---

5. his brother: *il fratello*. One would expect *cognato*(brother-in-law) here, since it is certainly Octavian (Augustus) to whom Fiammetta refers.

their troubles, gave vent to both hatred and grief at one and the same time in any way they could, hearing that they were considered wicked by their people, while being guiltless; but this is not happening to me. Towards me one feels compassion for something that gives me no grief, but I do not dare to reveal what does make me suffer. If I dared to do so, I have no doubt that just as a remedy has been found for all others in pain, one would also be found for me.

I also remember the sorrowful tears of Lycurgus and of his household, shed with good reason for the death of Archemorus, and they make me think of the tears of sad Atalanta, mother of Parthenopaeus, who was killed in the Theban battlefield, and their effect is so touching and I experience them in such a way that I could hardly feel them more deeply if I shed them myself, as I have already done before. I must say, these tears are full of immeasurable sadness; but each tear is portrayed in eternity with so much glory that it may be said to be happy; those of Lycurgus were honored by seven kings with magnificent obsequies and with innumerable games which they had instituted; and those of Atalanta were honored by the praiseworthy life and glorious death of her son. There is nothing that could turn my worthy tears to contentment, but if this were to happen, instead of calling myself—and being—the most unhappy of all women, I would come closer to asserting the opposite.

I also see before me Ulysses' long-lasting trials, the mortal dangers and the extravagant things that happened to him not without causing him the deepest mental anguish; but as I go over them in my mind they make me judge my own more severe, and now hear why. First and above all he is a man, therefore naturally stronger and more fit than I am, since I am young and delicate; he is vigorous and daring, used to difficulties and dangers as if he had been raised among them, so that labor seemed like downright rest to him. But fragile and accustomed to the amusements of sensual love in the softness of my bedchamber I find every small pain very burdensome; spurred on and taken everywhere by Neptune and Aeolus, he welcomed his labors, while I am plagued by this importunate love who molested and conquered as a master even those who harassed Ulysses, and if mortal dangers did not loom over him he would often seek them out, and how can one complain about finding what one seeks? But miserable as I am, I would gladly live in peace if I could and would flee from dangers, were it not that I was pushed towards them. Furthermore, Ulysses had no fear of death; rather he placed himself at its mercy; but I am afraid of it and once ran towards it only because I was driven by suffering and not without expectation of deep pain. He also was hoping to derive eternal glory and fame from his trials and dangers, but I am afraid that from mine I would derive only insults and shame if they were discovered. So indeed his trial did not surpass mine; rather, mine certainly surpass his, and even more so since what is written about his is more than what did happen, while mine are more than I can tell.

After all these, the tribulations of Hypsipyle, Medea, Oenone, and Ariadne strike me as if they were to be set apart from the rest for their great severity, and I find their tears and pains very similar to mine because each one was betrayed by her lover, as I was, and each wept, sighed, and suffered bitter and fruitless pain; but, as I have said, even though they suffered as I did, their tears ended with a fair vengeance, which mine do not have yet. Although Hypsipyle paid great honor to Jason and bound him to her through a law of duty, when she saw him taken away from her by Medea, she had as good reasons to lament as I can have, but the gods' providence, that watches over all things fairly, if not over my troubles, partially returned to her a much desired happiness when Medea, who had taken Jason away from her, was abandoned by Jason because of Creusa. Of course I am not saying that my misery would come to an end if the same thing happened to the one who took my Panfilo away from me (unless I were the one who took him away from her), but I gladly say that much of it would vanish. Similarly, Medea rejoiced in vengeance, although she became as cruel to herself as she was to her ungrateful lover when she killed their own children before his eyes and set fire to the royal dwellings and to his new woman. Oenone, who had lamented for so long, also learned in the end that her unfaithful and disloyal lover had received just punishment for the laws he had broken, and saw his land dreadfully devastated by flames because of the ill-chosen woman.[6] But I certainly prefer my pains to this kind of vengeance on my lover.

6. ill-chosen woman: Helen of Troy (see Glossary).

And Ariadne, too, after she became Bacchus' wife, from up in heaven saw Phaedra—who earlier, to belong to Theseus, had consented to Ariadne's being abandoned on an island—now maddened with love for her own stepson. Therefore, all things considered, I alone find myself achieving first place among suffering women, and I can do no more.

But if, my ladies, you still hold my arguments to be frivolous and consider them blind because they are from a blind, loving woman so that you regard other people's tears as more abject than mine, may this one and final argument be a supplement to all the others: if the envious one is more miserable than the envied, I am envious of all those people already mentioned because of their misfortunes since I consider them less disastrous than my own.

So, ladies, here I am, wretched because of Fortune's ancient deceptions, and besides this, she has acted not unlike a lantern that when almost extinguished gives out a brighter flash of light than usual, in that after giving me apparent relief, she then made me utterly miserable by giving me back the tears which she had taken away. In an attempt to convince you about these new troubles, I will postpone all other comparisons except one and say to you with that greater solemnity which wretched women like me can assert that my sorrows are at present more severe than they were before this useless cheerfulness, in the same way that fevers, bringing equal spells of cold and heat, customarily harm the relapsed patient more than they did at first.

Therefore, since I could offer you more pains but no new words, and because I have become compassionate of you and do not wish to annoy you by prolonging your tears—given that some of you perhaps have been or are weeping while reading—and in order not to waste any more time, that time which calls me back to weeping, I am deciding at last to be quiet, making it clear to you that there is no other likeness between my very true narrative and what I feel, than there is between the painted fire and one that truly burns. For this reason I pray to God that by either your prayers or by my own, He may quench this fire with soothing water through either my own death or the happy return of Panfilo.

NINE

In which Lady Fiammetta makes an end by speaking to her book and enjoining it in what dress it must go forth, when, to whom, and against whom to be on guard.

O dear little book of mine, snatched from the near burial of your lady, here it is that your end has come more quickly than that of our misfortunes, as is my wish; therefore, just as you have been written by my own hand and in many places damaged by my tears, present yourself to women in love; if, as I strongly hope, pity guides you, and if the rules of Love have not changed since we became miserable, those women will gladly receive you. Do not be ashamed to go to each one of them, no matter how mighty, in so lowly a garb as I am sending you in, as long as she does not refuse to have you. A garment made in any other way is not required of you, assuming that I wanted to give you one. You should be glad to show yourself similar to my disposition, which is so very unhappy that it clothes you in misery, as it does me.

Therefore, do not concern yourself with any ornamentation such as other books are accustomed to have, namely, with elegant covers, painted and adorned with various colors, with clean-cut pages, pretty miniatures, or grand titles; such things do not suit the grave lamentation you bear; leave these things to happy books, and with them the broad margins, the colorful inks, and the paper smoothed with pumice; it is fitting that you go where I am sending you discomposed, with your hair uncombed, stained and full of gloom, to awaken by my misfortunes blessed pity in the minds of those women who will read you. If it happens that through you the signs of such pity show in their lovely faces, give immediate reward for it, as best you can. Neither you nor I am so cast down by fortune that such signs—which are pronounced in us—may not be given, and they are nothing but those signs which Fortune cannot deprive any miserable person of, namely, the right to make oneself an example to those who are happy so that these people may set their affairs in order and avoid becoming like us; and you should demonstrate this point about me as well as you can, so that those ladies who are wise should become most sagacious in matters of love in order to avoid, for fear of our misfortunes, the hidden deceptions of young men.

Go then. I do not know whether a swift pace would suit you better than a slow one, nor do I know what places you should first seek out, nor do I know how or by whom you will be received. Proceed as fate pushes you along; your path cannot be at all preordained. The cloudy weather hides all stars from your view, but even if they were to appear, this violent fate left you no expedient by which to save yourself. Pushed here and there like a ship without rudder or sail, tossed about by the waves, let yourself go, and adopt different counsels as circumstances dictate.

If by chance you should fall into the hands of a woman who manages the affairs of the heart so well as to laugh at our sorrows and reprove us for being insane, bear the mocking with humility; it is the least of our troubles; remind her that Fortune is fickle and can very quickly make you and me joyous, and her like us, in which case we would return her laughter, mockery for mockery.

And if you find another who cannot keep her eyes dry as she reads but is sad and full of compassion for our misfortunes and multiplies your blotches with her tears, gather them within you along with my own, and consider them holy. Show yourself more pitiful and afflicted and humbly beg her to pray for me to the one who instantly visits the entire world with golden wings, so that perhaps implored by a more deserving voice than mine, and being more sympathetic to others than to us, he may alleviate our anguish. Whoever she may be, I pray from now on, with that voice that is made more moving in the wretched, that she may never reach such dejection and that the gods may always be receptive and benign towards her, and that her love affairs be made to last long and to be happy, as she wishes.

But if by chance, as you are passed from one hand to another within the loving throng of lovely ladies, you should fall into the hands of my woman foe, the usurper of our riches, immediately run away as if from an evil place; do not reveal any part of yourself to her thievish eyes, lest she rejoice a second time to have harmed us as she hears of our sorrows. But if it also happens that she should keep you by force, and should even want to look at you, show yourself in such a manner that not laughter but tears may be aroused in her by our misfortunes, with the result that by turning to her conscience she may give us back our lover. What a happy pity that would be, and how fruitful your labor!

Flee the eyes of men, and even if you should be seen by them, tell them this:

"You ungrateful sex, denigrator of innocent women, it is not suitable for you to perceive godly things."

But if you should reach the one who is the root of our misfortunes, scold him from afar and say: "O you who are more rigid than an oak, go away from here and do not violate us with your hands; the word you have broken is the cause of all my burden, but if you wish to read me with a humane mind, recognizing perhaps that you have offended the one who wishes to forgive you if you return to her, then look at me; but if you do not want to do that, you should not see the tears you provoked, especially if you persist in your original desire to increase them."

If perhaps some lady is astonished by your crudely composed words, tell her to dismiss them, because it is clear minds and serene and tranquil times that require ornate speeches. But tell her rather to feel admiration, since intellect and hand proved sufficient for that disordered little bit you are narrating, and considering that by stabbing me in various ways, love on one side and jealousy on the other keep my suffering spirits in a state of continual struggle and in murky weather, with contrary Fortune acting as an accomplice.

I believe you can proceed without fear of any ambush, since no envy will bite you with its sharp teeth; but if someone more miserable than you could be found—something which I do not believe possible—who might envy you as more blessed than himself, let yourself be bitten. I am not sure which part of you could still be wounded, since I see you torn all over by Fortune's beatings. He can scarcely offend you or pull you from high to low, since you dwell already in the lowest of places. Furthermore, let us also suppose that Fortune were not satisfied to have us levelled to the ground and were even trying to bury us under it: we are so experienced in adversity that on the same shoulders which have carried and are still carrying very great burdens we shall carry lighter ones; therefore, go into whatever place she wants you to.

Live then. No one can deprive you of this, and remain an eternal example to happy and unhappy people of your lady's anguish.

Here ends the book called ELEGY OF THE NOBLE LADY FIAMMETTA, *sent by her to all women in love.*

GLOSSARY

Abydos: A city on the shores of the Hellespont. When besieged by Philip of Macedon and faced with defeat, the inhabitants committed suicide rather than fall into the hands of their conqueror.

Achaemenides: A companion of Ulysses during his wanderings who was left behind in the cave of the Cyclops and was later found there by Aeneas.

Achilles: The son of Peleus and the sea-goddess Thetis and the greatest of the Greek warriors at Troy. When Agamemnon took his concubine Briseis away from him, he sulked in his tent and refused to join in the battle.

Actaeon: The son of Aristaeus and Autonoë. One day while on a hunt he spied Diana (Artemis) at her bath and gazed upon her, for which crime she changed him into a deer which his own hounds pursued and killed.

Admetus: The king of Pherae, in Sicily, whom Apollo served as a shepherd, in order to pursue his love for a young woman, who was, according to some sources, Admetus' own daughter.

Adonis: The son of Cinyras and Myrrha and a beautiful young man enamored of the hunt. Venus loved him, and when he was killed by a wild boar she changed him into an anemone.

Aegeus: The son of Pandion and Pelia, the father of Theseus, and legendary ruler of Attica. He married Medea after Jason abandoned her.

Aegisthus: Agememnon's cousin and lover of Clytemnestra, his cousin's wife. He helped her slay her husband.

Aeneas: The son of Venus and Anchises. He survived the fall of Troy and founded Rome. He is the hero of Vergil's *Aeneid*.

Aeolus: The guardian of the winds, whose six sons and six daughters lived with one another in incestuous union. When Aeolus learned of this, he drove them all either to suicide or into exile.

Aeson: The father of Jason. He was restored to his youth and vigor through the magic of his daughter-in-law Medea.

Agamemnon: The son of Atreus and the leader of the Greek army in the Trojan War.

Ajax: The son of Telamon and Periboea and a Greek leader in the Trojan War.

Alcmene: The daughter of Electryon and wife of Amphitryon. When her future husband returned after a series of exploits to marry her, she is said to have dressed herself in the most elegant clothes. Loved by Jupiter, who transformed himself into the shape of her husband to make love to her, she gave birth to Hercules.

Alecto: One of the Erinyes, or Furies.

Alpheus: A river god who fell in love with and pursued Arethusa, a nymph of Diana; when she asked the gods to save her, they turned her into a fountain.

Amata: The wife of Latinus and mother of Lavinia. She hanged herself after failing to marry her daughter to Turnus, king of the Rutulians.

Amphion: The son of Jupiter and Antiope. Having received a lyre from Mercury, he played it so well that at the fortifying of the city of Thebes his music caused the stones to assemble themselves into a wall.

Amphitryon: See Alcmene.

Apollo, or Phoebus Apollo: The god of light, prophecy, and music (especially the lyre), identified with the sun. He killed the Python which guarded the oracular shrine at Delphi.

Archemorus: See Lycurgus.

Arcturus: The chief star in the constellation of Boötes, prominent in the winter sky.

Argeia, or Argia: The wife of Polyneices, one of the Seven against Thebes, who was widowed by his death.

Argus, or Argos: A monster with one hundred eyes, whom Mercury (Hermes) slew after lulling him asleep with his lyre.

Ariadne: The daughter of Minos, king of Crete. She fell in love with Theseus and helped him escape from the Labyrinth after he had killed the Minotaur. Later, Theseus abandoned her on the isle of Naxos. According to some sources she was taken by Bacchus (Dionysus) to be his bride.

Aries: The Ram, the first of the zodiacal signs (March 21 to April 20).

Aruns: An Etruscan astrologer mentioned by Lucan (PHARSALIA I, 586 ff.), who says that he lived during the time of Julius Caesar in the ancient (and by then deserted) Etruscan city of Luna (now Luni), in the valley of Carrara, which is still known for its white marble. According to Dante (INFERNO 20, 46–51), Aruns lived in a cave somewhere in the mountains surrounding Luna.

Ascanius: The son of Aeneas and Creusa (2). He was renowned for his great beauty, and when Aeneas met Dido, Venus sent her son Cupid, disguised as Ascanius, to instill in Dido a passion for Aeneas.

Atalanta: The daughter of Iasus and Clymene. Swift of foot, she demanded that any suitor interested in marrying her would first have to defeat her in a foot race. Hippomenes tossed golden apples of Hesperides at her feet to distract her, won the race, and married her. She became the mother of Parthenopaeus.

Athamas: A king of Thebes and lover of Ino. When Jupiter became enamored with Semele and possessed her in the form of a lightning bolt, she died but gave birth to Dionysus. Semele's sister, Ino, took it upon herself to raise the infant god. Out of jealousy Jupiter's wife Juno punished Ino by driving Athamas mad.

Atreus: The son of Pelops and Hippodamia. His wife was unfaithful to him with his brother Thyestes, and out of revenge he killed Thyestes' sons and served their flesh to him at a banquet. For this crime the gods in anger made the night last two whole days.

Atropos: One of the three Fates. She cut the thread of each life span.

Ausonia: An ancient name for Italy, especially the southern region.

Avernus: A lake near Naples, regarded by ancient Romans as the site of the entrance to the underworld.

Bacchus (Gk. Dionysus): The son of Jupiter and Semele and the god of ecstasy, fertility, and wine.

Baia: A town on the Bay of Naples, famous since ancient times as a spa and resort. One of its ruins is the so-called Temple of Venus, in reality part of an octagonal Roman bath.

Boreas: The North Wind, associated with winter.

Byblis: The daughter of Miletus and Idothea. She fell in love with her own brother Caunus, who fled in horror when he discovered her passion. She went in search of him until she collapsed of exhaustion, and as she lay weeping on the ground nymphs transformed her into a fountain over which an ilex tree grew.

Byrria: See Geta.

Cadmus: The son of Agenor and Argiope (also called Telephassa) and the king of Phoenicia. He was sent by his father to find his sister Europa. After his companions were killed by a dragon, he sowed the dragon's teeth in the ground and from them sprang up soldiers who immediately turned against one another and slew themselves.

Callisto: The daughter of Lycaon. Jupiter desired her and transformed himself into the semblance of the goddess Diana to make love to her.

Canace: The daughter of Aeolus, god of the winds. She fell in love with her own brother Macareus and later killed herself.

Cassandra: The daughter of Priam. Apollo fell in love with her and granted her the gift of prophecy with the expectation that she would reward him with her love. When she scorned him he willed that all her prophecies would be ignored and she herself regarded as insane.

Cato the Censor: A Roman statesman (234–149 B.C.), famous for his opposition to contemporary luxury and for his hostility to Carthage.

Cato of Utica: A Roman statesman (95–46 B.C.), famous for his incorruptibility and devotion to the principles of the Roman republic.

Caunus: See Byblis.

Ceres (Gk. Demeter): The goddess of the harvest and of abundance and the mother of Proserpine.

Charybdis: A treacherous whirlpool on the coast of Sicily, in the straits of Messina, opposite the cave of Scylla (2).

Cincinnatus: Legendary Roman patriot (5th century B.C.) who left his farm to lead the Romans to a victory over the Volscians.

Cleopatra: The queen of Egypt and the last ruler of the Ptolemy dynasty. She fell in love with her brother, who imprisoned her because of her passion. Later, she had liaisons with both Julius Caesar, to whom she bore a son, and Mark Antony, whom she is said to have married.

Clotho: One of the three Fates. She spun the thread of each life span.

Clymene: Loved by Apollo, she gave birth to Phaethon, who was later killed while recklessly driving Apollo's chariot of the sun.

Clytemnestra: The wife of Agamemnon. She loved his cousin Aegisthus, and the two of them murdered Agamemnon upon his return from the Trojan War.

Cornelia: The widow of Crassus and later the wife of Pompey the Great. She was again widowed when Pompey was assassinated in Egypt by Ptolemy XIII of Egypt, who had his head cut off and his body thrown into the sea.

Creusa (1): The daughter of Creon, king of Corinth and the wife of Jason. She was killed by Jason's previous wife, Medea.

Creusa (2): The daughter of Priam and wife of Aeneas. As Aeneas was fleeing with his family from the ruins of Troy, she became separated from the group and was lost.

Croesus: The last king of Lydia, legendary for his wealth. Defeated by Cyrus the Great of Persia and condemned to death by fire, he called upon Apollo for help, was saved by a sudden rainstorm, and became Cyrus' friend and advisor.

Cumae: An ancient city on the coast of Campania, just north of Naples, and the site of the cave where the Cumaean Sibyl lived.

The Cumaean Sibyl: A prophetess who resided in a cave at Cumae in ancient times. She wrote out her prophecies on leaves that were then scattered by the wind and rendered indecipherable.

Cupid (Gk. Eros): The son of Venus and god of love, whose arrows wounded Apollo, among others.

Cyrus: Cyrus the Great (d. 529 B.C.), king of Persia. After he was defeated and killed by the Massagetae under Thamyris (or Tomyris), queen of the Scythians, she cut off his head and threw it into a skin filled with blood.

Daedalus: The legendary craftsman of Athens who built both the famous Labyrinth in which to house the Minotaur and also the wings by which to escape from it after he and his son Icarus had been imprisoned in it by Minos.

Danae: The daughter of Acrisius of Argos and Aganippe. She was shut up in a brass tower, but Jupiter, appearing in the form of a shower of gold, possessed her.

Danaus: The son of Belus and Anchinoë. At his orders all but one (Hypermnestra) of his fifty daughters (the Danaides) killed their bridegrooms on their wedding night so that he could remain the sole heir of his kingdom. For this crime the Danaides, except for Hypermnestra, were sent to Hades and condemned to the task of emptying a river with water jars full of holes.

Daniel: The heroic figure of the Old Testament book named after him.

Daphne: The daughter of Peneus. She was pursued by Apollo, who desired her, and at her own request her father, a river god, changed her into a laurel tree.

Darius: Darius the Great (521–485 B.C.), king of Persia, who extended the boundaries of the Persian empire but was defeated by the Greeks at Marathon.

Deianeira: The daughter of Oeneus, king of Calydon, and Althaea. Hercules married her but later abandoned her for Iole.

Deidameia: The daughter of Lycomedes of Skyros, in whose household Achilles lived for a while disguised as a girl. When Ulysses and Diomedes heard that Achilles was hiding there, they brought ornaments and jewelry to show the women but also a few weapons, and by showing his interest in the weapons, Achilles betrayed his identity. Deidameia bore Achilles a son, Pyrrhus (also called Neoptolemus).

Deiphobus: A son of Priam and Hecuba. He married Helen of Troy after the death of Paris. She later betrayed him to the Greeks and he was killed by Menelaus.

Deipyle: The mother of Diomedes and wife of Tydeus, one of the Seven against Thebes. She was widowed by his death.

Demophon: See Phyllis.

Diana (Gk. Artemis): Sister of Apollo and goddess of the hunt and of virginity, sometimes called Phoebe and identified with the moon.

Dido: The widowed queen of Carthage, who loved Aeneas and killed herself after he abandoned her.

Diomedes: The son of Tydeus and Deipyle and one of the Greek leaders in the Trojan War.

Dis: Another name for Pluto, king of Hades.

Dionysius: Here probably Dionysius the Elder (405–367 B.C.), tyrant of Syracuse.

Dryope: The daughter of Eurytus, king of Oechalia, and the sister of Iole. She was loved by Apollo, bore him a son, and was later changed into a poplar tree.

Elissa the Sidonian: A legendary princess of Tyre whom Virgil identifies with Dido of Carthage.

Erysichthon: Son of Triopas of Thessaly. Out of contempt for the gods, he cut down an oak sacred to Ceres, who inflicted him with an insatiable hunger, so that he ended by gnawing on his own flesh.

Etruria: An ancient name for that part of Italy ruled by the Etruscans and now known as Tuscany and Umbria.

Europa: The daughter of Agenor, king of Phoenicia, and Argiope. She was loved by Jupiter, who assumed the shape of a bull and carried her across the sea to Crete.

Eurydice: The wife of Orpheus. She died after stepping on a serpent and went to Hades, from where Orpheus tried unsuccessfully to retrieve her.

Evadne: The wife of Capaneus, one of the Seven against Thebes. Widowed by his death, she flung herself upon his funeral pyre.

Ganymede: A beautiful shepherd youth whom Jupiter became enamored with and took to Olympus to be his cupbearer.

Geta: He and Byrria appear as servants in Plautus' *Amphitryon*. They are also protagonists in a popular medieval poem by Vitalis of Blois called *Geta*.

Glaucus: A fisherman turned sea creature who fell in love with Scylla(2).

Hannibal: The chief Carthaginian general during the Second Punic War. After a series of defeats at the hands of the Romans, he committed suicide.

Harpies: Legendary creatures with the body of a vulture and the face of a woman, considered loathsome and thought to be harbingers of evil.

Hecate: A goddess associated with night, the underworld, and witchcraft.

Hector: The son of Priam and Hecuba and the greatest of the Trojan warriors. He was slain by Achilles.

Hecuba: The wife of Priam, king of Troy, who saw her husband and children die in the Trojan War.

Helen, or Helen of Troy: The wife of Menelaus, king of Sparta. Loved by Paris, he led her away to Troy, an act which led to the Trojan War.

Hercules (Gk. Heracles): The son of Jupiter and Alcmene. Among his Twelve Labors, he killed the Nemean lion, slew the giant Antaeus, dragged the three-headed dog Cerberus out of Hades, and held the world up momentarily for Atlas. He fell in love with Iole, daughter of Eurytus, king of Oechalia.

Hero: See Leander.

Hesperia: A legendary land in the west, which the Romans sometimes identified with Spain.

Hesperus: The Evening Star or the Morning Star, depending on the season of the year.

Hippolytus: The son of Theseus and Hippolyta. His stepmother Phaedra fell in love with him and when he spurned her advances, she accused him before Theseus of having taken her by force. Theseus believed her, and as Hippolytus was fleeing along the coast to escape his father's wrath, a sea monster rose out of the surf, frightened the horses of his chariot, and he was dragged to his death over sharp rocks.

Hippomenes: See Atalanta.

Hydra: The nine-headed monster of the Lernian Spring, in Argolis, which Hercules killed as one of his Twelve Labors.

Hymen: The god of marriage.

Hypsipyle: The daughter of Thoas, king of Lemnos. She bore Jason two sons but was abandoned by him for Medea.

Icarus: The son of Daedalus. He accompanied his father in his escape from the Labyrinth in Crete by means of wings which Daedalus had devised, but in his pride he flew too near the sun, which melted the wax on the wings, and he fell to his death in the sea. That part of the eastern Aegean sea which surrounds Samos was said to be the site of his death and so was called the Icarian sea.

Inachus: King of Argos and father of Io.

Ino: The daughter of Cadmus and Harmonia and the wife of Athamas. After Athamas had killed their own son Learchus in a fit of madness with which Juno afflicted him, Ino took their other son, Melicerte, into her arms and plunged into the sea.

Io: The daughter of Inachus, king of Argos, and Melia. She was loved by Jupiter, who changed her into a heifer so she could escape the watchful and jealous eye of his wife Juno. Goaded by a gadfly sent by Juno, she wandered over several continents until she reached Egypt, where, according to some sources, she recovered her human form and married the god Osiris, an act which led to her sometimes being identified with the goddess Isis.

Iole: The daughter of Eurytus, king of Oechalia, became Hercules' concubine after he killed her father.

Iseult: See Tristan.

Ixion: The son of either Phlegyas or Mars and the king of the Lapithae. He was punished in Hades for insolence towards the gods by being fastened to a burning wheel.

Jason: The son of Aeson and Alcimede. After recovering the Golden Fleece from Colchis, he abandoned his wife Medea for the love of Creusa (2), whom Medea then killed, as well as her own children by Jason.

Jocasta: The wife of Laius and mother of Oedipus. She unwittingly married her own son after her husband's death.

Jugurtha: King of Numidia (ca. 156–104 B.C.). He murdered his two cousins to become sole ruler. Later, defeated by the Romans, he was taken a prisoner to Rome and starved to death.

Juno (Gk. Hera): Sister and wife of Jupiter and protectress of marriages. She disguised herself as Beroe, an aged nurse, to take revenge on Semele by advising her to ask Jupiter to appear before her in all his splendor. Semele followed her advice and was consumed to ashes.

Jupiter (Gk. Zeus): The son of Saturn and chief Olympian god. Among his many transformations, he changed himself into a swan to make love to Leda and into a bull to make love to Europa.

Lachesis: One of the three Fates. She measured the thread of each life span.

Laodameia: The wife of Protesilaus, who was the first Greek to be killed at Troy.

Leander: A youth of Abydos, who fell in love with Hero of Sestos and was drowned one night while swimming across the Hellespont to meet her.

Leucothoe: The daughter of Orchamus and Eurynome. Apollo desired her, and by transforming himself into the likeness of her mother gained access to her.

Lycurgus: The legendary king of Nemea. He became distraught with sorrow when his infant son Archemorus was fatally stung by a serpent.

Lyssa: A personification of madness or frenzy and associated with the Erinyes, or Furies. It appears in Euripides' *Bacchae* and *Heracles.*

Mars (Gk. Ares): The god of war. He fell in love with Venus and was trapped with her in a net devised by her husband Vulcan.

Medea: The daughter of Aeëtes, king of Colchis, and Idyia. She was the wife of Jason, whom she helped in his quest for the Golden Fleece. A magician, she could transport herself in a chariot driven by dragons.

Megaera: One of the Erinyes, or Furies.

Menelaus: The son of Atreus, husband of Helen, and Greek leader in the Trojan War.

Mercury (Gk. Hermes): The messenger of the gods, one of whose duties was to guide souls at their death to their appropriate place in Hades.

Midas: The king of Phrygia, who prayed to Bacchus to turn everything he touched into gold, a request which the god granted, so that even the food which Midas touched turned into gold.

Minerva (Gk. Athena): The daughter of Jupiter and goddess of wisdom.

Misenus: The trumpeteer of Hector. After the fall of Troy he travelled with Aeneas and was drowned on the coast of Campania. Some legends identified his grave site, rather than the Lake of Avernus, as the entrance to the underworld.

Mount Barbaro: Apparently Mount Barbara, in Campania, near Naples.

Mount Falerno: In Campania, near Naples.

Myrrha: The daughter of Cinyras, king of Paphos, and Cenchreis. She fell in love with her own father and from that union gave birth to Adonis. She was later transformed into the myrrh plant.

Narcissus: The Greek youth who fell in love with his own reflection in the water and was changed into the flower that bears his name.

Neptune (Gk. Poseidon): The brother of Jupiter and god of the ocean. He fell in love with the daughter of Nycteus of Thessaly and granted her wish that she might be changed into a man.

Nero: Roman emperor (A.D. 54–68), notorious for his cruelty.

Nisida: An isle in the Bay of Naples.

Oedipus: The son of Laius and Jocasta. He unwittingly killed his father and married his mother. Upon discovering his fate, he blinded himself and went into exile.

Oenone: A young Trojan shepherdess on Mount Ida whom Paris fell in love with, married, and deserted. She witnessed his return later in the company of Helen, and when he received his fatal wound at Troy she refused to heal him, but after he died she experienced remorse and flung herself on his pyre.

Orpheus: A legendary poet of pre-Homeric Greece, said to be the son of the muse Calliope or of Apollo himself. He descended into Hades in an attempt to retrieve his wife Eurydice, charmed Pluto and the other inhabitants of the underworld with his lyre, but failed to rescue his wife.

Paris: The son of Priam and Hecuba. He judged Venus rather than Juno or Minerva to be the fairest of the goddesses and awarded her the golden apple, for which favor she gave him in return the most beautiful woman on earth, Helen, the wife of Menelaus, an act which led to the Trojan War.

Parnassus: A mountain in Boetia, on which flowed a fountain sacred to the Muses.

Parthenopaeus: The son of Atalanta, queen of Arcadia. He was famous for his beauty and one of the Seven against Thebes. He was killed during the siege of the city when a rock hurled at him shattered his skull.

Parthenope: An ancient Greek name for Naples.

Pasiphae: The wife of Minos, king of Crete. She fell in love with a bull and placed herself in a wooden cow built by Daedalus so that she could satisfy her desire, and from this union she gave birth to the Minotaur.

Penelope: The daughter of Icarius and the wife of Ulysses. For twenty years she faithfully awaited his return from the Trojan War.

Perdix: The nephew of and apprentice to Daedalus. His own skill as a craftsman drew the envy of his uncle, who threw him from a great height to his death.

Perseus: The son of Jupiter and Danae. After a career of heroic exploits, such as the slaying of the Gorgon, some sources say he went to Asia and founded the kingdom of Persia, which bore his name.

Phaedra: The wife of Theseus. She fell in love with her stepson Hippolytus, and when he spurned her advances, she falsely accused of him of raping her and hanged herself.

Phaethon: The son of Apollo and Clymene. One day he received permission from his father to drive the chariot of the sun, only to lose control of the horses, and when the earth was thereby threatened with conflagration, Jupiter killed him with a lightning bolt. His two sisters, Phaethus and Lampetie, wept so profusely for him that the gods turned them into willow trees.

Phoebe: See Diana.

Phoebus: See Apollo.

Phyllis: The daughter of Sithon of Thrace. She was loved but abandoned by Demophon and then killed herself and was turned into an almond tree.

Pithecusae: An ancient name for a small island near the Bay of Naples, now called Ischia.

Pluto: The brother of Jupiter and king of Hades, the underworld. He abducted Proserpine from a field near Enna, in Sicily, while she was gathering flowers and made her his wife.

Polydorus: The youngest of Priam and Hecuba's sons, slain in the Trojan War.

Polyxena: The daughter of Priam and Hecuba, loved by Achilles.

Pompey the Great: Roman general (106–48 B.C.). He was a member of the First Triumvirate and was later defeated by Julius Caesar at Pharsala, after which he fled to Egypt, where he was assassinated.

Portia: Daughter of Cato of Utica and wife of Brutus. After hearing of her husband's defeat at the battle of Philippi, she committed suicide by swallowing live coals.

Pozzuoli: An ancient city on the Bay of Naples, known in Roman times as Puteoli.

Priam: The king of Troy and father of Hector, Paris, Cassandra, Creusa (2), and Polyxena, among others.

Procne: The sister of Philomela and wife of Tereus. When her husband raped Philomela, he cut out her tongue so she could not reveal the identity of her ravisher. After Philomela informed Procne of the crime by means of a tapestry she wove, the two sisters killed Tereus' son Itys and served his flesh to him at a banquet. When Tereus discovered what he had done, he pursued the two sisters with sword in hand, but as they were fleeing, Philomela and Procne were transformed into, respectively, a nightingale and a swallow.

Proserpine (Gk. Persephone): The daughter of Ceres. While gathering flowers in a field near Enna, in Sicily, she was abducted by Pluto and taken to the underworld to be his wife.

Protesilaus: See Laodameia.

Pyramus: A Babylonian youth who loved Thisbe. They both died from suicide after a series of errors and mischances.

Pyrrhus (1): The son of Achilles and Deidameia. As Troy was being overrun by the Greeks, he slew Priam. Also known as Neoptolemus.

Pyrrhus (2): The king of Epirus (c. 318–272 B.C.), who was defeated by Rome.

Saguntum: A city in Spain loyal to Rome and besieged by the Carthaginians under Hannibal during the Second Punic War. When faced with imminent defeat the inhabitants of the city immolated themselves rather than fall into the hands of their enemy.

Sardanapalus: The last king of Assyria, notorious for his luxury and effeminacy.

Saturn (Gk. Cronos): The ancient pre-Olympian god who was displaced by Jupiter.

Scaevola: A legendary Roman statesman famous for his courage and wisdom.

Scipio Africanus: Either Scipio Africanus Major (234–183 B.C.), who defeated the Carthaginian general Hannibal, or Scipio Africanus Minor (185–129 B.C.), who also gained important victories over the Carthaginians.

Scylla (1): The daughter of Nisus. She fell in love with Minos, king of Crete, who was at war with Nisus, and to please Minos, she cut off her father's head and presented it to him.

Scylla (2): A beautiful nymph loved by Glaucus, or, as some say, by Neptune. Because of the jealousy of her rival (Circe, Juno, or Amphitrite, according to different versions of the story) she was transformed into a sea monster with six heads that terrorized mariners by seizing and devouring them as they sailed past its lair, a cave situated on the straits of Messina opposite the whirlpool of Charybdis.

Semele: The daughter of Cadmus and Harmonia. Loved by Jupiter, he appeared to her in the form of a lightning bolt that killed her as she was giving birth to Bacchus (Dionysus).

Semiramis: A legendary queen of Assyria and founder of the city of Babylon. The wife of Ninus, she fell in love with her own son.

The Seven against Thebes: Seven Greek leaders, including Oedipus' son Polyneices, who besieged and captured the city of Thebes, all of whom were killed in the struggle, except Adrastus, the leader of the expedition.

Socrates: The famous Greek philosopher (d. 399 B.C.). He died in prison by drinking hemlock.

Sophonisba: The daughter of Hasdrubal, the Carthaginian general, and the wife of Syphax, king of Numidia. When Syphax was defeated and killed by Masinissa, a Nubian prince, the latter proposed to marry Sophonisba but was ordered to turn her over to Scipio Africanus Major. To save her from captivity, Masinissa offered her a bowl of poison from which she drank. According to other sources, she poisoned herself to keep from marrying Masinissa. Still others say she did marry Masinissa but poisoned herself the following day.

Spurinna: A beautiful and chaste Athenian youth who disfigured his own face lest his beauty lead others into sinful desire.

Styx: One of the four rivers of Hades; its name in Greek means "hateful" or "gloomy."

Tantalus: The son of Jupiter. He was punished in Hades for a crime against the gods by being afflicted with an intense thirst and placed up to his chin in a pool of water which receded every time he bent to drink. He was also given a great hunger that he could not gratify because the fruit dangling from a branch overhead would spring away as he reached out to pick it.

Taurus: The Bull, the second of the zodiacal constellations (April 20 to May 21), sometimes identified with Jupiter.

Telethusa: A young woman of Crete who had raised her daughter Iphis as a boy so that the child would not be killed by her husband Ligdus, who had wanted a male. When Iphis grew up and was betrothed to the girl Ianthe, Telethusa prayed to the Egyptian goddess Isis to change Iphis into a man so that the marriage could be consummated, a request which Isis granted.

Tereus: See Procne.

Theseus: The son of Aegeus and Aethra and the king of Athens. He was loved by Ariadne but abandoned her. He later became the husband of both Phaedra and Hippolyta, the queen of the Amazons.

Thisbe: See Pyramus.

Tisiphone: One of the Erinyes, or Furies.

Tityus: A giant of great beauty, he attempted to seduce the goddess Juno, who punished him for his impudence by condemning him to Hades, where vultures continually fed on his liver.

Tristan: Tristan and Iseult were tragic lovers of Arthurian romance.

Troilus: The son of Priam and Hecuba, he was slain in the Trojan War.

Ulysses (Gk. Odysseus): The Greek leader whose wanderings lasted for ten years after the fall of Troy. Though married to Penelope, he slept with the enchantress Circe and lived with the nymph Calypso on the isle of Ogygia.

Venus (Gk. Aphrodite): The goddess of beauty and love, the wife of Vulcan, and the mother of Cupid. Born out of sea foam, she first stepped ashore on Cyprus and so was often associated with that island.

Vulcan (Gk. Hephaestus): The god of fire, the blacksmith of Olympus, and the husband of Venus.

Zephyrus: The West Wind, associated with spring.

SELECTED BIBLIOGRAPHY

Primary sources

Alighieri, Dante. *La Divina Commedia*. Edited and annotated by C. H. Grandgent. Boston: D. C. Heath & Co., 1933.

_____. *The Divine Comedy*. Translated by Charles Singleton. Princeton: Princeton University Press. The Bollingen Series, 1970–75.

_____. *La Divina Commedial*. Edited by C. H. Grandgent. Revised by Charles Singleton. Cambridge, MA: Harvard University Press, 1972.

_____. *The Divine Comedy*. Translated by L. G. White. New York: Pantheon Books, 1948.

_____. *Vita nuova*. Milano: Garzanti editore, 1979.

Apuleius, Lucius. *The Golden Ass*. Translated by Robert Graves. Middlesex, England: Penguin Books, 1964.

Boccaccio, Giovanni. *Fiammetta*. Codice De' Rossi 2806, c.XIV o XV. Parma: Biblioteca Palatina.

_____. *Amorous Fiammetta*. Translated by Bartholomew Young. London: T. Gubbin & T. Newman, 1587.

_____. *Fiammetta, opere del Boccaccio*. Edited by J. Heitz, introduction by G. Gigli, Strasburgo, 1910.

_____. *Amorous Fiammetta*. Translated by Bartholomew Young, introduction by Edward Hutton. London: Navarre Society, 1926.

_____. *L' "Elegia di Madonna Fiammetta", con le chiose inedite*. A cura di V. Pernicone. Bari: Laterza e Figli, 1939.

_____. *L'Elegia di Madonna Fiammetta*. A cura di Salvatore Battaglia. Milano: Bompiani, 1944.

_____. *Decameron, Filocolo, Ameto, Fiammetta*. A cura di E. Bianchi, C. Salinari, N. Sapegno. Milano-Napoli: Ricciardi, 1952.

_____. *Elegia di Madonna Fiammetta*. A cura di Pia Piccoli Addoli. Milano: Rizzoli, 1962.

_____. *Tutte le opere*. A cura di Vittore Branca. Verona: A. Mondadori editore, 1964.

_____. *Opere*. A cura di Bruno Maier. Bologna: Zanichelli editore, 1967.

_____. *Opere minori in volgare*. A cure di Mario Marti. Milano: Rizzoli, 1969.

_____. *Opere di Giovanni Boccaccio*. A cura di Cesare Segre. Milano: Mursia, 1978.

_____. *The Decameron*. Translated by M. Musa and P. Bondanella, introduction by Thomas Bergin. New York: New American Library, 1982.

Capellanus, Andreas. *The Art of Courtly Love.* Translation and introduction by John L. Parry. New York: F. Ungar Co., 1964.

Juvenal. *Satires.* Edited by F. G. Hardy. London: Macmillan, 1970.

Lucan. *Pharsalia.* Translated by Robert Graves. Harmondsworth: Penguin Books, 1956.

Marie de France. *The "Lais de Marie de France."* Translated by R. Hanning and J. Ferrante. New York: E. P. Dutton, 1979.

Ovid. *Metamorphoses.* Translated by Mary M. Innes. Middlesex, England: Penguin Books, 1977.

————. *Heroides and Amores.* Edited by W. Heinemann and translated by Grant Showerman. Cambridge: Harvard University Press, 1986 reprint of 1977 edition.

Plato. *The Collected Dialogues.* Edited by E. Hamilton and H. Cairns. Princeton: Princeton University Press, 1961. 1984 reprint of 1961 edition.

Plotinus. *The Enneads.* Translated by S. McKenna. New York: Pantheon Books, 1959.

Plutarch. *The Lives of the Noble Grecians and Romans.* Translated by J. Dryden. New York: Modern Library, 1930.

Ruiz, Juan. *The Book of the Archipriest of Hita.* Translated by M. Singleton. Madison: University of Wisconsin, Medieval Studies of Hispanic Seminary, 1975.

————. *The Book of Good Love.* Translated by R. Magnani and M. A. Di Cesare. New York: State University of New York Press, 1970.

Seneca. *Four Tragedies.* Translated by E. F. Watling. Middlesex, England: Penguin Classics, 1972.

Statius. *Statius.* Translated by R. Fitzgerald and D. Fitts. New York: Harcourt, Brace & Co., 1949.

Terence. *The Comedies.* Translated by Betty Radice. Middlesex, England: Penguin Books, 1964.

————. *Les poemes de Tristan et Iseult.* Translated by G. Bianciotto. Paris: Librairie Larousse, 1968.

Virgil. *The Aeneid.* Translated by A. Mandelbaum. New York: Bantam Books, 1972.

Critical Writings and Related Works

Arrowsmith, W. and R. Shattuck. *The Craft and Context of Translation.* Austin: University of Texas Press, 1961.

Baddeley, St. Clair. *Robert the Wise and His Heirs, 1278–1352.* London: William Heineman, 1897.

Barilli, Renato. "La retorica nella narrativa del Boccaccio: *L'Elegia di Madonna Fiammetta.*" *Quaderni d'Italianistica.* Autumn 1985.

Bassnett-McGuire, Susan. *Translation Studies.* London: Methuen, 1980.

Battaglia, Salvatore. "Il significato della *Fiammetta.*" *La Coscienza Letteraria.* Napoli: Liguori editore, 1965.

_____. *Giovanno Boccaccio e la riforma narrativa.* Napoli: Liguori, 1969.

Becker, B. Marvin. *Florence in Transition.* Baltimore: Johns Hopkins Press, 1969.

Bergin, Thomas G. *Boccaccio.* New York: Viking Press, 1981.

Billanovich, Giuseppe. *Restauri Boccacceschi.* Roma: Edizioni di Storia e Letteratura, 1947.

Bodkin, Maud. *Archetypal Patterns in Poetry, Psychological Studies of Imagination.* London: Oxford University Press, 1951.

Boer, Charles. "Poetry and Psyche." *Spring.* New York: Spring Publications, 1973.

Bowden, Betsy. "The Art of Courtly Copulation." *Medievalis et Humanistica* 9 (1929):67.

Branca, Vittore. *Boccaccio Medievale.* Firenze: Sansoni, 1964.

_____. *Giovanni Boccaccio, profilo Biografico.* Firenze: Sansoni, 1977.

_____. *Tradizione delle opere di Giovanni Boccaccio.* Roma: Edizioni di Storia e Letteratura, 1958.

_____. "Un quarto elenco di codici." *Studi sul Boccaccio,* vol. 9. Florence: Sansoni, 1975–76.

Brehier, Emile. *The Middle Ages and the Renaissance.* Chicago and London: University of Chicago Press, 1965.

Brower, Reuben. *On Translation.* Cambridge: Harvard University Press, 1959.

Brucker, Gene A. *Renaissance Florence.* New York: J. Wiley & Sons, 1969.

Bundy, Wright Murray. *The Theory of Imagination in Classical and Medieval Thought.* Urbana-Champagne: University of Illinois Press, 1927.

Burckhardt, Jacob. *The Civilization of the Renaissance in Italy.* New York: Harper & Row, 1958.

Campbell, Joseph. *The Hero with a Thousand Faces.* Princeton: Princeton University Press, 1973.

Carnasciali, Franca. "Boccaccio chiosatore di se stesso." *Da Dante a Cosimo I, ricerche di storia religiosa e cultura toscana nei secoli XIV–XV.* A cura di D. Maselli. Pistoia: Tellini, 197.

Carswell, Catherine. *The Tranquil Heart.* New York: Harcourt, Brace & Co., 1937.

Cartford, J. C. *A Linguistic Theory of Translation, an Essay in Applied Linguistics.* London: Oxford University Press, 1959.

Constable, Giles. "Twelfth-century Spirituality and the Late Middle Ages." *Medieval and Renaissance Studies.* Chapel Hill: University of North Carolina Press, 1971.

Cook, A. S. "Boccaccio, *Fiammetta* Chapter One, and Seneca, *Hippolytus.*Act One." *American Journal of Philology* 28(1907):200–204.

Corazzini, Francesco. *Giovanni Boccaccio,le lettere.* Firenze: Sansoni, 1877.

Cottino-Jones, Marga. *An Anatomy of Boccaccio's Style.* Napoli: Cymba, 1968.

Coulter, Catherine C. "Boccaccio's Knowledge of Quintilian." *Speculum* 31(1958):490–95.

———. "Statius, *Silvae* V.4 and *Fiammetta*'s Prayer to Sleep." *American Journal of Philology* 70 (1959):390–95.

Crescini, Vincenzo. *Contributo agli studi sul Boccaccio con documenti inediti.* Torino: Loescher, 1883.

———. "Il primo atto della *Fedra* di Seneca nel primo capitolo della *Fiammetta* di Boccaccio." *Atti del Regio Istituto Veneto di Scienze, Lettere e Arti* 80 (1920–1921).

Delcorno, Carlo. "Note sui dantismi nell'*Elegia di Madonna Fiammeta.*" *Studi sul Boccaccio,* 11:251–94. Firenze: Sansoni, 1979.

De Sanctis, Francesco. *"La Fiammetta e il Corbaccio."* Antologia Critica sugli Scrittori d'Italia, 1:394–97. A cura di Luigi Russo. Firenze: Vallecchi, 1933.

———. *Storia della letteratura Italiana,* vol. 1. Milano: La Universale Barion, 1946.

Di Pino, Guido. "Una estate barocca per Fiammetta." *Italianistica* 5:1–19.

Donato, Clorinda. "Nota sull'*Elegia di Madonna Fiammetta* e la possibilita' di una triplice analisi psicoanalitica: autore, personaggio, pubblico." *Carte Italiane* 3 (1981–82).

Downing, Christine. *The Goddess, Mythological Images of the Feminine.* New York: Crossroad, 1981.

Durand, Gilbert. "Exploration of the Imaginal." *Spring.* New York: Spring Publications, 1971.

Eco, Umberto. *Opera Aperta.* Milano: Bompiani, 1980.

Edel, Leon. "Hawthorne's Symbolism and Psychoanalysis." *Hidden Patterns.* New York: Macmillan, 1966.

Eliade Mircea. *Myth and Reality.* New York: Harper & Row, 1975.

Felstiner, John. *Translating Neruda, the Way to Machu Picchu.* Stanford, California: Stanford University Press, 1980.

Fletcher, Angus. *Allegory, the Theory of a Symbolic Mode.* Ithaca, N.Y.: Cornell University Press, 1964.

Foucault, Michel. *The History of Sexuality.* New York: Pantheon Books, 1978.

Franz, M. L. von. *Apuleius' Golden Ass.* New York: Spring Publications, 1970.

Frazer, James G. *The Golden Bough, a Study in Magic and Religion.* New York: Macmillan, 1973.

Freud, Sigmund. *The Basic Writings.* New York: Modern Library, 1938.
_____. *The Interpretation of Dreams.* New York: Avon Books, 1965.

Frye, Northrop. *Anatomy of Criticism.* Princeton: Princeton University Press, 1973.

Gathercole, P. M. *Tension in Boccaccio: Baccaccio and the Fine Arts.* Jackson: University of Mississippi Press, 1975.

_____. "Boccaccio in English." *Studi sul Boccaccio,* vol. 7. Firenze: Sansoni 1973.

Gigli, Giuseppe. *Antologia delle opere minori volgari.* Biblioteca Scolastica di Classici Italiani diretta da Giosue' Carducci, 1907.

Givens, Azzurra B. *La dottrina d'amore nel Boccaccio.* Firenze, Messina: Editrice G. D'Anna, 1968.

Grant, Michael. *Roman Myths.* New York: Charles Scribner's Sons, 1971.

_____. *Myths of the Greeks and the Romans.* New York: New American Library, 1962.

Graves, Robert. *The Greek Myths.* Middlesex, England: Penguin Books, 1977.

Griffin, Robert. "Boccaccio's *Fiammetta:* Pictures at an Exhibition." *Italian Quarterly* 17–18 (Spring 1975):75–111.

Gruppe, Otto. *Geschichte der klassischen mythologie und religionsgeschichte wahrend des mittelalters im Abendland.* Leipzig: Teubner, 1921.

Haight, Elizabeth H. "Apuleius and Boccaccio." *More Essays on Greek Romances.* New York: Longman, Green & Co., 1945.

Harding, M. Esther. *The Way of all Women, a Psychological Interpretation.* New York: Longman, Green & Co., 1945.

_____. *Woman's Mysteries, Ancient and Modern.* New York: Harper & Row, 1976.

Hauvette, Henri. *Boccace, etude biographique et litteraire.* Paris: Armand Colin, 1914.

Hay, Denis. *The Italian Renaissance.* London: Cambridge University Press, 1963.

Hillman James. *Suicide and the Soul.* London: Hodder & Stoughton, 1964.

_____. *Insearch: Psychology and Religion.* London: Hodder & Stoughton, 1967.

_____. *The Myth of Analysis, Three Essays in Archetypal Psychology.* Evanston, Ill.: Northwestern University Press, 1972.

_____. *Plotinus, Ficino and Vico as Precursors of Archetypal Psychology.* Roma: Istituto dell'Enciclopedia Italiana, 1973.

_____. "Anima." *Spring.* New York: Spring Publications, 1973.

_____. "Anima II." *Spring.* New York: Spring Publications, 1974.

_____. *Re-visioning Psychology.* New York: Harper & Row, 1975.

_____. "Anima Mundi, the Return of the Soul to the World." *Spring.* Dallas: Spring Publications, 1982.

Hollander, Robert. *Boccaccio's Two Venuses.* New York: Columbia University Press, 1977.

Hough, Graham. "Poetry and Anima." *Spring.* New York: Spring Publications, 1973.

Huizinga, J. *The Waning of the Middle Ages.* Garden City, N.Y.: Doubleday & Co. 1954.

Hutton, Edward. *Giovanno Boccaccio.* London, New York: John Lane Co., 1910.

Iannace, M. F. *La religione del Boccaccio.* Roma: Trevi, 1977.

Iannucci, Amilcare. "L'*Elegia di Madonna Fiammetta* and the First book of the *Asolani:* The Eloquence of Unrequited Love." *Forum Italicum,* vol.10, *1–2* (1976).

Jacobson, Howard. *Ovid's "Heroides."* Princeton: Princeton University Press, 1974.

Jacobson, Roman. *The Framework of Language.* Madison, Wis.: Michigan Studies in the Humanities, 1980.

Jung, C. G. *Two Essays on Analytical Psychology.* London: Rutledge & Kegan Paul, 1953.

_____. *Psychological Types.* London: Rutledge & Kegan Paul, 1962.

_____. *The Structure and Dynamics of the Psyche.* (C.W.V.8). Princeton: Princeton University Press, 1976.

_____. *Symbols of Transformation.* (C.W.V.5). Princeton: Princeton University Press, 1976.

_____. *The Archetypes and the Collective Unconscious.* (C.W.V.9). Princeton: Princeton University Press, 1977.

_____. *Misterium coniunctionis.* (C.W.V.14). Princeton: Princeton University Press, 1977.

Kirk, G. S. *Greek Myths.* Middlesex, England: Penguin Books, 1980.

Kirkham, Victoria. "Reckoning with Boccaccio's 'Questioni d'Amore'." MLN 89 (1974):47–59.

Klein, Viola. *The Feminine Character.* Urbana: University of Illinois Press, 1975.

Kristeller, P. O. *Renaissance Thought.* New York: Harper & Row, 1961.

Kuriyama, C. B. "The Mother of the World: A Psychonalytical Interpretation of Shakespeare's *Anthony and Cleopatra.*" *English Literary Renaissance* vol. 7, 3 (Autumn 1977).

Lacan, Jacques. *Ecrits.* New York: W. W. Norton & Co., 1977.

———. *Feminine Sexuality.* New York: W. W. Norton & Co., 1982.

Ladner, B. Gerhart. "Medieval and Modern Understanding of Symbolism: A Comparison." *Speculum,* vol. 54, 2 (1979).

Layard, John. *The Virgin Archetype.* Zurich: Spring Publications, 1972.

Lederer, Wolfgang. *The Fear of Women.* New York: Harcourt, Brace, Jovanovich, 1969

Levy, Jiri. "The Translation of the Verbal Art." *Semiotic of Art.* Edited by L. Mateika and I. R. Titunik. Cambridge: MIT Press, 1976.

Lipking, Lawrence. *Abandoned Women and Poetic Tradition.* Chicago, London: University of Chicago Press, 1988.

McManus, Francis. *Boccaccio.* London: Sheed & Ward, 1947.

Marcuse, Herbert. *Eros and Civilization, a Philosophical Inquiry into Freud.* London: Sphere Books, 1972.

Marti, Mario. "Per una metalettura del *Corbaccio:* il ripudio della Fiammetta." *Giornale Storico della Letteratura Italiana* 153 (1976):60–85.

Mazza, Antonio. "L'inventario della 'Parva Libreria' di Santo Spirito e la biblioteca del Boccaccio." *Italia Medievale e Umanistica,* vol. 9. Padova: Antenore, 1966.

Mazzaro, Jerome. *The Figure Dante, an Essay on the "Vita Nuova."* Princeton: Princeton University Press, 1981.

Miller, Jean Baker. *Towards a New Psychology of Woman.* Boston: Beacon Press, 1976.

Moreschini, Claudio. "Sulla fama di Apuleio nel medioevo e nel rinascimento." *Studi filologici Letterari e Storici,* vol. 7. Padova: Antenore, 1977.

Mott, Freeman Lewis. *The System of Courtly Love.* New York: Haskel House, 1965.

Muscetta, C. and A. Tartaro. "L'*Elegia di Madonna Fiammetta:* epistola narrativa in prima persona." *La Letteratura Italiana Storia e Testi,* vol. 2. Bari: Laterza, 1972.

Neumann, Erich. *The Great Mother.* Princeton: Princeton University Press, 1972.

———. *Art and the Creative Unconscious.* Princeton: Princeton University Press, 1972.

———. *Amor and Psyche, the Psychic Development of the Feminine.* Princeton: Princeton University Press, 1973.

Nida, Eugene. *Towards a Science of Translation.* Leiden: E. J. Brill, 1964.

———. *The Theory and Practice of Translation.* Leiden: E. J. Brill, 1959.

Olson, Glending. *Literature as Recreation in the Middle Ages.* Ithaca, N.Y.: Cornell University Press, 1982.

Osgood, Charles C. *Boccaccio on Poetry, being the Preface and the Fourteenth and Fifteenth Books of Boccaccio's "De Genealogia Deorum Gen-*

tilium." Indianapolis and New York: Bobbs-Merrill Co., 1955.

Otto, Walter F. *The Homeric Gods, the Spiritual Significance of Greek Religion.* Boston: Beacon Press, 1964.

Pabst, Walter. *Venus als heilige und furie in Boccaccios "Fiammetta" Dichtung.* Krefeld: Scherpe-Verlag, 1958.

Panofsky, Erwin. *Renaissance and Renaissances in Western Art.* New York: Harper & Row, 1972.

_____. *Studies in Iconology, Humanistic Themes in the Arts of the Renaissance.* New York: Harper & Row, 1967.

Petroff, Elizabeth. "Medieval Women Visionaries: Seven Stages to Power." *Frontiers,* vol. 3, 1.

Pound, Ezra. *Literary Essays.* Edited by T. S. Eliot. New York: A New Direction Book, 1935.

_____. *Translations.* Westport, Conn.: Greenwood Press, 1979.

Quaglio, Antonio Ezio. *Le Chiose dell'"Elegia di Madonna Fiammetta."* Padova: Cedam, 1957.

_____. "Un nuovo codice della *Fiammetta." Studi sul Boccaccio,* vol. 5. Florence: Sansoni, 1969.

_____. "Per il testo della *Fiammetta." Studi di Filologia Italiana,* vol. 15. Florence: Sansoni, 1957.

Ramat, Raffaele. "Indicazioni per una lettura del *Decameron. Scritti su Giovanni Boccaccio.* Reprinted from *Miscellanea Storica della Valdelsa,* 69, 2 e 3 (1963).

Rastelli, Dario. "La modernita' della *Fiammetta." Convivium,* n.5 e 6, Torino: Societa' Editrice Internazionale, 1947.

_____. "Le fonti autobiografiche nell' *Elegia di Madonna Fiammetta." Humanitas* 3 (1948).

_____. "Le fonti letterarie del Boccaccio nell'*Elegia di Madonna." Saggi di Umanesimo Cristiano,* 4 (1949).

_____. "Spunti lirici e narrativi, motivi stilistici nella *Fiammetta* di Giovanni Boccaccio." *Lettere Italiane* 3 (1951).

_____. "Boccaccio retore nel prologo della *Fiammetta." Saggi di Umanesimo Cristiano* 3 (1947).

Renier, Rodolfo. *La "Vita Nuova" e la "Fiammetta", Studio Critico.* Torino e Roma: E. Loescher, 1879.

Robinson, Taylor, A. *Male Novelists and Their Female Voices: Literary Masquerade.* Troy, N.Y.: Whitston Publishing Co., 1981.

Rogers, Robert. *The Double in Literature, a Psychoanalytic Study.* Detroit: Wayne State University Press, 1970.

Rose, H. J. *A Handbook of Greek Mythology.* New York: E. P. Dutton, 1959.

Rossetti, Dante G. *Poems and Translations, 1850–1870.* New York: Oxford University Press, 1968.

180

Scaglione, Aldo D. *Nature and Love in the Late Middle Ages*. Berkeley: University of California Press, 1963.

Sebeok, Thomas A. *Myth, a Symposium*. Bloomington: Indiana University Press, 1968.

Segre, Cesare. "Strutture e registri nella *Fiammetta*." *Strumenti Critici* vol. 18 (1972).

Serafini-Sauli, J. P. *Giovanni Boccaccio*. Boston: Twayne Publishers, 1982.

Seznec, Jean. *The Survival of the Pagan Gods, the Mythological Tradition and its Place in Renaissance Humanism and Art*. Princeton: Princeton University Press, 1972.

Singleton, Charles S. *An Essay on the "Vita Nuova."* Baltimore: John Hopkins University Press, 1977.

———. "Dante: Within Courtly Love and Beyond." *The Meaning of Courtly Love*. Edited by F. X. Newman. Albany: State University of New York Press, 1968.

Smarr, Janet Levarie. "Boccaccio and The choice of Hercules." *MLN* 92 (1977).

———. *Boccaccio and Fiammetta: The Narrator as Lover*. Urbana: University of Illinois Press, 1986.

Spivack, Charlotte. "The Elizabethan Theatre: Circle and Center." *Centennial Review* 13 (1969).

Stein, Robert. *Incest in Human Love, the Betrayal of the Soul in Psychotherapy*. Baltimore, Md.: Penquin Books, 1973.

———. "Body and Psyche: An Archetypal View of Psychosomatic Phenomena." *Spring*. New York: Spring Publications, 1976.

Steiner, George. *After Babel, Aspects of Language and Translation*. London: Oxford University Press, 1975.

Strouse, Jean. *Women and Analysis*. New York: Grossman Publications, 1974.

Symond, J. A. *Giovanni Boccaccio as a Man and Author*. New York: AMS Press, 1968.

Tripp, Edward. *The Meridian Handbook of Classical Mythology*. New York: New American Library, 1970.

Tuchman, Barbara W. *A Distant Mirror, the Calamitous 14th Century*. New York: Ballantine Books, 1979.

Waley, Pamela. "Fiammetta and Panfilo continued." *Italian Studies* 24 (1969).

———. "The Nurse in Boccaccio's *Fiammetta*: Source and Invention." *Neophilologus* 56 (1972).

Warner, Rex. *The Stories of the Greeks*. New York: Farrar, Straus & Giroux, 1967.

Will, Frederic. *The Knife in the Stone*. Paris: Mouton, 1973.

Wind, Edgar. *Pagan Mysteries in the Renaissance.* New York: Norton Library, 1968.

Wolf, Diana K. "The Concordance of the *Elegia di Madonna Fiammetta.*" Ph.D diss., University of California, 1984.